THE CLOSING

A NOVEL BY

DAGMAR MARSHALL

RABID PRESS *AUSTIN, TX 2005*

Rabid Press, Inc.
P.O. Box 4706
Horseshoe Bay, TX 78657

The Closing

www. rabidpress.com

Design and layout by Peterson Design
petersondesign@mn.rr.com

Library of Congress Control Number: 2004096669
ISBN 0-9743039-1-7
ISBN 978-0-9743039-1-8

Printed in the United States of America
First Edition, November, 2005

ACKNOWLEDGEMENTS

Thanks to Susan Malone, Editor, not enough kudos for her expertise; a great teacher and friend.

David Baker, Editor-In-Chief and Keith Baker, Marketing Director, Rabid Press, Inc. for their belief in the novel and for giving me the opportunity to work with them and the staff at Rabid Press.

My ever-present family support and the Blue Ridge Mountains for their constant inspiration.

Bouquets to Paul Cossman, a dear friend and owner of a remarkable book store, Humpus Bumpus. His tireless efforts on behalf of the O'Georgia State Wide Writing Contest was a huge influence on my desire to write.

*Dedicated with love to Gordon, my husband
of forty-eight years who died January 23, 2004*

*He was my dearest friend, my biggest fan,
an incredible father and grandfather.*

I miss him more than I can say.

THE CLOSING

PROLOGUE

The rotors whipping the air around the helicopter created pounding reverberations that bounced off the surrounding mountains.

Burke McGuire paused in taking pictures when he noticed Jimmy break into a sweat. He knew Jimmy didn't like navigating so deep into valleys. The helicopter hovered low enough that the tall grasses beneath were pushed flat to the ground of the valley floor. Mountain air currents were unpredictable, and Jimmy – by his own admission – was not the daredevil type, especially flying a million-dollar helicopter that didn't even belong to him. Burke had already decided to push Jimmy as far as he could.

"Jimmy, this is the goddamndest, most beautiful site for a golf course I have ever seen. Over to the right more," Burke McGuire, camera clicking again, yelled over the thrumming of the rotors.

"Burke, jeez, we're too low. I want out of here. You've been shooting this valley for an hour." Cords of tension rose on Jimmy's sinewy forearm and on the back of the hand holding the stick. "We can't stay much longer. I don't know of any chopper fuel stations up here, old buddy."

"Okay, okay." Burke flashed a thumbs-up sign and Jimmy started gaining altitude. Burke gazed down at the rolling, lush grass covering the valley floor, the crystal clear creek

1

running along the long tree line of the valley, and began drawing mental pictures of golf holes.

WHACK!

"Jeez almighty. We've been hit by something." Jimmy steadied the helicopter and pushed it higher. He stared intently at the instruments.

"Maybe a bird. We okay?" Burke took a deep breath.

"I see no indicated damage. She's handling fine." Burke exhaled.

Jimmy cocked his head. "Wait. Look over there."

Burke followed Jimmy's line of sight. "Smoke. Looks like smoke. Could be a forest fire. Let me take some shots. Rangers might need them. Can you get a little closer?"

"Damn! No! That's from a shotgun. That's a damn puff of smoke from a shotgun! Some damn fool's shooting at us! We're goin' bye, bye." Jimmy banked sharply away and gained altitude rapidly. "Bet those boys were making white lightin' and they think we're spying on 'em. Whaddya bet?"

Burke nodded. "We got crazy swamp folks in Florida. They got crazy mountain folks here in the beautiful Blue Ridge."

Jimmy landed the helicopter at Peachtree-Dekalb Airport. He showed Burke a crease in the skin of the helicopter, just in back of the pilot's door.

"Man," Jimmy said, "look at that. Good damn thing we weren't any closer to those boys. We were target practice, today. I get the feelin' they might do more damage than this next time."

And there will be a next time, Burke thought as he and Jimmy headed for the Hearn Guilford corporate jet, its engines already screaming readiness for takeoff.

Leaning back in the plushness of the custom seat, Burke

sipped a Beefeaters on the rocks. He briefly admired the elliptical-shaped crystal glass in his hand, etched with the initials HG. Jimmy sat beside him, sucking on a beer.

Burke also enjoyed the luscious Bridgette's retreating and very shapely backside. Even the hostess on this plane was custom-built. Only the very best for Hearn Guilford. He hoped Bridgette had missed Jimmy's slap-happy drooling look down her substantial cleavage. But, she was no doubt used to it.

Jimmy asked, "You think that's the property you want for the golf course?"

Burke smiled. "It's not a matter of thinking I want that property, I know I want that property. It's right. It's perfect."

"Burke, we've been shootin' a lot of property up there in those mountains and you have to fall for the one place they're shootin' back at us. Damn."

Burke grinned, "You don't get successful by backing down from a little gun-shot activity. After 'gators, rattlers and poachers, a few moon shiners might be a relief."

"Sometimes, McGuire, you scare the hell out of me with your semi-truck-rollin' down-a-hill-with-no-breaks attitude."

Burke toasted his old friend. "Someone's gotta do it and I am that someone."

CHAPTER 1

Canty O'Neil paced around her desk, lifting and pulling at her phone cord until she could get close enough to the county map on her wall. She identified a location on the map and gasped. Dear God!

"Hello?"

Canty clicked her thoughts back to the voice in her ear. "Joanna, sorry. Who did you say wants this property?"

"Hearn Guilford Golf Designs. They are the leading golf course design company in the world."

Canty took a deep breath and traced over the map. Joanna had named the plat book and pages and there was no doubt about it. Someone named Hearn Guilford wanted the Ponder property... *for a golf course.*

Canty gripped the phone tighter. "Tell me one more time, Joanna."

Joanna's voice became edgy and impatient. "Look, Guilford Golf Course Designs wants eight-hundred to one-thousand acres of mountain land to develop into an ultra-posh golf club community. There – in Wynton, Georgia. They know where it is. They need a broker to package the property for them. I told them, Canty O'Neil of O'Neil Properties was the only broker I would recommend. Is there a problem?"

"No, Joanna. I just wasn't expecting this. How do they know about the property?"

"Guilford Designs has been doing aerials of the property and surrounding properties for the past six months. Burke McGuire will be in touch with you by fax this afternoon."

"Who is Burke McGuire? Do you know him?"

"Only by phone. The man is strictly business and wants answers quickly. Hearn Guilford Designs depends on him for all their acquisitions and golf designs. This is a big one, Canty. Really big. I'm their main referral arm, so please, don't turn me down."

Canty tucked a hank of hair behind an ear. "Not a chance, Joanna. The Orlando Connection and O'Neil Properties are on their way up. Way up."

"Keep me informed. The usual referral structure will be applied. Bye for now."

The click was resounding.

Canty perched on her desk and stared at the wall map. She shook her head, her dark heavy hair whooshing by her cheeks.

"The dadgum, screwed-up Ponder property. I've got to package that land, complete with three nutcases and a whacked out woman who considers herself ruler, sell it as golf course property and deal with people who probably have no conception of how anything works up here. This may be impossible."

Canty slid off the desk. Her trim, athletic body crackled with energy.

"This sale," Canty poked her finger at the designated property, "could be the end of in-the-red for O'Neil Properties. This could let Pop kick back and relax for the first time in all his fifty-eight years. This sale could change lives here and a lot of those lives may not be for it. I hope this Guilford Designs man knows what he's doing and will listen to me because we could all be full of buckshot holes if he won't."

Canty headed for the front door. "Willodene," she spoke over her shoulder to her secretary, "I'm going to review some property. I'll be back in about an hour or so. I'm expecting a very important fax. If you have to leave, just put it on my desk. Make sure no one sees it except you."

★   ★   ★

Canty drove her Jeep up the steep gravel road, dodging ruts and grimacing at the pinging and hammer-like blows the loose stones made on the undercarriage. She pictured oil dripping and transmission fluid flowing from the bowels of the Jeep.

"Just a little further," she said and yelped when her teeth snapped shut on the edge of her tongue. "Dammit!"

Canty gunned the Jeep the last few yards to the crest of the hill. She braked and pulled a tissue out of the mashed box beside her, holding it to her mouth to stop the trickle of blood coming from her tongue.

"Thanks, old thing," she garbled to the Jeep and patted the steering wheel.

Another wound in the line of duty. Real estate was a bloody business, by God. She found herself already aggravating the sore place with her teeth, still tasting the iron flavor of her blood.

Maybe Queen Ponder is into her soaps and won't spot me, she thought. Canty stepped out on to the gravel road. A canopy of hardwoods and pines over her head turned the daylight down to dusky gray. Just a few yards beyond she could see tatters of soft blue, hazy sky. She reached the edge of the tree line.

The vista was overwhelming in its sweep. The tumbling haze that dressed the Blue Ridge Mountains dipped and rose creating a dramatic progression of light and shadows on the old hills. Canty never tired of the beauty of the mountains. They surrounded her life, as protective as family and friends.

Down below her feet stretched a lush valley, containing close to three hundred acres of fertile bottomland. Ever changing patterns of light and dark shifted amongst the tall valley grasses. Secret Creek, fed from springs emanating from the mountains, edged the eastern side of the valley. Even from Canty's perch, she could see diamond–clear shards of water being tossed into the air as the creek dashed through its rocky bed on the way to Lake Mist, a mile away.

As a young girl, Canty and her father had climbed as far back as they could into the hills to find the source of the creek. They discovered waterfalls and rapids and wild life but never the source.

"Canty, honey," Pop had said, "that ol' creek don't want us to know where it's comin' from. My great-granddaddy named it Secret Creek and never found its source, either."

Mr. Burke McGuire must be a very smart man to have chosen this property for development. Too bad it belonged to the Ponder family. Wonder how smart he'll be about understanding the minds of a thieving, uneducated, incestuous mountain family. Please don't be in a big hurry, McGuire.

Canty turned toward a screeching voice coming across the valley to her left. "I hate you, go away, I hate you, go away!"

"Dammit Queen, you and your damn nasty talking bird. You're both out on that porch, just waiting for fools like me." The crack of a rifle shot startled Canty and she dropped to the ground. She heard the whine of a bullet and an unmistakable thud as it found its mark in a tree beside her. Dust and shredded bark stung her eyes.

"Okay, okay, I'm leaving," she yelled out. "By God, Queen, you're true to your word." Canty stayed low, scooting around to the driver's side of the jeep and scrambled in quickly. She gunned the engine and executed a fish-tailing U-turn to head back down the road.

"I hate you, go away!" continued to echo in her ears.

Canty breathed a sigh of relief as she pulled onto the main road back to town. She checked her watch. More than two hours had passed since she talked to Joanna Stark. The fax should be in by now.

She hummed along with the radio and tapped the wheel lightly with her fingers in rhythm with a rocking "Pretty Woman" by Roy Orbeson. How to approach Queen Ponder about selling? Maybe she should decide on a few alternative properties to show Mr. Burke McGuire, just in case Queen and her merry band of idiots made mud pie out of the idea.

Burke McGuire, I don't know you, yet, but I do know every bit of dirt in this county and the areas around it and by God, if we can't work with that property, we'll find another. Canty sighed. There was no other like it and she knew it.

Just past the city limits sign for Wynton she saw the marked sheriff's car in her rear view mirror. She slowed quickly, but not quickly enough. The flashing blue lights drew steadily closer.

Damn, Tully Jones. She pulled over and the Sheriff's car stopped behind her. Rolling down her window, Canty looked up into the smiling brown eyes of Sheriff Tully Jones.

Canty and Tully had grown up together, gone to school together, laughed together, cried the blues to each other, and lived through each other's happy times and sad times. Everyone knew them and they knew everyone. The town had waited for a marriage that never happened and Canty knew was about as possible as snow in July. She'd attended the University of Georgia to study business and finance in the hopes to help Pop expand his lumber and building business and give him some relief from his normal fourteen to sixteen hour days. Her real dream was to marry Tully Jones.

Tully, in turn, had earned a degree in Criminology at Georgia State. He'd joined the police force in Atlanta, and played the rough game of an undercover investigator for five years, finally returning home to become sheriff of Morgan County.

By the time Canty came back home to Wynton, her life had changed dramatically. She'd earned her degree in business and finance but found herself an unwed mother-to-be. She needed friends, not suitors.

"Hey, Tully." Canty tried her best to look innocent.

"Won't work, Canty. You were going fifty-five in a thirty-five miles per hour zone." His voice spoke with authority but she could see the mischief in his brown eyes.

"But Sheriff, I hadn't had a chance to slow down. I just barely passed the city speed limit sign."

To her annoyance, the Sheriff kept on writing. "License, please."

"You know who I am, Tully."

"Of course I know who you are, Canty O'Neil, but I haven't had time to memorize your driver's license number. However, if you continue to flaunt the law, I just might. Proof of insurance, please, ma'am." He held out his hand.

She shuffled through her glove compartment and passed the card to him, smiling and still feigning innocence.

Canty's smile faded as he kept on writing. Finally, Tully snapped the ticket off his pad and handed it to her with her license and insurance card.

"Thanks, Sheriff." Canty barely moved her lips.

Canty watched in her rear view mirror as the tall, lanky sheriff returned to his car. Tully Jones, you may be a good looking dude and you may love being sheriff more than anything but you are a pain. She looked down and saw a scribbled note on a small scrap of paper with her license. Dinner tonight? Seven?

Wanting to shoot him the bird, she instead gave him a thumbs up sign. He pulled by, a big grin crinkled and softened his rugged, stern looks. He was still the best friend she ever had.

DAGMAR MARSHALL

CHAPTER 2

Willodene was tidying her desk and preparing to leave when Canty returned. She shook an accusing finger, "I was gettin' worried about you. Where've you been and why didn't you have your cell phone on?"

"Willy, if I told you I had been shot at while checking out the Ponder property and then got a speeding ticket on the way back to the office, from none other than Sheriff Tully Jones, would that clear up matters?"

Willodene squinted at Canty. "I believe everything you're sayin' but you still haven't answered why you didn't have your cell phone on, 'specially prowling around Ponder property."

"Actually, I forgot." No sense in saying anything but the bottom-line facts.

Willodene lightened her tone. "Okay, but Canty—"

"I know, it was stupid. We're all so happy to have the darn phones so we can keep track of each other and I rendered this little sucker absolutely helpless." Canty tossed her phone down on Willodene's desk.

Willodene picked it up, pressed the On button and handed it back to Canty. "There!"

Canty's smile evolved into a deep earthy chuckle. "Willy, you are definitely a 'can't live with you, can't live without you' kinda friend."

"I hear you." Willodene ran her fingers through her

13

curly salt and pepper hair. "I also need you to know we received a pages-long fax from Hearn Guilford Golf Designs, Incorporated. The one you was waitin' for."

Canty started toward the fax machine.

"It's on your desk where you told me to put it." Willodene yanked off her reading glasses. Her round blue eyes lasered in on Canty. "And who is Burke McGuire? He called here awhile ago and he sounded like a bear chewin' briars."

Things were happening a lot faster than she imagined. "Willy, we might just be getting into the greatest opportunity for O'Neil Properties ever. That's why I was out at Ponder's, and that's why I got a speeding ticket, and that's why I forgot my phone."

Canty related the phone call of the morning and how much she felt the whole project could mean to the town, the county, and O'Neil Properties. "Willy, I'm dying to see that fax. Want to read it with me?"

"No need to ask twice," Willodene hurried to Canty's office with her.

The pages contained a history of Hearn Guilford Golf Designs, Incorporated, the origin of the company, the goals and achievements of the company, and the names and brief biographies of the current management teams' members.

Six teams, Canty noted, and all answered to McGuire. Included was a brief financial statement. Hearn Guilford Golf Designs, Inc. showed it was not only a profitable firm, but into the billion-dollar range profitable.

The last page of the fax was a letter addressed to O'Neil Properties, Wynton, Georgia, Attention, Mr. Canty O'Neil.

Canty chuckled, "Willodene, this man's in for a big surprise. Mr. Canty O'Neil, indeed."

Willodene snorted, "Oh, yes, indeed. Read on."

Canty read the letter out loud. It stated that extensive study had been conducted during the past year and a half in order to find the right surroundings for Hearn Guilford Golf Design, Inc. to build its first mountain-area golf resort and country club. Results of the study showed the area surrounding Wynton, Georgia was ideally suited for the project. O'Neil Properties was the first choice for pursuing the purchase of the chosen property to be developed. The study showed that O'Neil Properties had an in-depth knowledge of the area and a solid reputation for integrity in business.

"Well, la de da," Willodene remarked.

Canty tucked a lock of hair behind each ear and exhaled. "You know, Willy, this fax and this letter are big stuff for little old O'Neil Properties."

"Nothin' you and your Pop can't handle."

Canty cleared her throat and read on. "Mr. O'Neil, please contact me through Orlando Connection. Joanna Stark will be waiting to hear from you. Should you have any reservations about handling the purchase and sale of property for the project, let her know immediately. Otherwise, we'll be in contact within a week. Looking forward to working with you, Mr. O'Neil. We'll have a lot to discuss before either of us commits to the final Client/Broker relationship. By the way, are there any places to stay in Wynton, Georgia? Joanna Stark will make reservations wherever you say. Sincerely, Burke McGuire, General Manager."

"Why was Burke McGuire calling?"

"He wanted to make sure we got the fax, and he wanted to know when you would be replying to Joanna Stark. My answers were 'yes' and 'soon as she can.'"

Canty laughed. "No wonder he sounded growly. People like that want specific answers, as in 'now'."

"I know that but he just took me back when he sounded so grumpy. Course maybe he always sounds like that."

Willodene shook her head. "Why, we might not want to deal with that man at all."

"Willy, I've got to talk to Pop about this. I just need to hear what he thinks of the concept and our involvement."

"He'd be the first one I'd talk to, that's for sure." Willodene nodded. "When you talk to Clower O'Neil, tell him I said 'hello.' He's been so busy building houses lately, I can't even get him over to the house for dinner."

"Willodene Bert, you and Pop need to get your stuff in order and tie the knot."

Willodene spread her fingers and gazed at her cotton candy pink nails. "Canty, honey, you know I've been in love with your Pop since right after he was widowed and you was only three. He is so dear to me, but you know he thinks he's too old for me. Poof, he's nine years older, and that ain't much. My Momma and Daddy were twenty years apart."

Canty laughed. "He's a warm hearted man with cold feet! You know he thinks Toby makes the sun rise and the moon set but I think he's using him and me as an excuse not to make a commitment. He'd run you down the aisle in a Chinese second if I ever got married. That age thing is a bunch of hooey. He just feels so responsible for us."

"Oh, honey," Willodene squared her narrow shoulders, "I know it and I admire him so much for it. Not many daddy's would take on a pregnant, unwed daughter with such total, unquestioning devotion. God knows that was a hard time for you and Clower."

"Indeed it was, Willy. Can you imagine that was over ten years ago?"

"I know one thing, Tobias O'Neil is the luckiest little boy in the world to have a momma like you and a grandpa like Clower to raise him. He's a fine young man too, even though all he wants to do is play baseball."

Canty snapped upright. "Good grief, Willy, you just reminded me. I've got to pick up Toby from ball practice right now. You want to come with me?"

"Not tonight. You get on your way, I'll close up shop. Here," she handed Canty the folded pages of the fax, "I'll be lookin' forward to hearin' what Clower O'Neil thinks about all this golf course stuff."

"Me, too, Willy. Me, too."

CHAPTER 3

Canty headed out on the road leading to Toby's school and the ball fields. She noted with dismay that the traffic swirling around the town square was increasing at a startling pace. The by-pass road, under construction, couldn't be finished soon enough. Many of the townspeople were upset about the 'big road' but without it, constant gridlock would stifle the square very soon. The mountains of North Georgia had ceased to be a secret.

Canty's thoughts raced as she drove down a side street in an attempted short cut. Visualizing a golf course and country club in the area was exciting enough, but the spin-offs could change the whole complexion and standards of the area. An amenity like that would attract more people here on a permanent basis. The results would be new sub-divisions, shopping villages, churches, restaurants, medical facilities, new schools, movie complexes. Plus, a lot of upset people, and a lot of opportunists.

She glanced down. She was traveling several miles an hour over the speed limit. "No, no," Canty lightened her foot on the gas pedal, "not twice in one day. This whole thing has me moving at warp speed."

She pulled into the parking area next to the ball fields. A boy, dark hair blowing, arms and legs pumping hard, dashed toward the Jeep before she could come to a full stop.

"Ma! I hit a homer! It was great. I put it over the left field fence. Everyone was yellin'. Man, it was great. You shoulda seen it." The still tenor tone of youth bounced happily in Canty's ears."

"You should have seen it," she said lightly.

"Yeah, right." Toby dashed around to the passenger door and plopped beside her with a bounce.

Canty leaned over and gave the smooth cheek streaked with ball-field dirt and sweat, a quick kiss. Toby turned his face to her and grinned. "What's for dinner?"

She tweaked his ear. "Food, is that all you can think of?"

"Ma, when a man hits a home run, he's gotta have good food so he can hit another one." Toby held a pretend bat and swung his arms, his gray eyes shone.

Canty contained a burst of laughter and swallowed hard. In the excited face of her son she saw herself as a child. Toby had her dark brown hair, thick and straight, her gray eyes surrounded by thick black lashes and accented by straight dashes of black brows. His nose was small like hers and just slightly tilted up. His wide mouth was wider, but the smiles were identical, big and bright. Toby's smile was still filled with teeth too big for his face. The touch of freckles across his nose, accented by the sun were identical to her own. And, that quick and indefatigable energy that belonged to the O'Neils was his, too.

Canty thanked God on a regular basis that Tobias Clower O'Neil looked so much like herself and her pop.

They drove back around the small square and on out the other side to the road leading home.

"Ma, can I call Pop, please? I gotta tell him about my home run." Canty smiled and handed him her cellular phone. She didn't worry about correcting his grammar this time. He was too excited to listen anyway. He dialed quickly, and fortunately Pop was home.

"Ma, Pop's all excited, too. He can't wait for us to get home so he can hear more."

"Tell Pop we're about ten minutes away." With dusk approaching quickly in the mountains, Canty flicked on her headlights. "Also, tell him I have something important to talk to him about."

Toby relayed the message and, for the rest of the way home, asked what was so important.

The sun's rays were still visible as red orange streaks of light, quickly growing smaller behind the mountains as they climbed O'Neil Ridge Road.

The O'Neil property covered most of the ridge, down to the bottomland that was rimmed by a bold stream, and the next mountain. The family property consisted of one-hundred and fifty acres of bottomland and one thousand acres of mountains. According to an old and yellowed deed, Great-grandpa O'Neil had owned an incalculable amount of the surrounding acres, but no one had ever positively identified the boundaries. Canty could remember her Grandpa pointing north and declaring the property line extended to that big old pine "way up top of that ridge, east to that notch in the mountain peak, only visible on a very clear day, south to where the stream disappeared into the rocks, and west to where the sun sets." It seemed to Canty as a child, that the O'Neils owned the world.

Then, the United States Government came by and began purchasing mountains and forest lands all around them. Grandpa O'Neil figured no one could do much with whole mountains anyway so he kept one mountain and the good bottom land. "Yup, Canty, honey," he'd say, "you can tell all them flatlanders you meet, your family owns a mountain, used to own three, cut back to just one." Then, he'd spat out a stream of tobacco juice and laughed. "But, sugar, I made sure the best land for growing and grazing stayed right here with us. Now, no one can do nothing with the rest of it 'cause you can bet the United States Govmint ain't goin' to give nothing away or even sell it. You and yours have a lifetime o' living right here if you so choose."

Canty was always spellbound by her Granddaddy's stories of the land and his pride in his mountains. True to the O'Neil heritage, Pop also thrived on the O'Neil land. She knew, no matter what she said, he worried that now that she was college educated and had a son, she might want to leave Wynton for another life. Canty had no intention of leaving her beloved mountains. But now, she found herself worrying that Toby might grow up to look for another world.

Canty parked the Jeep under the old carport. Pop was sitting on the porch, puffing on his pipe and rocking in his favorite chair. She loved seeing him sit there. He wasn't a man to be still and relax but when Toby was coming home he watched and waited right there.

Toby dashed up to Pop, waving a fist and chanting "home run, home run!" Pop grinned. Nearly sixty, he was wiry and tough as leather. Making a living and raising a family in the mountains was not easy work. Between farming and the O'Neil lumber mill, which Pop had hatched and nurtured into a continuously growing business, every minute of every day was full.

Canty leaned back on a porch post and smiled as Pop lifted Toby on his lap and tousled his hair. She couldn't help but think how far they'd come. Canty's mother died when she was only three, so Pop had the double duty of making a living and raising a daughter. When Canty came home pregnant, unmarried and deserted after graduation from the University, Pop never hesitated to welcome her home with open arms, and love.

Toby's birth brought a huge measure of joy to Canty and Pop. Toby was only three months old when Canty took over the book-keeping at the lumber mill. Toby had a special place beside her desk where he was constantly scrutinized by all.

At first Pop wasn't too sure she and Toby should be around the mill. The men who did business there were rough and not always careful about their speech or manners. But, Canty was born to the mountains and the mountain people and understood them, and their lives. She had also known almost every one of them since childhood. The men had an unwritten law around Canty and Toby, no cussin' or spittin'. They all fell in love with the little dark-haired, gray-eyed, boy.

One night when Canty and Pop were driving home, he marveled at how things were running much smoother at the mill now that Canty was there.

"Pop," she swelled up with pride, "it's only because now you have time to watch over those orders more closely. Don't forget, I was a business major at the University. I know how to do the numbers and you sure know how to get the work orders out and done right."

"It's been good, Canty and it's goin' to get better. You've made me look around and open my eyes to the changes these mountains are in for. From what I can tell, we're going to have to be ready to meet it head on or sink. Been thinking about starting a little home building thing on the side, test the waters, so to speak. Been thinking that you gettin' your real estate license might be a good idea."

"Pop! What a super idea. What a fantastic, super idea. You just let me handle the real estate end of your building business. You build 'em, I sell 'em. O'Neil Properties!"

Toby was so startled by her outburst he let out a yell.

"Canty, that boy of yours is everything to me. I, by God, want to leave him more than just a mountain and some bottom-land. He's gonna need it. By the way, how many years you gonna wait to tell him why he don't have a daddy?"

Canty was shocked into silence.

"Well, Canty girl, you got to have been thinkin' about it. Ol' Toby's goin' to be asking questions, soon."

"Well," Canty took a deep breath, "here's what I plan to say because it's the truth. 'Toby,' I'll say one day, 'your daddy is dead. He died before you were born. He was killed in an automobile accident. It was so long ago, and because I came home to Pop, I decided you should stay with the name O'Neil.'"

Saying it outloud had brought another huge twinge of pain to Canty's heart. She had loved Toby's father with passion and fire. The passion got away with her one night after too many beers and promises of undying love and marriage, and Toby was conceived. After graduation, Toby's father left for his home on Long Island vowing to call. He did not. Two months later, Canty called him to tell him she was pregnant with his child. He promised to send for her as soon as he broke the news to his parents. He extracted her solemn oath not to call him, he would call her. He did not call. Canty did not break her oath.

Toby's cries of "home run" snapped Canty out of her brief reverie. Happiness is now, she thought.

. Canty sat down in a rocker next to Pop and Toby, and dug into her brief case for the fax. She was bursting to tell Pop all about the news but wouldn't dream of interrupting the man-to-man talk between Toby and Pop. No detail was omitted. The pitch; the swing; the hit; were described in great detail. Their relationship could not be closer if Pop were his father instead of his grandfather. In fact, she often thought, very few fathers had the wisdom and patience of a grandfather. Finally, Pop looked to her and asked about her day.

"I have had a most extraordinary day. It started with a call from Florida, continued on to being shot at by Queen Ponder, received what could be the most important fax of my lifetime, even though the sender thinks I'm Mr. O'Neil, and topping it off, picking up my son only to find out he had hit one over the fence."

"My, my." He settled back. "Seems I've heard the end of the day before the beginning. Is that right, Toby?"

"My, my," echoed Toby. "But the end is the best part."

"You got that right, young man. Now, Mr. O'Neil, it's your turn." Pop grinned, the weathered face crinkling into brown corduroy.

Canty laughed. "Okay, men, get ready." She briefly described the eventful day and handed the fax to her father as a finale.

Pop read the whole text and Canty waited, jittering with anticipation.

"First, Canty," gray eyes met gray eyes, "don't want you messin' around with Queen Ponder. She might decide to actually take aim one day and you could be in the way. Second, the golf course idea may be a little ahead of its time. Folks here don't play much golf. It's goin' to take awhile to bring enough people here permanent to keep a golf course floatin'."

Canty tucked a lock of hair behind each ear and hoped Pop didn't notice the twitch in her left eye.

"However, and don't you look so sulky just cause you don't like what I'm sayin'. It's gonna depend on what this McGuire fella is all about, and how much he knows about us and what's all around us." He leaned toward Canty and she could see a silver sparkle in the gray eyes that only came when he was excited. "Canty, girl, you don't have to do nothin' but get that land packaged and close the deal. Then, it's up to that McGuire fella. I'm trusting that you are sure it's the Ponders' land and hoping not, because it's goin' to be hell to put it together and could be dangerous, too. Those Ponder men are mean and slick as grease, and Queen is crazy if ever anyone was. It's not goin' to be an easy thing. You'll earn your money, hope you live to spend it."

"Pop, you can't mean that." But she knew he did. She too, knew the Ponders. "But, don't you think the risk is worth it? Don't you see the benefits to the whole county by working through this and building a main attraction up here?"

He stopped rocking and leaned close to her again, his voice soft and firm. "Canty, you gotta have a need or be able to make one. Like I said, it'll all depend on what the McGuire fella knows. I like the idea, Canty, don't get me wrong there. Sounds like the company in Florida has a lot of experience and money. Shoot, anytime the O'Neils stand to make some money selling land, you don't think I'd turn my back, do ya?"

"I know, I know." She took a deep breath. Her left eye stopped twitching. "We'll just have to take one step at a time. We're just going to have to see exactly what Mr. Burke McGuire has in mind."

They rocked quietly and watched the final wisps of sunlight disappear in behind their mountain.

"I just feel there's something big about this Pop," Canty whispered.

Pop reached out a hard, callused hand and Canty took hold. "I do believe you're right. Your instincts are true." He chuckled. "I'm just playing devils advocate here so you don't go off half-crazy and then find out it's a bust."

"I hear you, Pop." Canty sighed with relief. I have never wanted anything to be so right.

"Don't get your hopes up too high and keep after something that can't happen. Promise me you'll drop this project if it gets dangerous."

Canty squeezed Pop's work-tough leathery hand. "But how can I promise that when dangerous will be your interpretation, not mine."

Pop's gray eyes glinted with mischief. "An O'Neil to the core." He kissed her cheek and called Toby to come on in for dinner.

★　★　★

Canty was starving. Pop and Toby had eaten dinner and were settled down with Toby's homework. Tully had called at seven saying he'd be a little late, "emergency to handle". It was now nearly eight and Canty was ready to start chewing on the porch railing.

At last, she saw automobile lights flashing in and out of the trees as a car drove up the ridge. Tully was out of the car and up the porch steps, grinning and offering a bouquet of somewhat wilted daisies. Canty smacked the back of her right hand on her forehead, declaring she was too weak to even get up.

"Don't know how I'll even make it to the car. I am famished to the point of fainting. Why, my poor head is so light, I am smothered in dizziness."

"Bull," Tully reached down, pulled her to her feet, and threw her over his shoulder in a fireman's carry.

"Quit! Tully Jones, you quit that. Put me down!" Canty yelped. Pop and Toby came dashing out to the porch.

"It's okay, Mr. O'Neil. Canty's a little upset 'cause I'm late but I'll take good care of her. Got to feed her before she gets any more out of control." Tully swung around, headed for his car and dumped her into the passenger seat.

Canty asked him to step-on-it before she took a bite out of his arm.

"Canty, I'm not going to speed just because you're hungry. You realize you are asking the elected sheriff of Morgan County to break the law? Shame on you. That reminds me, why were you speeding this afternoon?"

"Wouldn't you like to know? Better yet, I know you would like to know." Canty smiled, wanting to make him squirm a little.

"You stinker!" Tully pulled into the parking lot of the Sizzlin Steak House. He strode around to the passenger door and opened it with a flourish. "Welcome to the Ritz-Carlton of Morgan County. As a recently ticketed speeder, it would only seem right that the sheriff escort you to dine. Someone has to keep your butt out of trouble."

Canty zigged around Tully and hit the swinging front doors of the Steak House at a trot. She grabbed a handful of pretzels from the wooden bowl on the bar, and headed for the kitchen. "Two sirloins, medium, two of the biggest baked potatoes you have, with sour cream, two orders of corn on the cob, and house salad, please!"

"You got it!" came from within.

As Canty slid into the booth across from Tully, he bent toward her and put one of his large, rough fingers under her chin. "I believe I see fire in those gray eyes, fire so hot this place may spontaneously ignite and burn down." He leaned back, waiting.

"Tully, what would you think if I said that a very big golf course design company wants to put a course in Wynton, Georgia?"

"I'd think that now I know why you were speeding this afternoon. You were having hallucinations and lost control of your right foot."

"Not so funny, old buddy." Canty reached across the table and put a hand on Tully's arm, speaking with exaggerated slowness. "I am dead-level serious. This is going to happen and put this little town on the map. People will be clamoring to live in Wynton, formerly known as 'I've Never Heard Of It, Georgia' Oh, thank goodness. Food."

The plump, gum cracking waitress broke the spell as she placed salads and rolls on the table declaring the steaks nearly ready.

"Patsy, honey," Tully said, "you better not be lyin' or you may find yourself being sliced up and devoured. I'm here with a starving lunatic, suffering with delusions."

Patsy squinted at Canty, and pointed at Tully. "Canty, this man isn't very nice, sometimes. Don't know why you want to hang around with him."

"Patsy, when I'm hungry, there's no one not nice enough for me. What's new?"

Patsy smacked her gum. "Wish you'd been here sooner, Sheriff. Terrell and Smith Ponder were in here and actin' mean."

Tully's smile faded. "What were they doing?"

Patsy leaned closer. "I'm telling you what, they was looking for trouble like always. Liquored up and making nasty remarks to me and Sally. Cook was getting ready to call you when they just up and left. Spun their wheels so some stones knocked paint off the front door. God, them boys is mean and ugly."

Canty dug into her salad. "Hope they get a little more cooperative, real soon. They have a real treat coming their way."

Patsy turned back to the kitchen. Tully put his fork down. "What?"

Canty related what she knew so far, including the fact that the Ponder property would be perfect for a golf course. She also admitted that she had been screamed at by Queen's bird and shot at by Queen herself that afternoon. "Thus," she hinted at a smile, "I was speeding, away from my doom!"

"Dammit, Canty, you stay away from those Ponders." Tully's voice was a low rumble. "There's plenty of other property around here for a golf course. They'll never sell and you'll be putting yourself in danger."

"Tully," she said calmly, breaking open a biscuit and buttering it with deliberation, "I realize there could be some huge problems, believe me. However, the very biggest problem, as I speak, is that Burke McGuire, Hearn Guilford's nearly-in-charge-of-everything main man," Canty leaned close to Tully, "has already been up here and chosen the Ponder property."

"Kee-rap!" Tully grabbed up his ice-water and took a huge swallow.

30

CHAPTER 4

Sleep was elusive. Canty's mind would not shut down. Tully's and Pop's concerns about the Ponders were justified. They could be vicious, mindless monsters.

She rolled from her side, sprawled on her back and willed her body and mind to be still. Queen Ponder ruled, and was the only one of the bunch that had any clarity of mind. Old Queen spent so much time trying to protect her backasswards, stupefied brothers, she stayed sober. She'd never win a Miss Congeniality vote, but at least she hadn't fried her brains in white lightning like the rest of them.

I can only hope money talks to Queen Ponder and her brothers as it does to everyone else, she thought as she ran her tongue against her teeth and felt the soreness.

A not-so-pleasant reminder of her latest encounter with Queen Ponder.

She could easily remember back to her first encounter with Queen. After the last picnic with Pop and another futile search for the source of Secret Creek, Canty determined she could find it. Pop just wouldn't keep going long enough. Pop declared the creek tunneled up near the top of Ponder Ridge and if the source is on the Ponder side of the ridge, nobody's going to find it as long as there is a Ponder. She was forbidden to wander on Ponder property and had heard story after story of how strange the Ponders were. The townspeople declared they spoke a foreign language and they all had shiny green eyes and long bushy hair. Some said they didn't wear clothes. Some said they slept in the trees. Some said the men always carried loaded shotguns or rifles and prowled the mountains at night "killing things." It was said that if you wandered onto Ponder property, you would be snatched up and forced to live as a Ponder for the rest of your life. Ponder sightings were a continuous source of gossip and the stories grew more frightening with every telling.

Canty O'Neil wasn't afraid because she didn't believe the stories. Pop never said whether he thought they were true or not but "just don't wander on their property because they have made it clear, they don't want company. Period."

At age ten, Canty O'Neil made a pact with herself that she would find the source of Secret Creek, all by herself. Then, she could lead Pop right to it and he would be so proud of her. She set out one Saturday morning, walked the two miles to Secret Creek and then took the familiar route upstream. Canty had been climbing for nearly one hour and she was tired. She sat down on mossy ground in front of a huge old maple tree. Leaning back she closed her eyes and listened to the sound of the tumbling creek, whispering and splashing over the rocks.

"Looka here, Terrell. I found me a little girl. Danged if it ain't Canty O'Neil from town. Now ain't she a sweet thing." Canty opened her eyes and Smith Ponder slapped a hand over her mouth. Canty yanked his hand away.

"You Ponder boys, leave me alone. This isn't your property." She scrambled to get up but Terrell joined his brother and grabbed her ankles. He jerked her down hard. Canty felt the sting of tears hit her eyes. "Stop it. My Pop is right behind me and I can tell you, he's got a rifle."

Terrell and Smith both snorted with laughter. They each spit, one slimy glob landing on Canty's pants leg. Canty willed herself not to scream. She felt vomit rise in her throat. Terrell ran his hand up between her legs. "Ohh, pretty. Can't wait to get into those jeans." He started tugging at her belt. "Smith, you see Pop anywhere?"

"Sure'n hell don't. Hey, give me a feel." Smith spider walked his fingers up Canty's other leg. His slobbering mouth grinning, he walked further, up across her chest and with a quick yank, ripped her blouse open, buttons flying. "Shit, girl don't even have titties yet. Gimme a kiss."

Canty could smell his liquored breath and felt her stomach roil. "You probably don't have anything between your legs yet, either. Stupid, ugly boys."

Smith grabbed her face between his calloused hands. "Yum, yum." He stuck his tongue in her mouth. Canty bit down, hard. Smith howled and backed off. Terrell smacked her hard across her cheek and she tumbled sideways and lay still.

"Terrell, time to show this little bitch somethin' about life." He began pulling down his jeans. Smith bellowed and followed suit. Canty froze on the ground hugging her knees to her chest. Her throat was so constricted she couldn't make a sound.

Canty heard a loud, raspy voice. "You scum, put your useless peckers back in your pants and move out!"

She managed to open her eyes to the sight of a tall, skinny woman. Long black hair streamed around her shoulders, coal black eyes gleamed from her scraggly face and her lips were painted scarlet. She had a rifle aimed at Terrell and Smith.

Terrell and Smith yanked their pants up. Terrell whined. "We's only kiddin', Queen. Why, we wouldn't hurt Canty

O'Neil. Not us. Don't you shoot us, don't you do it!" The two boys took off running and disappeared into the woods. Queen whistled a bullet in their direction.

Canty unlocked her body and sat up slowly. She was shaking so hard, she could hardly pull her blouse closed.

"So, you be Canty O'Neil," the raspy voice said. "Well, I'm Queen Ponder and those are my disgustin' twin brothers. They's only twelve but they look eighteen and got the brains of a chicken."

"Queen Ponder. Thanks." Canty bit her lip hard and fought back tears.

"Now, you come with me, little girl. We're goin' back to my house and I'm goin' to sew back your buttons. Pick 'em all up, now."

Queen sewed on Canty's buttons, she washed her face and gave her some sweet tea. "Canty, you git on home, now, straight home. Don't ever want to see you walkin' around up here alone again. You git too close, you're goin' to feel the heat of a bullet by your ear. You hear me?"

Canty never told Pop what had happened. She was afraid he'd go after the whole family with his shot-gun and none of them were worth spending a lifetime in jail. She had recurring nightmares of being chased through woods, her clothes being ripped from her body by unseen hands and laughing, faceless mouths with blackened teeth sucking on her face and chest and legs. A huge shotgun that grew long, black hair blasted the air around her and she awoke screaming. Pop would rush in to comfort her and hold her until she fell back to sleep.

He asked her over and over again about the bad dream, but Canty always said she couldn't remember. It was just a scary, bad dream.

Canty never went searching for the source of Secret Creek again. If Pop wanted a hike in the woods, she always thought of other areas of the mountains she wanted to explore. If she ever saw the Ponder's in town, she hurried away in another direction.

Two years after her encounter, while she was walking from a store on the square, she felt something hard hit her back and turned to see Terrell and Smith pointing at her and laughing. She picked up the rock they had thrown at her.

"Creeps!" she yelled. She stood her ground and stared at them. They laughed and scratched their crotches.

"Problem, Canty?" Tully Jones had loomed in back of her.

She remembered how relieved she was that her friend, now sixteen and a muscled 6'4", had arrived. "Why, no, Tully. Nothing I can't handle."

Tully strode over to Terrell and Smith, towering over them. "I'm saying this once. Don't ever fool with Canty O'Neil." He grabbed their shirt fronts and pulled them up close, each size fourteen boot standing hard on one foot of the brothers.

"Hell, Jones," Terrell sputtered, "we already checked her out. She ain't got nothin' we want. Get your big feet off us."

"Next time, the big feet might be on your ugly faces. Could make an improvement, but I doubt it." Tully stepped back and let go of them. They turned and ran, laughing.

Tully put big hands on her shoulders and forced eye-contact. "Canty, you're not stupid but you just did a stupid thing, baiting those boys."

"They threw a rock at me and they're creeps and I'll tell 'em again if they come near me."

Tully shook her gently. "You're lucky I was here today but I can't follow you around all day."

"Tully Jones," her chin was up and her gray eyes were flinty, "I don't want anyone following me around all day, even you."

Tully shook his head and pulled her into the drugstore for an ice-cream soda.

Canty smiled at that memory. It was the day I fell as madly in love as a twelve year old can be. Tully Jones was my hero and I adored him.

The Ponder boys rarely ever came to town after that and Canty was sure it was all because of Tully Jones. Her nightmares ended.

CHAPTER 5

The telephone was ringing as Canty unlocked the office door and rushed to pick it up.

"O'Neil Properties, Canty speaking. May I…"

"Canty, so glad you are there. It's Joanna. Burke McGuire just called and wants a reservation at someplace in Wynton, for tonight. I didn't dare tell him you hadn't replied yet. Why haven't you?"

Because I had to talk to Pop, she answered silently. "Joanna, we are all ready to go here. Sorry I didn't get back to you sooner."

The voice crackled with impatience. "Canty, Burke is in his car as I speak and will be there in about four hours. He started before the sun came up."

Early riser equals plus one for you, Burke McGuire. "It's okay, Joanna. Is he a B&B type or Best Western type?"

"Dear God, Canty. No frilly Bed & Breakfast place. I know how absolutely cute those mountain places can be. Best Western it is. That's it?"

"Well, the foundation is in for a Days Inn." Canty laughed.

"Dear God."

"God is not going to finish the Days Inn in time for choices, Joanna."

"Canty, I'm sorry. This whole thing is so big and that damn man just does things without giving anyone a chance to think."

"By the way, I hope the damn man knows he is dealing with Miss Canty O'Neil and not Mister as he put in his fax. Didn't you tell him?"

"Dear God."

"Joanna!"

"Sorry." Joanna's voice calmed back to her professional timbre. "I honestly didn't realize he thought you were Mister. Can't worry about that now and honestly, I don't know him well enough to know whether it would matter. It may be a surprise, but matter? I don't know."

Canty tucked a lock of hair behind her ear. "Now you are making me really nervous, Joanna."

"All this man knows is you are the best, so relax. It'll be fine. Just go ahead with the reservation. He has directions to your office, and maps of everything up there."

"How many nights? "

"Don't know that either. Just do one night for now."

"Okay Joanna. I'll take care of it. Thanks."

Would Burke McGuire be anxious to see the Ponder property right away? Well, she thought, the fact was, he'd have to drive it and walk it before we work out a proposal to purchase. That would take several days, aerials or no. I don't even know how much land he really needs and if it's all Ponder.

"What'd Clower say, Canty?" Willodene appeared at her office door with the morning blessing of two cups of steaming hot coffee.

Canty grinned at her friend, and gratefully accepted the coffee. "Pop said he's not sure the area is ready for such an undertaking. He says it all depends on how much this McGuire fella knows. We are not exactly the golf capital of the world. But, he likes the idea and the prospect of O'Neil

Properties making some money."

Willodene nodded. "Sounds like conservative Clower all right, but he does have a good point. After you take away all the initial excitement, what do you have? Have you ever played golf? Do you know anyone here who plays golf? Do you know anyone here who even talks about golf?"

"That's the scary part, but I cannot begin to think that a company like Hearn Guilford would build a golf course just because the land looks pretty and the mountains are here." She sat back and sipped Willy's brew. "God, Willy, I've heard of being able to stand a spoon in the cup but this stuff, you couldn't even get the spoon in the cup."

Willodene pursed her mouth. "Hey. That's my famous Willodene Espresso. I really like it. It's called Macadamia."

"It's different, I give you that much. When in the world did you get into Espresso? We've never had Espresso before. Don't tell me O'Neil Properties paid for you to buy this tar."

Willodene placed her cup carefully on Canty's desk, pinky finger extended, the cotton-candy nail polish winking, "Dearest Canty, if Wynton is going to be the new golf capital of the world, we need to acquire a taste for the finer things in life. You wouldn't want people coming here and thinkin' we're a classless group of mountain goats."

"Golf capital of the world. Right. Willodene Bert, you are a nut and I love you." Canty started laughing. "We haven't even collected a dime and you are headed for high society. Poor Dad, he doesn't know what he's in for."

"Clower O'Neil will love trying Espresso," she paused, lips pursed, eyes flashing at Canty over her granny-style reading glasses. "He may not like it but he'll try it. Too bad his close-minded daughter can't see beyond the freckles on her nose."

"Clower O'Neil will think you have lost your marbles for sure. I want to be there when you serve him this stuff." Canty threw her hands up in mock disgust. "But just for you, and only for you, I will sip a little more. I will try desperately to be more open-minded about the finer things in life. By the way, that Burke McGuire man is on his way as I speak. He should be arriving about lunch time."

"You are kiddin' me. Oh, Canty, how exciting. What do I need to do?"

"Quick, build me a Ritz-Carlton hotel."

"Mind if I call it the Best Western?" They both laughed.

CHAPTER 6

Burke McGuire gunned the Jaguar through another hairpin turn on Blood Mountain and grinned at the road-hugging feel, and superb handling of the car. The overhanging trees dappled the forest-green hood with sketches of leaves and dashes of sunlight.

I must have died and am on the road to the Pearlies, he thought. Now, this was how to find one's way to the Gates.

A semi-truck swooped around the turn up ahead, hugging the mountain.

"Whoa!" Burke yelled, down shifted into a more controlled speed, and gave the truck driver a big smile and a thumbs up as they met and passed. Burke waited for the back draft to push at the Jaguar, and lightly positioned his hands in a different place on the leather steering wheel.

"Didn't even budge you, baby. You slipped on through his wash like squeezing soap through a wet rubber glove. You are something else." Burke continued to coil and uncoil the Jaguar around the tight curves.

I do believe, he thought, that this machine likes the mountain roads a lot better than those boring Florida concrete paths. Here we have some roads to challenge a car like this. I will definitely enjoy working in these mountains.

As Burke turned a curve, he was forced to slow dramatically behind an RV as wide as the lane. He pulled his cellular phone from his pocket and quickly dialed.

"The Florida Connection, Joanna Stark."

"Joanna. Burke. Do I have a place to stay?"

Joanna swallowed. "Yes, Mr. McGuire but I told O'Neil Properties you would stop there first so they can meet with you and—"

"Joanna, just don't tell me I'm booked into one of those cutsie B&B's with the ruffled curtains and the pseudo early American maple furniture."

"No. I put the kibosh on that sort of accommodation."

"Nice, lady. One more favor before I land in Wynton?"

"Your wish is my command, sir."

"Please call O'Neil Properties and give them a fix on my location and ETA. I'm passing a sign that says Neal's Gap."

"Will do," she said.

Burke clicked off. The RV had mercifully pulled into a camp. He accelerated through the next turn, and glanced down into a deep gash in the mountains. "Can this little boy from the orange groves of central Florida build a golf course in the Blue Ridge Mountains, and I mean a serious golf course?"

Burke smiled as he remembered sneaking around the golf course that bordered his family's property...

"Hey, boy, whatcha doin?."

Twelve year old Burke McGuire made a quick decision not to run. The man coming at him had a twelve gauge shotgun tucked under his arm. "I'd like to unload some buckshot at your butt, son. Go ahead and run."

Burke held still. No sense giving him the target he wanted, he thought. "Didn't mean any harm, sir. I just live over there on the other side of the fence. I was just lookin' at the pretty grass and stuff."

The man loomed over him and laughed, showing yellow teeth and a plug of tobacco tucked back in his jaw. "This here's private property. You gotta belong to be walking around. Don't reckon any citrus grower's brat could be a member here. I'm bringing' you up to the office of the head professional here. He'll want to talk to your daddy about your trespassin'. You got a daddy, ain't ya?"

Burke just stared at the man.

"Come on, kid." The man grabbed at his arm.

"I'll come. No need to pull at me." Burke made his voice stay even. No way would he let this gross bully know his stomach was churning with dread. Talking to the head professional person would be easy. Talking to his daddy about getting caught trespassing would not.

Burke kept the man slightly in front of him as they walked, hoping he would catch any homicidal moves before they happened and could deflect the gun. They finally reached the club house and the man pushed him into the office labeled "Hearn Guilford, Head Professional."

The big man was all smiles. "Finally caught the little shit, boss."

A tanned, youthful face, framed in brown curly hair and touched with a half-smile met Burke's eyes. "Well now, young man, Hank's been tracking you for sometime now. Several of our members have reported seeing a boy hanging out along some of the fairways. Doing nothing. Very curious. You have a name?"

The head professional had a slow, easy way of speaking. Burke relaxed a little. "Yes, sir. Burke McGuire. I just like looking at the golf course. It's the prettiest piece of land I've ever seen. I just been trying to figure out what grasses you use and fertilizers and stuff."

"Well, I'll be damned." The head pro leaned back in his chair. "What do you make of that, Hank?"

"Believe our boy here is lyin'. Probably finding golf balls to sell back to the members. Had some other kids try that last summer. They paid the price, just like you will, son."

Burke pictured the man lining up the other kids and blowing them away with his twelve gauge. Then he'd spit a nasty stream of juice, and start laughing. Burke turned his back on Hank and lined up his face with the head professional.

"Sir, that's the truth. I told Mr. Hank, here," he managed a quick incline of his head toward the man, "I live right on the property next door. Me and my family's been growing oranges since way back and my uncle owns a feed and seed in town. See, I really like the land and I've been watching your men working out there to make it pretty. I have a few ideas about your land."

"Little snot mouth. Mr. Guilford, I say we call this boy's daddy and maybe the Sheriff."

"It's okay, Hank. I have to hear the rest of this story. Best ever." Hearn Guilford turned to Burke. "Son, I am most eager to hear your ideas."

Burke took a deep breath. "I've seen some bad drainage problems over on hole nine and I know how to fix them. I've also seen a problem on the fourth tee box. The rainy season's coming and that nice little pond you got by the tee box will flood for sure, and your tee box will be gone. I know how to solve that problem, too. Number eight is too hard. I've watched people tee off and almost all the time, they hit that creek. I mean you got to be perfect not to hit that creek. You could easily make a landing area on the tee side of that creek with very little diverting of the creek. Then, folks could have a choice to go for it or play safe. They'd like that. I can tell by what they're saying."

"Whoa, whoa, whoa!" Hearn Guilford stood up. "Son, you have been trespassing on private property for quite some time or you sure wouldn't know all you know about this golf course."

"Yes, sir. But, what do you think about my ideas?"

"Well, I'll be damned." Hearn sat down, a wide grin on his youthful face. "Burke McGuire, I am going to call off the dogs, meaning Hank, of course. As a matter of fact, I am going to tell Hank to let you walk around this place anytime, providing you don't bother anyone, and providing you don't get hit with any golf balls. Tell your daddy that I would like to have you work over here on the maintenance crew anytime he can turn you loose. How's that sound?"

"Great, sir."

"Now, I want to know about any other ideas you have, anytime. You just come on by. Hank, I can't thank you enough for catching up to this youngster. I see a great future here and I want to be part of it."

"If you say so, Mr. Guilford." Hank glowered at Burke. "Mind you don't start bringing any of your snot-nosed friends around with you. This is private property." He stroked the barrel of the twelve gauge.

"Yes sir, Mr. Hank. Thank you, Mr. Guilford." Burke walked stiffly from the room, feeling Hank's eyes on his butt. He closed the office door behind him and thanked God he hadn't wet his pants.

The rest of Burke's formative years were spent sweating in the orange groves and using every other spare moment sweating on the golf course. He learned about golf courses. He earned a full scholarship to Florida State University to study agronomy. Burke went on to study engineering, landscape architecture, and land planning. His insatiable desire to learn all he could about designing golf courses led him to continue pursuing in-depth knowledge of turf maintenance and irrigation. By the age of twenty-eight, Burke had designed and implemented two courses for his friend, Hearn Guilford, and was a respected member of the ASGCA, the American Society of Golf Course Architects. Hearn Guilford had chosen wisely.

Burke accelerated through a hairpin turn and groaned when he saw a tractor-trailer barely hauling up the next grade. A sign read Speed Zone Ahead One Mile. He eased the Jaguar to the yellow line, peering ahead as far as he could to spot any on-coming traffic. The road looked clear and flat as far as he could see, which was plenty far enough for the car to accelerate past the truck. The yellow line was broken.

"All right. Go!" Burke thrilled at the awesome acceleration of the Jaguar and gave a happy wave to the truck driver as he flashed by. He pulled back in just as the broken line became solid again. Another sign read Speed Zone Wynton City Limits, 40 mph. Parked just in front of the City Limits sign was a white sedan with a blue light bar on the roof. The blue light bar was flashing. The letters S-H-E-R-I-F-F were stenciled in big black blocks across the back of the trunk.

Burke automatically lifted his foot from the gas pedal. The speedometer needle slowly moved down from eight-five miles per hour to fifty-five miles per hour and as he passed the Sheriff's car, it said forty-five miles per hour. The siren whooped.

Damn and double damn. Burke pulled over and stopped a few yards in front of the Sheriff's car. "Stupid, stupid idiot." He whacked the steering wheel in frustration. The shadow of a man loomed by his side and then the man himself. Tall, rangy, and armed.

"Nice car you got there, boy."

"Thank you, Sheriff." Shit, the last person who ever called him "boy" was carrying a twelve gauge and looked mean as hell. This guy's carrying a large pistol and also looks mean as hell. Not good to be called "boy". Not good.

A low growl emitted from the tight lips of the man. "Where you headed?"

"Wynton, Sheriff."

"Well, you're about there. Got a place to stay?"

Burke couldn't read the man's eyes through his dark glasses.

"Yes."

"Now where would that be?" A slight smirk played across his face.

"Well, to be honest, I'm not sure. It's been arranged." Great, Burke. Very impressive.

"Well, then, may I ask why are you going to Wynton?"

"Buying property, Sheriff."

The smirk spread just a little. "Figures. Just happened to note your Florida license plates."

Yeah, right. "Guess you have a lot of folks coming up from Florida buying land?"

"We do. Would you by any chance be meeting with a real estate agent. Hard to find property up here without one." The smirk stayed.

"Yes, Sheriff, I have an agent to work with."

"Would you by any chance have a name for that real estate agent?" Smirk getting larger.

"Yes, Sheriff." Burke took his time shuffling through a folder of papers on the seat beside him. He pulled out a paper and read slowly down the lines. "I will be working with a Canty O'Neil of O'Neil Properties. Know the man?"

"Happen to."

Burke strained to look at the Sheriff's face. His reaction to the name sounded sarcastic.

"Now. In case you are wondering why I stopped you," the Sheriff held up his ticket pad and clicked on his ball point pen, "you were driving speeds well in excess of the limits for the last ten miles."

"I know and I'm sorry." How in hell could the sheriff know. Educated guess. Bullshit.

The Sheriff filled out the ticket. Burke handed him the obligatory license, insurance card, and car title upon request. He was relieved when the man returned them and handed him the ticket.

"How long will you be staying, boy?"

"Several days." Call him boy one more time and Burke knew he'd be in his jail for as long as the sheriff saw fit.

"Not a very informative fella, now are you? Several days should do. This is Monday. You can pay your fine at the court house Wednesday morning. You didn't contest, so I'm letting you off easy on the fine, this time. I suggest you lighten up on the gas. Car like that one is real easy to pick out. Anywhere."

The Sheriff finally turned and started walking to his car. "Say hello to Canty O'Neil for me," he said over his shoulder, the smirk turning to a big grin.

"You bet, Sheriff." Burke waited again until the Sheriff pulled in front of him and followed his car at a discreet distance into Wynton.

CHAPTER 7

"Canty, relax for heaven's sakes. Your pacing around like that is driving me crazy. Well, I'll be blessed. Would you look at that car?"

Canty halted her incessant motion and looked out of the front window. "Wow. Willodene, wow. What is it?"

"It's expensive, I can tell you that." Willodene stepped from her desk and the two women watched as a forest-green Jaguar convertible, top down, driven by a man with sandy red hair swirled past her office.

"Did you see the license plate, Willy?" Canty strained her eyes to follow the back of the car as it distanced itself from the building.

"Florida."

"You're kidding. You don't suppose it could be that Burke McGuire man, do you? It's one–thirty, just about the right time. Here it comes again around the square and it's pulling into our parking lot."

Willodene laughed out loud, startling Canty. "Girl, get away from the window. What will he think if the big boss lady is standing at the window hopping from one foot to another like a kid waiting for Christmas?"

"He's getting out of the car. It has to be him. He just looks like a Burke McGuire. Look at him."

"Canty."

"Right. I'll be in my office." Canty whirled away from the window and retreated. She checked her hair and applied fresh lipstick. She checked her desk and aligned papers. She checked that all the maps and pictures were straight. She checked out the window from her office.

She watched as the man she was sure was Burke McGuire walked to the office entrance, a large roll of papers tucked under one tanned, muscular arm. He took only a moment to glance at the office building and the surrounding locale. He looked square all over. He had a flat top. Unbelievable, a flat top. He had a square jaw. His shoulders were wide and square. His sport jacket hung ruler straight giving his body an even more square look. He looked determined.

Canty's intercom buzzed. "A Mr. Burke McGuire to see Mr. O'Neil." She could hear the laughter bubbling in Willodene's voice and hoped he wouldn't notice.

Canty wanted to say, "Send him in," but couldn't deny Willy the chance to see his face when he met Mr. O'Neil.

She walked into to the reception area as casually as her tense nerves would allow. "Mr. McGuire, how nice to meet you. I'm Canty O'Neil."

A quick flicker in his ice blue eyes betrayed his surprise but only for a second. He held out a large, square hand and smiled hugely. "Well, I'll be damned."

"Hopefully not." Canty put her hand in his and enjoyed his firm, warm grip.

They both turned at the sound of Willodene's unexpected whoop of laughter. "Sorry, Mr. McGuire, but we've both been waiting for your reaction to Mr. Canty O'Neil."

"Willy!" Canty tried to sound annoyed but laughed, instead.

Burke McGuire joined with a deep chuckle. "Okay, ladies, you got me. Never checked. Just assumed. Something

I thought I had learned never to do. Sorry about that. He focused on Canty. "I know one thing, you are a hell of a lot prettier than any Mr. Canty O'Neil could ever be."

Canty gave thanks that Burke McGuire had a sense of humor.

"Come on in my office, Mr. McGuire. I'd like to see what you have rolled up under your arm. Rumor has it, you've been flying around doing aerials. By the way, nice car you have there." Canty gestured toward the Jaguar as they entered her office.

"Right and right. Your Sheriff thought so too."

Canty whirled around and met his eyes. She was startled at the weakness and tingling that shot through her body. She took a deep breath and one step backwards. He grinned. Damn, he's quick.

"You don't mean you met my friend Sheriff Jones? Not surprised. We don't see many Jaguars in Wynton. Where'd you two meet?"

"About three miles out of town. I was moving a little faster than the sign said I should."

Damn it, Tully. He would have to be there. She smiled. "Speeding is one of the few crimes that keeps the Sheriff busy. I have been on the receiving end of a few of the Sheriff's handwritten notes myself. Welcome to Wynton."

"It's okay. I earned it. Now, let me show you what Hearn Guilford Golf Course Designs, Inc., has been doing." At the conference table, Burke began spreading out sheets of blueprints and aerial photography. He scanned the plat maps wall and placed a thick square finger directly on the area of the Ponder property. "That's it. Beautiful. How about the folks that own it? Ponder. Hope money talks to them. They have right at eight-hundred acres and two-hundred are in North Carolina which is perfect. We're going to need an airstrip and an inn that can get a liquor license. That's where North Carolina comes in."

"Burke, I agree about the beauty of that property and I want to hear more about the inn and so forth. But you need to know that dealing with the Ponders is going to be hell."

"I figured that when we were being shot at in the helicopter."

Canty felt her knees tremble. Shooting at the helicopter? "No! When did that happen?"

"Last week. Jimmy, my pilot, and I were so low, we probably looked like we were going to land. Something hit the 'copter and we got out of there fast. After we landed, Jimmy figured we were spotted as revenuers and there was no doubt in his mind the damage he discovered behind the cockpit was shotgun fire.

Canty shook her head. "That kind of harassment had to be the brothers. Burke, those brothers are vicious and sneaky. One of them is so retarded you could cry, except he will do anything the other two tell him. They are so twisted and sick it's scary. Money may talk to them but I'm not sure. It may take a while to pull that package together."

Well, Canty, you probably just blew the whole deal right out of town, she thought. "I believe the only way we can get through to the brothers is by way of Queen Ponder. She truly does rule those lunatics but she is getting old and caring less about their behavior."

"And?"

"So, I will see Queen. She's known me and my family all our lives, but don't get your hopes too high. She doesn't give a hoot about us or anyone, for that matter. She'll shoot at me as quick as anyone. She uses a rifle. In fact," Canty laughed, "I was target practice just yesterday."

Burke's voice hardened. The ice-blue eyes flashed on Canty's face. "Look, I want that property so bad I've been dreaming about it at night for months. I've done research up the ying-yang and have plans drawn and ready to be put in the dirt. You were recommended as the person who could close the land package. I may just have to ask this Queen for a dance myself."

"Wait just a minute, I am probably the only one who can reach that woman."

"Probably?" He just kept looking at her with the square-set jaw look of a tenacious bulldog.

"All right, definitely. I'm here to help you, and I can, but not if you don't believe in me. This is going to take a lot of patience. I'm so excited about the project and what it can do for this town that I fully intend to face the whole whacko clan of Ponder. But, I have to do it my way."

Burke McGuire smacked the table with his hand and hooted. "All right. I like your directness and your attitude. The patience part is going to be a son-of-a-bitch but I'll give it my best. I believe we can work together. What do you say?"

"I say, let's get on with it. Follow me to the Best Western and we'll check you in and get some lunch." Canty had to grin. This man could be so totally disarming. She had just determined the whole dream to be broken and in one second, he put it all back together.

"Got a better idea. Ride with me in my fancy 'mobile and show me around. Let me know where your friend Tully hides out so he won't catch us."

"I'd love to ride in your fancy 'mobile. I'll fill you in on the Ponder family and our Wynton as we go."

Burke McGuire was a very good listener. Canty showed

him the small town square and explained that the old brick courthouse was on the Historical Register. She talked about the new by-pass road that would relieve the increasing congestion. She pointed out the shops and told him the shop-keepers names and a brief history of their lives in Wynton. She directed him to the compound of grammar, middle and high schools built on a plateau overlooking Wynton and surrounded by breathtaking views of the mountains.

Burke grumbled, "Beats looking at orange groves. I could have dreamed bigger just looking at the damn scenery. I would have liked living in these mountains, lady."

Canty smiled at him, relieved at his obvious approval of Wynton.

She filled-in the history of Wynton, built by hard-working Scotch-Irish immigrants, over one-hundred years ago.

They stopped at the sandwich shop and took hoagies and lemonade to Wynton's only park. There were several old wooden picnic benches placed close to the tumbling Etowah River. Huge trees hung precariously on the banks, their lower branches dipping into the river.

"What do you think of Wynton so far?" Canty asked, purposely when he had a mouthful of sandwich.

He continued chewing, swallowed, and took a long drink of lemonade before replying. The man was imperturbable, she thought.

"How do the hard-working people of Wynton react to change, as in progress? How do the hardworking people of Wynton accept new concepts, new roads, and new people, excluding the Ponder family."

"Reluctantly, reluctantly, and also, reluctantly. However, if whatever it is makes sense, then with grace and good manners." Canty sighed. "The Ponder family live in their own bubble. I doubt their thinking about anything has changed since the first Ponder set foot in Wynton. They were originals then and haven't changed. They'll be tested for the first time."

Burke waited.

Canty explained that the Ponder family had arrived in the Wynton area nearly a hundred years ago. A large and reclusive family, they socialized only when one of them was supposed to find a spouse and propagate. They were very well off materially and so were able to bring outsiders into the family quite easily. At one time, there were seven blood Ponder families living on the property.

Burke chuckled. "That's a frightening thought. How many are there now?"

"Four, and I mean, four individuals. Queen and her three brothers, Terrell, Smith and Pauly."

"Good God, what in hell happened to them?"

Canty absently brushed a crumb from Burke's chin. He acted startled, then grinned. Canty looked away from him, annoyed at the flush she felt on her cheeks.

"Well, gradually, they drew a line around themselves that no one could or wanted to cross. The men were having no luck finding women who wanted to live in such isolation. Then, cousins married cousins…"

"Come on, you're not talking good old incest now are you?" Burke shook his head.

"You got it, smart man. So, over many years, the weak genes flourished. Lack of education and trust kept them from doctors or any kind of immunization from disease. Outsiders began to be afraid of associating with them and the results are evident. The family has literally died out. Queen holds together the last of the Ponders."

"Long live the Queen!"

Canty laughed. "Indeed. She has to be in her seventies, at least, and no one has laid eyes on her in years. All anyone knows is she sits up there in her little house on the mountain and watches TV. However, her major entertainment is firing her deer rifle at anyone she sees setting foot on Ponder land. Somewhere and somehow, she acquired a mynah bird who sits with her and yells at her targets. Fortunately, she is a crack shot so we figure she's just having fun scaring people away. If Queen wanted to make holes in people, she could and would."

"I believe I have met some of the Ponder relatives in Florida hanging out with the 'gators in the land of the trembling earth."

Canty smiled. "Well, then, perhaps you would be just the person to negotiate with the family."

"After you put the package together." He paused and she saw the sparkle in his blue eyes, "When can we do a little hiking? My feet are just burning to touch the hallowed Ponder land."

Canty pointed to the Jaguar. "You're kidding."

"I never said in that car. We'll go get your Jeep." He strode toward his car without a glance behind him.

Canty could barely stifle a giggle, acknowledging with amusement, the looks and waves of many of Wynton's finest who openly gawked at the Jaguar as it growled its way through town.

She asked Burke if he realized he and his car were a spectacle.

"Sure. Not many people have seen a Jaguar C-type. This is a 1953. Only fifty-four C-types were ever produced. The 1951 and this model each won at Lemans. Hell of a car."

Well, excuse me." Canty said with a laugh.

After they picked up her Jeep, Canty drove Burke around the circumference of the Ponder property and to a few view areas she knew were not visible from the house.

Burke brought his camera and clicked off shots incessantly. In between pictures, he pointed and asked questions. Canty did her best to answer but found his thoroughness and total absorption unnerving.

Dusk was settling in when Canty and Burke stopped at her office. He waved off her offer to show him the way to the motel.

"Just directions, please ma'am. Can't be far."

Canty watched him drive off. "Burke McGuire is the most self-contained, smart pain-in-the-butt I've ever met."

Pop and Toby were bursting with questions when she arrived home. "I'm afraid all I have are answers," she said and laughed. "But not the answers you are looking for right now, my dear men. Burke McGuire wore my brain out with questions, questions, questions."

"Mom," Toby demanded, "we've got to know if he's nice and what he looks like."

"He's square in build, crew cut sandy red hair, about six feet tall, and drives a 1953 forest green Jaguar C-Type convertible."

"Wow! A Jaguar. Oh, man." Toby's face lit up. "I gotta see it, Mom. Can he come over for dinner? Did you ask him to come?"

"You don't even know whether I think he's nice and you want him to come for dinner?" Canty tried to sound horrified. "Judge a man by his car, do you?"

"Well, Canty, I by darn want to hear your answer about nice." Pop rocked and grinned at Toby.

"You know, I really can't say much. I can't say he isn't nice. I just haven't ever met this personality, man or woman. I've been so busy answering his questions I really don't know anything about him except he was very intense and determined. I'll be out most of the day with him tomorrow and I expect I'll have a more complete report tomorrow night. Okay?"

Pop stopped rocking. He reached for Canty's hand. "This must be one interesting fella if Canty O'Neil hasn't gotten him figured out yet. There was only one other that you had blinders on about. Hope this isn't the same kind."

CHAPTER 8

Burke asked the desk clerk for directions to the nearest fast-food palace. The clerk looked at him crooked but mentioned the three in town. He chose the Taco Bell about a mile from the motel. Burke parked the Jaguar close to the entrance door and noted the flat-out stares and open-mouths of the locals. He nodded at several and went in, ordered take out, picked up the local newspaper, and nearly collided with the sheriff on his way out.

Coincidence? Oh, yeah. "Hello, Sheriff. Hope you had a good day."

"Why, it's Mr. MugWire." Tully dragged out the name derisively.

Lousy actor. Doesn't even show a modicum of feigned surprise.

"How're you doin' boy? Thought that was your car out front. You enjoy meeting Mr. O'Neil, did ya? Right purty fella, if I do say so." He bellowed and walked on in.

Burke contained the desire to put a fist in the man's gut. He strode to his car and noticed a piece of paper on his window. "Damn, this a follow up ticket?" He pulled the paper off the windshield. It had been stuck on with bubble gum. It said, "Go back to Florida" in barely discernible letters, printed with a red crayon.

On the way back to the motel, Burke toyed with the idea of showing it to the sheriff and then reconsidered. "Hell, no, he'd probably think it was funny. I'll save it to show to Mr. O'Neil."

Burke locked the Jaguar, unlocked it, fingered the bubble-gum paper in his pocket, changed his mind and locked it again. He went into his room and opened the curtains just wide enough so he could see the car. The outside light shone on it like a laser beam. He went back to the car, unlocked it, put the semi-automatic pistol that normally stayed in the glove compartment into his pocket, and locked the car again. Hearn Guilford had given him the pistol and insisted he learn to use it and carry it in the Jaguar.

"I've seen a hole-in-one cause less excitement than when that Jag comes snarling into view. Some people won't hesitate to send you to the big sand hazard in the sky if you don't have some protection. Someone will want that car."

Burke disagreed. If someone wanted the car that bad, they could have it, he thought. Shooting at someone over a car didn't make sense.

"For a smart man, sometimes you act dense, Burke. You drive down into swamps, you're always out in the middle of nowhere trying to cut a deal on land, you talk to people who haven't ever been taught about having a conscience and would knock you off just to take a joy ride. That car is a main draw, man. Get with it."

Burke was reluctant but took the time to go to a shooting range to learn to fire a handgun. He had handled shotguns and rifles all his life, a necessity around the orange groves for holding down the snake and vermin population and didn't take long to become a decent shot. The pistol stayed unloaded and locked in the glove compartment along with his permit to carry. He carried ammunition in a small metal container in his traveling golf bag.

Burke poured himself a Beefeaters on the rocks from a flask in his travel bag. He held up the scratched motel glass to the light and spoke directly to it. "No etched initials and very little ambiance surrounds us, but you will taste just fine." He sat back in the scratchy vinyl recliner.

Burke began pouring over the plans and aerials for the golf course. He had designed and redesigned every hole over and over again. Just how close to reality would he be when he could set foot on the land and really finalize the design? The mountain course was a totally new experience and he devoured the opportunity to use what he knew and learn more.

He found himself moving back to the window to check his car periodically. He checked his pants pocket for the note, wrapped around the gum. He wanted very much to show it to Canty O'Neil.

"That is one self-contained, smart pain of a woman," he said to no one, "and I need her to get this job done. Well, hell, you don't even know if she's married or what. That sheriff dog acts very personal about her. She saw me react to her little pull away in her office. I invaded her aura and she wasn't sure whether she liked it or not. Liked it, I think. Oh well, love 'em and leave 'em, the McGuire way. Never have found a woman I didn't want to leave after awhile. Dysfunctional family raises dysfunctional son in orange groves of middle Florida. See you in the morning, Canty O'Neil."

CHAPTER 9

When Canty arrived at the office the next morning, Burke had already spread renderings and photographs on the conference table. She watched as he precisely arranged his work, and was again struck by the sheer intensity of the man. She doubted if he even realized she was watching him.

"I see you already have some coffee, Burke. Willodene is very proud of her Macadamia Espresso. I think it's terrible. Want some Tums?"

He turned away from the table and welcomed her with a heart thumping smile. "I liked it fine." He held up a crumpled piece of paper. "By the way, this represents the second piece of paperwork I've received since coming to Wynton. This directive was attached to my windshield with chewing gum, which I've artfully covered by folding the paper. You are welcome to examine it and interpret its content. It won't stick to your fingers."

Canty extended her hand and he dropped the paper into her open palm. She opened the crumpled ball enough to read the scrawled, crayoned message.

"Burke, I'm sorry about this but any strange car in town with Florida license plates, receives similar notes. It's almost become a past-time for some folks. It's nothing serious."

Burke raised his eyebrows. "I believe it is."

"No." Canty dropped the note into her wastebasket.

"Wynton folks are not thrilled with what they call the Florida Intrusion, but you'll be surprised how accepting they will be once they get to know you."

"I'll be very surprised. However," he reached down into the basket and retrieved the wadded note, "I'd like to keep this as a souvenir. It goes well with my speeding ticket. Memories of Wynton."

No comment on that remark would be smart, she thought. Angry is an understatement. Canty took a deep breath and picked up one of the photographs. "Let's see what you have here."

"Canty, have you ever played golf?"

"No. Unless you count the times Toby, Pop, and I played the Putt Putt Course in town."

"Doesn't count. Toby your husband?"

"No, Toby is my son. He's ten."

Burke flinched ever so slightly. She bet those wheels were turning. Canty caught that he wanted to know more, but wouldn't ask. Was he being a gentleman or didn't he care enough?"

Burke flipped through his papers. "Are you ready for the big picture?"

"Absolutely."

"What I plan to put in the ground is one of the most exclusive golf clubs anywhere. The course will be spectacular, winding along the creek and up into the mountains. There will be no parallel fairways. There will be views to make you forget you just double bogeyed." He paused and looked at her, a lopsided grin on his lips, "I'll explain double bogey later. The golfer will have a caddie-driven cart and will be pampered for eighteen holes with instructional assistance, new balls when necessary, and clean clubs as you go. The cart itself will contain whatever food and drink the golfer orders plus a few incidentals like a comb and brush, sun block, god-forbid insect repellent, and mist fans for the unexplainable hot day. In other words, total luxury, which will extend to the most incredible clubhouse ever built. I'll go into more details on that building but it will contain approximately sixty-thousand square feet of total but completely tasteful extravagance. He stopped abruptly. "Questions?"

"I have no idea of what to ask. Sixty-thousand square feet for a club house? Good grief, that's huge. How many people will live there?"

"Only a few major employees. The clubhouse will contain the pro-shop, spas, indoor pools, squash courts, a bowling alley, a doubles tennis court, the latest in hi-tech exercise equipment plus physical trainers, hairdressers and barbers, boutiques and a restaurant and grille, plus a small but always staffed infirmary for minor mishaps. Anything paramount I haven't mentioned will be included as soon as I think of it. The ground surrounding the course will be platted for homes. All lots will be at least three to five acres, more if necessary. Total privacy for the homeowner."

"Wait. My mind is boggled. Your plans are so far out from what I expected. Who in the world will build homes there? I've worked with some very wealthy people from Florida and the mid-west but I'm not sure I've met anyone with the kind of money it'll take to live within a plan like this one." Canty watched Burke's expression for any signs of exasperation at her comments.

The lopsided grin evened and spread. "That, Canty, is where the marketing and research people with Hearn Guilford Golf Designs come in. They've already spent months contacting the many very wealthy people who already belong to Guilford communities and in fact, to any upper-level golf and country club. We're offering all the amenities those people are accustomed to with a few added perks and the response has been positive. Canty, these are the kind of people that most people never have a reason or opportunity to meet. These are the kind of people who live in a bubble of wealth beyond the Mr. & Mrs. Everyday's capability to fathom. These are the kind of people who demand this kind of luxury and relaxation. See up here," he ran his heavy square hand across the top of the plat that extended into North Carolina, "this is the site for the landing strip." A thick finger moved quickly down and to a ridge. "This is the site for the clubhouse, which, as you know, will have a phenomenal view. The golf course itself, will be all through this area. The homes will be placed so that they will be screened from view from the golf course but homeowners can choose a site with a view of the golf course and mountains."

He turned to Canty. "With me so far?"

"Yeah, I think so, but my head is spinning. It's very impressive. Hearn Guilford has already spent a lot of money, but there is a lot of work to be done. You don't even have the land, yet. How can you show the people of Wynton that this project will be beneficial to them? They may not be able to belong to your dream up there but you'll want their overall approval." Canty felt her lower lip tremble and grimaced to control it.

Burke stepped closer and once again she felt a rush of weakness down to her toes. "Canty, I know this whole thing is sudden to you but as we go along, you'll see that all those factors have been taken into account. Hearn Guilford has never disrupted the life-style of a community. He has added to its economic base and given people choices and opportunities. No forceful changes will take place in Wynton. This project will take close to three years to complete and that does not include the homes. We already know the perimeter road will be completed by then and be more than enough to satisfy our clientele. We'll have our own water system and waste plant. We'll even have a recycling center and a landfill." Burke strode over to a window looking out at the square. "I guarantee that this town can look exactly as it does today when our whole project is complete. I can also assure you that if Wynton changes to any great degree, it will be because the people will wake up and grab at opportunities they didn't know existed."

Canty leaned up against her desk and took a deep breath. She looked out her windows and she envisioned shopping malls, apartments, high rise office-buildings and gridlock. She wanted to scream at Burke McGuire to go away and leave Wynton alone.

She surprised herself. Her voice was even and soft. "I knew I didn't know exactly what to expect, but this," she pointed at the renderings and photographs, "is beyond anything I could have imagined. I do have a very special request before we go any further."

"And..."

Canty breathed deeply. He has the most annoying habit of keeping conversations at warp speed. No pause, just go. "And," she said, "in order to make me credible to Queen Ponder and the people of Wynton, I'm asking you to bring me facts, numbers and pictures on previous Guilford communities. The before and after of the areas. I would like to—"

"Canty, I knew you were smart. I'm beginning to find out just how smart. I'll send you a package containing the information you want and need as soon as I get back to Orlando. I'm sure the last three communities will cover it."

"Only if they are comparable to Wynton."

He shook his head. "Can't produce a mountain town for you, but you will see two small towns in Florida and one in Alabama. You'll also receive names and telephone numbers of the local government officials of these towns and I'll be happy to tell them you may be calling."

Oh, no you don't. "No, please don't call ahead for me."

Burke's ice-blue eyes narrowed. "Well, I'll be damned. You don't trust me."

Canty's skin prickled. "Mr. McGuire, I just heard of this project yesterday. You've had all the up-front time you needed to prepare. I've had none. One thing I'm sure of, you're sincere and serious about the project. I prefer to initiate any research on your prior golf course communities on my own. It's just the way I work."

Burke walked back to the conference table and began gathering his materials. "I do believe I have just received another 'go back to Florida,' message."

"No!"

Burke turned and smiled but the smile did not reflect in his eyes. "I'm getting too many mixed signals, here. You're either going to help package that land for Hearn Guilford or you're not. I need that answer. I am a buyer. I didn't come here to hire you to make any decisions for me on this project. I know it's important that you're informed and I'm doing my best to accomplish that. I'm glad you love your town and its people but you can't play God. Just get me the land." He dragged out the last sentence as though instructing a belligerent child.

Canty's joints felt like wet grass. "I'll be in touch with

Queen Ponder as soon as possible. I didn't mean to make you so angry." Damn, she had screwed this up so bad. "I guess I had my own ideas about what you might be doing and what you are doing is far from what I thought. I'm trying to re-group my thinking. I don't intend to play God. I'm still the right person to get that land pulled together for you."

Canty stepped to the topo map and drew an invisible line with her finger. "This is Ponder property. The section that falls into North Carolina may have some other families involved. I'm not sure about that, yet. I would like some idea of what Guilford is willing to pay."

"Here's what I want you to do for me." His tone was clipped and precise. "Contact those people. Tell them you have an interested purchaser and let them tell you if they will sell, and what they want for their land. The less you know about how much Guilford will pay right now, the better off you'll be."

"Thanks for the vote of confidence." Canty walked quickly back to her desk and faced Burke. "The first big thing I need to do is find out whether the land is held jointly by all the family members or if it has been parceled out. The Ponders won't tell me any of that nor whether they will sell, much less how much they would want for the land. They'll wait for an offer. As I speak, they probably have no clue as to what the land is worth but by the time Hearn Guilford makes an offer, they'll know."

His face was rock solid impassive. "You going to tell them?"

"First I need to know that O'Neil Properties is representing Hearn Guilford and that you won't be bringing another agent in to write the contract and negotiate the terms once I do all the leg work. Land here can go for one-thousand an acre up to ten thousand dollars an acre. A parcel that large will fall somewhere in the middle or slightly less. It wouldn't matter if I did tell them, they wouldn't trust anything I said anyway. The Ponders will make their own decisions and believe it, they will negotiate and they will be hard-headed."

Burke took one more look at the topography maps and picked up his brief case. "I'll be leaving first thing in the morning after I pay my speeding ticket. Keep me posted on your progress. As soon as you have something solid, I'll be back and we'll write that contract. Right now, I am going to take the charming Willodene for a ride in that fancy car. With your permission, of course. And then, I'll be headed back to Orlando."

"Go away and take Miss Espresso with you!"

A smile began, in his eyes this time.

★   ★   ★

Canty, Toby, Willodene and Pop surrounded Pop's special; country ham, creamed corn, hash browns, butter beans, and corn bread made in the big iron skillet.

"Pop, I tell you what's the truth." Toby talked through bites. You could have been a famous Southern chef. Wouldn't have been half as hard as the work you do now."

"Toby O'Neil, what have I told you about talking with your mouth full?" Canty gave him her most intimidating narrow-eyed look.

"You told me not to but now look," Toby kept chewing, "you're asking me a question and how can I answer with my mouth full?"

Pop grinned, "Don't forget who made the creamed corn.

No one can make creamed corn better than you, Willodene."

Willodene sparkled. She patted the back of Pop's hand with her small one, the nails now shining, cherry red. "Clower, I believe you to be the kindest man I've ever known."

Canty shook her head, and cleared her throat with a swallow of butter milk. "Now, I want you all to eat quietly while I paint you a picture, a big picture."

Canty related all the facts she had from Burke about the project. She also emphasized that she would be contacting several other completed Guilford projects for feedback. "I want to know how the towns affected have handled the impact of a large project like a Guilford Community. I want more information on the quality of the project, the good parts and the bad. All of it."

Pop stopped eating.

Canty continued. "I just can't picture this multi-million dollar thing up there on Ponder property," Canty continued. "I imagined a really nice middle-of-the-road, welcome-to-all golf course, and maybe some summer homes. I imagined lots of work and lots of opportunities for the people in Wynton, but I think this type of thing will absolutely exclude any areas they could participate in. Linda's Cut and Curl and Sally Jo's dress shop aren't what those people will be coming down the mountain to see. The thought of some of our people putting up money to open places that might get customers from up there doesn't make sense. Those people won't be living here all year round and there could be some sad failures in town. And, if the project falls flat, you know who would be hurt the most? Wynton would. We'd be a joke. I just don't see it."

"My turn, Canty." Pop reached for a second helping of ham, "I see your side and I'm surprised at the concept

Guilford is following. I don't know that I agree with your gloomy side, though. Doesn't matter." He carefully cut a piece of ham, and chewed. "However, I don't recall you telling me that this McGuire fella asked for your approval on what he's planning. Seems like all he wants is for you to pull that property together. As for me, I don't want you dealing with those Ponders anyway and it sounds like you're close to pulling out on dealing with Guilford. Okay with me. But, I believe this McGuire fella's going to get that land, with you or without you. You and Mr. McGuire ain't buttin' heads too hard now, are you?"

"Pop. This O'Neil won't miss an opportunity. Burke McGuire accused me of playing God, just like you are with your sideways psychology. I told him and I'm telling you, I am the only one who can deal with those Ponders and I intend to do just that."

"Just a minute, Canty," Willodene spoke up. "Clower, I've met Burke McGuire, in fact I've been out for a ride in that fancy Jaguar of his, how about that?"

Toby swallowed his food. "Miss Willodene, can you get me a ride? Can you?"

Willodene smiled a small smile. "I'll do my best, Toby boy. 'Course your momma may run him off before I get the chance."

"Willy! Who's side are you on?" Canty sputtered.

Willodene winked at Pop. He winked back. "Clower, I want you to know that Burke McGuire is a fine man. I believe he can outsmart anyone in this town, including the sneaky, nasty Ponders. I believe he goes straight after what he wants, and gets it." She chuckled. "I also believe Canty O'Neil and Burke McGuire are going to do some good business together if they don't crack their heads too often."

Canty bit off her words. "Willy, you've been listening outside my office."

Willodene took a deep breath and patted Clower's hand again. "Couldn't help but hear you two buttin' heads as Clower said. Probably anyone within fifty yards of the office heard that conversation. And, besides, Canty, I heard him say he liked my macadamia espresso just fine."

Canty groaned then burst out laughing.

Pop rared back and hooted. "Now, that's more like it. I can't see that this project will hurt this town. Wynton will work through it and do just fine. The O'Neil versus McGuire situation is another story, however. We'll just have to wait to see how it ends.

CHAPTER 10

Canty spent the next three days attempting to make contact with a Ponder – any Ponder. She tracked their haunts and spread the word that she wanted to speak to Queen, as soon as possible.

She received two packages from Burke McGuire. She was very impressed with the quality of the brochures, and detailed information of the promised reports.

Canty and Willodene dug in, and devised a very searching questionnaire to be answered by the various entities involved with Hearn Guilford Golf Designs, Inc. Canty then contacted listed recipients to ask for their cooperation when they received her mail. She still had no idea whether or not Burke had called ahead, but something told her he would respect the way she wanted to handle it. Not agree necessarily, but respect.

"You don't trust me." She remembered his voice sounded like he'd just eaten a razor blade.

Touchy, touchy, Mr. McGuire.

Canty smiled at Willodene as she entered her office. "Willy, I've been on this phone for an hour and I've talked to five of the contractors on Burke's list. Not one had anything but good words about the Hearn Guilford projects they worked on."

"Why am I not surprised?" Willodene replied.

"And, the best part is none of them said there were any major problems within the towns that were affected by the project. I had no one refuse to fill out the questionnaire."

"Why am I not surprised?" Willodene replied.

Canty laughed. "You are so bad, Willy." Good thing I love you. Now, I'm debating on whether or not to send a copy of the questionnaire to Burke or just let him see the information when we have it all together."

"Canty, honey, you want this man to trust you and know that you trust him. If any of those folks decide to send him a copy of your research and he doesn't even know…"

"Right, Willy." Canty smiled. "If there is one thing Mr. McGuire and I have to do is trust each other."

Willodene squinted and pointed a finger with a perfect, cherry red nail, "What are you grinning about, Canty O'Neil?"

"Not a very innocent question, Willodene Bert. Very thinly disguised, I might add. The answer to your question is, when I think of Burke McGuire, I smile, that's all."

Later that afternoon, Canty received a call from O'Dell Myers, the owner of the Shell station on the square. He had just seen the Ponder boys and relayed her message. Their reply was that they would talk to Queen about bringing a visitor. "They also got gas and didn't pay. Mean boogers."

Odds were a refusal, Canty thought. Please, please, please, give me a chance, Queen.

Burke called Canty the next morning. He spoke rapidly and gruffly and Canty held back a strong urge to snap back at him. He simply couldn't understand why she hadn't seen Queen Ponder yet.

"I told you how difficult it would be. I have made enormous progress just getting the boys to say they will relay the message. It will happen, Burke. I'll let you know as soon as I hear just when I can see her."

"Going to take the sheriff with you?"

"Why?"

His voice lightened a notch. "Because you are my procuring agent and I need to keep you bullet-hole free. Also, I received the copy of your questionnaire. How long did it take you to decide you better send me one?"

Twit! Canty could feel her stomach tighten unpleasantly. "No time at all. It's the professional way to conduct business. Mutual trust is very important if we are going to make this work."

Burke laughed. "Have you changed your thinking about me?"

"I never said I didn't trust you. You just misunderstood how I like to work."

"You're good, very good. I'll try to be more understanding. What's your schedule next week? I want to send my architect and decorator up there."

"But Burke, there's nothing to see."

"They'll know what to look for, don't worry. I want them to smell that clean mountain air, tour the town, get as close to the property as possible without being shot at, and in general soak up the atmosphere. It's invaluable time for them. What's a good day for you?"

Canty flipped through her calendar. "Any day but Wednesday, and if all of a sudden I get the chance to meet with Queen..."

"Don't worry. If you get that chance, do it. They'll be fine. I'll tell them to see you Tuesday. Ask my espresso woman to get them two-one night reservations at your four star, under my name. In the meantime, keep me posted."

"Right." They both hung up without saying goodbye.

"You're grinning again, Canty." Willodene startled Canty from her thoughts.

"You scared me, sneaking up on me like that. I'll grin anytime I please."

"I wasn't sneaking up on you, just bringing you some coffee like I always do." Willodene placed a steaming cup on Canty's desk. "I like that Burke McGuire. There's just something about him that's special. Oh, my God, here they come!"

Canty followed Willodene's pointed finger. Strolling up the walkway to the office door were three specters of men, heavily black-bearded with hair hanging to their shoulders They all walked bowlegged in turned-over cowboy boots. Their clothing looked as though it had been brutalized by a bear. The man on the right cradled a shotgun. The man on the left had to keep tugging the sleeve of the middle man to keep him in line. The middle man was at least a head taller and half-again as wide as the others. He kept turning around and wandering off.

Canty and Willodene stared, transfixed. Willodene was the first to snap back. "I'm goin' to lock the doors and call the sheriff."

"No!" Canty had to grab her arm to keep her from bolting toward the entrance door. "We'll be all right. We just haven't seen those Ponders for so long, we forgot how gross they look. I know how to deal with them and I have to talk to them."

"I'm not letting those scum into your office," Willodene hissed. "Talk to them out by the door."

By the time the Ponders reached the front entrance, Canty and Willodene had opened the door.

"Well, hello there. Good to see you, Terrell. You can leave the shotgun outside, thank you." Canty stretched her five-foot six inch frame to the limit. She still didn't feel very intimidating. "Smith, you're looking well. Could use a little trim on that beard. Pauly, come on in here where I can see you better. You need to get Queen to sew you a few buttons on that shirt."

"Shiiiit, Pauly don't need no buttons. He'd only swallow 'em. Probably choke hisself." Terrell stepped in, the shotgun still resting on his arm. Smith and Pauly followed and Pauly immediately started poking around Willodene's desk. Pauly hit a key on her computer and it beeped. He yelped and backed away.

"Pauly, Pauly, it's all right. Sit down here." Canty led Pauly to the nearest chair, loathing being so close to the man. The strong smell of urine on him made Canty's nose tingle and her eyes tear. She carefully looked at his hand. "It's all right, Pauly."

The big man slumped down in the chair, sobbing. Canty could hear Willodene gasping, "Oh, my God" and prayed Terrell and Smith didn't hear her.

"Terrell, I said you could leave the shotgun outside." Canty stuck her hands in her jeans pockets, hoping to stop the trembling.

"Hits broke. You can see that. Don't plan on shootin' anythin'." He grinned, his mouth slimy and close to toothless. Smith guffawed and scratched at his crotch. Pauly sat crunched up in the chair, looking at the opposite wall, tears drying on his bloated cheeks.

"Now that's good to know. I expect you are here to tell me when I can talk to Queen."

"Sort of. First she wants to know why you want to talk to her 'fore she gives you visiting time. Ain't that right, Smith?"

Smith quit scratching. "What's that?"

"Queen wants to know why Miss Canty here wants to talk at her. Ain't that right?" He shifted the shotgun to his left arm and punched Smith hard below his ribs. Smith stood gasping for breath. A gutteral sound came from Pauly. He pushed the chair off his hips and stumbled toward Terrell and Smith.

"Sit back down, Pauly!" Terrell yelled at him as though he were deaf. Pauly hauled his gross body back to the chair and again enveloped it with his haunches.

Canty and Willodene were wide-eyed. Terrell uttered a high-pitched screech that Canty hoped was laughter.

"Now, Canty O'Neil," Smith said, "why is it you want to talk to Queen? She needs to know." Smith had recovered enough to join Terrell in a stare down with Canty.

Canty turned and whispered to Willodene to go sit down behind her desk. "Look cool, Willy. Don't take your eyes off them. Just do it." Willodene walked around the hulk of Pauly, now rocking slowly in the chair and took her seat behind the desk. She narrowed her eyes and kept the Ponders in clear sight.

Canty spoke low. "Terrell Ponder, you are lying." She heard Willodene's sharp intake of breath. "My bet is you haven't even asked Queen if I can talk to her, yet. Will you ask her and will you let me know?"

Terrell switched the shotgun back to the crook in his right elbow. He and Smith stepped closer to Canty, so close she could smell their stinking, unwashed bodies. She swallowed hard and rooted her feet to the floor.

"Gentlemen," she heard Willodene cough and wanted to throttle her, "I have known you since I was a little girl. You love to scare, and cheat folks. I don't scare, so quit. All I need you to do is ask Queen when I can speak to her."

Terrell spoke, his foul breath making her eyes water. "Okay, I'll ask her. We's just havin' fun. You know us. We'll be back or get word. Come on, Pauly." They were nearly out the door when Terrell turned his head. "You know, we should jes get married. We need some of your blood in the Ponders, by God. How about it?"

"In your dreams, Terrell. In your dreams."

"Stupid bitch." He slammed the door behind them.

Canty turned and saw Willodene, looking like it would take a blow torch to thaw her out, her face a pale mask of disbelief.

"I don't believe what I just saw or heard, Canty O'Neil. Are you gutsy beyond belief or..."

"Or, a stupid bitch?"

Willodene laughed and began opening the windows. "Phew, phew."

★   ★   ★

Canty had just gotten home with Toby when Tully's car with Willodene riding beside him, pulled up to the front porch, spewing dust.

Tully took the three porch steps in a stride. "Canty O'Neil, we gotta talk. I mean, you and me, Pop, Willodene, and Toby."

"Tully, what is it?" Canty knew.

"Those Ponders were at your office carrying a shotgun. I told you not to fool with them if I'm not there. Willodene says they were scary as lightin' and Terrell asked you to marry him. God damn, Canty. Stay away from those animals!"

"Tully, you stop right there. I wanted to see them. I need them to get me a time to talk to Queen. They were nasty but they never threatened us. Look, I promise when they let me know about seeing Queen, I'll tell you. I won't go without you."

Tully's broad shoulders slumped and he sat down hard

in a porch rocker.

"Willodene," Canty turned to her friend, "I'm not happy with you."

Willodene pursed her mouth. "Canty, I'll not apologize for telling. Sheriff needs to know these things."

Toby came out of the house, slapping a baseball into his glove and tossed another glove into Tully's lap. "Catch?"

Tully pulled his long body out of the rocker. "You got it, Toby." He stared down at Canty for a brief second and mouthed, "Promise?" She nodded.

Pop came out with a tray of fruit jars packed with ice, and a tall pitcher of sweet tea. Willodene took the tray from him and flashed him a big smile. "I'll handle this for you, Clower. You just sit. Man works as hard as you do, needs some rockin' time."

"Willodene Bert, you make a man feel mighty good. Hope you don't ever get as bossy and headstrong as my daughter. Don't know what kind of man will want to deal with her mind on a permanent-type basis."

Willodene sat down in the chair next to Pop and they began a quiet rocking together. "I expect there's one."

"You two stop talking about me like I wasn't here," Canty huffed. She stepped off the porch to join Toby and Tully. "By the way..." she turned and saw Pop reach out and take Willodene's hand. They were both grinning and rocking like two little kids, she thought. Better yet, her body flooded with warm tingles, like lovers.

CHAPTER 11

A white Mercedes sedan pulled up to the office of O'Neil Properties and out stepped a shimmering goddess in white, followed closely by a short, small-boned man dressed in sagging khakis.

Canty listened to the voices outside her door.

"Hello. My name is Diamond, and my friend here, is Max. Is Canty O'Neil here?" The woman calling herself Diamond stood six feet tall in her three inch spike-heeled silver sandals. She had a halo of platinum hair, artfully locked into a wind-blown look. She had huge dark brown eyes fringed with long black lashes and a wide scarlet mouth that surrounded gleaming white teeth. Her white silk pantsuit was studded with gold. She was the most startlingly beautiful woman Willodene Bert had ever laid eyes on.

"Yes," Willodene found herself whispering, "I'll get her. Would you like some coffee, you and your friend?"

"How lovely." Diamond flashed a perfectly manicured hand, dressed with two large diamond rings. "Max, darling. Coffee?"

"Quite definitely, Diamond, dear."

Canty strode out into the small reception area. "I'm Canty O'Neil and you must be the architect and decorator from Hearn Guilford. Hello, and welcome to Wynton."

Canty had never met a more electrifying looking person in her life. Diamond filled the room with light. Canty expected white hot electric sparks to fly from her fingers. Max barely reached Diamond's shoulder. His milky blue eyes peered through smeary glasses. He had dull brown hair just long enough to be pulled back into a stubby pony tail and his pale hands constantly tapped on his thighs. Canty waved them into the two small chairs opposite her desk.

"Max, darling, stop that incessant twitching." Diamond's eyes riveted on the man. He ceased all movement. "You must understand, Canty darling, Max is the most brilliant of all architects and is totally uncomfortable anywhere but at the drawing board or touring one of his creations. But he is a darling. He really is."

"Does he speak?" Canty asked.

Max burst out laughing. Canty was relieved. She smiled at him and he returned her look with a twisty grin that she liked. He removed his smeary glasses and began polishing the lenses with a bright blue handkerchief that appeared in his hand like a magic trick.

Canty briefly explained that she hadn't known exactly what time they were to arrive and apologized for not greeting them at the door. Willodene entered with her tray of coffee and stood while they took their first sip. Diamond's cup rim was immediately ornamented with scarlet. Max looked up at Willodene and she, too, received the twisty grin.

"Canty, darling, we had a marvelous stay in Atlanta last night. Your Ritz-Carlton is lovely. I know Burke was so busy he didn't give you a time and I apologize to you for not calling ahead this morning. Max and I spent several hours last night pouring over the photographs and plans Burke gave us, for the one-millionth time, I might add."

Diamond's pitch-perfect voice melted around Canty's ears. Her gestures were expansive and emphatic but controlled.

"Max has already begun work on the clubhouse design. We are trying to coordinate our thinking on the decor so it will all fit the aura of the club as well as the new community."

Canty was totally fascinated. "Diamond. Is that your real name?"

Diamond uncrossed her long legs and leaned slightly toward Canty. "I earned the name when I went into my own decorating and design business, darling." She almost whispered. "A diamond is hard, brilliant, and worth a lot of money." She sat back, a very slight smile flickering across her lips.

"Don't ever doubt that Diamond is all that, plus the woman was born with an overactive creative gene." Max spoke in a total monotone. "She is unparalleled in her field."

"Do you have a schedule for us, darling? We need to see the town and the property involved. Pictures are wonderful but Max and I need an up-front and personal look at this stage. We need to mingle with the local people just a little. I snatch ideas from the merest contact with the culture of an area."

Canty would drive them as close to the actual site as possible but could not promise they would set foot on the property. As for seeing the town and meeting some of the local people, that would be easy.

Diamond's big brown eyes widened. "Burke warned us. He said something about the property owner being quick on the trigger and actually having been shot at while doing aerial photography. I can't believe that lifestyle still exists." Diamond sighed. "Well, Max and I have no intention of being shot at, do we darling? We will check into our suites at your motel and then be off for a tour. Is that suitable?"

"Absolutely. I think the best thing to do would be to follow me to the motel. I would rather we take our little tour in my Jeep. You may want to change into something more casual."

Diamond narrowed her eyes. "Canty, darling, on you, jeans and boots are divine. My body needs sheathing in only the finest of flattering fabrics and I would feel terribly awkward in denim. I may put on my white leather boots, though. We'll see."

Canty strode through the office in the wake of Diamond and Max. Willodene stared until Canty glared at her.

"Oh, Canty. Clower has a big delivery late this afternoon. Can you pick up Toby from practice? I told him not to worry. One of us would be there."

Canty thought a moment and decided it would be fun to bring Diamond and Max to the practice field. She wanted some local color, she'd get local color. Besides, she wanted to see Toby's face when he laid eyes on Diamond.

"Okay, folks. Let's check into your suites." She led the way out of the office.

Canty directed Diamond and Max to the front desk of the Best Western. It was all she could do not to burst into laughter at the astonished look of the desk clerk.

"Dear boy, reservations for Diamond and Max, please." Diamond turned on her bright-lights super-dazzle smile.

Canty was willing to bet the clerk would wet his pants momentarily. He flipped through several pages and began to frown.

Canty spoke up, "Look under Burke McGuire."

The clerk nodded, and picked two keys from the room key board. He put the keys in front of Diamond and Max and Canty saw him put his shaking hands quickly into his pockets. The laughter in her body was about to bubble out.

Canty waited in the Jeep. Diamond appeared from her

room, smiling, now wearing spike heeled white patent boots. Canty groaned. Max appeared, still in his rumpled shirt and slacks and scruffy moccasins.

She had never seen two such polar opposites in her life. How in the world they gee-hawed at all was astounding, but her impression was that they were good friends, as well as business associates. Whatever makes the world go round, she mused.

Diamond ensconced herself in the seat beside Canty wreathed in a cloud of musky perfume. Max wordlessly hoisted himself into the back seat. Canty sneezed. She quickly cracked her window and prayed she would not have an embarrassing fit.

"Rooms all right?" she asked.

"Perfectly charming, darling," Diamond replied.

"Perfectly," Max mumbled.

"Good. Not only is it the best motel we have, it is the only motel we have which of course..."

Max leaned forward and literally blew into her ear. "Makes it the best."

Canty jerked in surprise.

"Don't mind Max, Canty darling. He was born with a very unusual sense of humor and utterly atrocious timing. Only his illustrious talent as an architect saves him from my wrath. You, of course, do not have to put up with him as I do, so feel free to take him down a notch anytime. As for your problem with my perfume, I'm sorry."

Deciding silence was golden, Canty drove to the highest point possible for a view without setting a tire on the Ponder property. They all got out and surveyed the valley.

Max was the first to speak. "Burke McGuire, you have done it again only better. I'll be damned if this isn't the most magnificent sight I've ever had the good fortune to see." He gestured toward the highest ridge. "There, just as I thought. The clubhouse. It will site perfectly. Members will be able to see for miles plus nearly half of the golf holes. Do you know anything about golf, Canty?"

His question blind-sided her. "Excuse me, oh, no, I really don't."

"Some advice then." Max looked directly into her eyes. "Learn all you can as fast as you can. Burke has a hell of a time communicating with people who don't understand golf. He eats and breaths the game and golf courses. He is considered one of the foremost golf historians in the world. A word to the wise, Canty."

Canty was immobilized. The quiet Max was suddenly the in-charge Max telling her how to deal with Burke McGuire.

"Max, I don't feel that my knowledge or lack of knowledge about golf has anything to do with getting this property sold to Hearn Guilford. You know architecture, Diamond knows design, Burke knows golf course design, and I know the land. It all starts right here and no one moves until the land belongs to Hearn Guilford Golf Designs, Inc." Canty returned his direct gaze and held his eyes until he looked away.

"Bravo, Canty! That's putting old Max back on his own track. He also has a dictatorial streak in him among his other bad habits. I see I do not have to offer any further advice on Max's personality. He is so lucky to be such a brilliant architect." This time Canty was sure she saw sparks flying all around Diamond.

"Let's continue this tour, people. I want you to see something of Wynton before dark." Canty headed to the Jeep.

Max stood rooted, gazing out into the valley and the surrounding mountains. He had pulled a small pad of paper and stub of a pencil from a pocket. He looked, jotted notes, and looked some more.

"Max, darling," Diamond spoke gently to him as though he was a child, "we really must go."

Max broke his deep concentration and smiled his twisty grin at Diamond and Canty. "Ready," he uttered, and walked quickly toward the Jeep.

They took their places and Canty started the engine. Diamond gasped. Canty glanced around and saw the Ponders approaching the Jeep. Terrell cradled the shotgun and Canty set her jaw, cursed under her breath, and waited.

"Why, looka here," Terrell sputtered, "thought you was hangin' out with a angel. Look at that woman, now just look Smith and Pauly. Next to you, Canty O'Neil, that's the pee-darndest purtiest sight I ever have seen."

Pauly came close to the Jeep, grinning and drool-ing, and reached a massive, thick hand out to touch Diamond's sleeve.

"Get your damn hand off me." Diamond ordered. Pauly yelped and jumped back.

"Now, that ain't nice talkin' to Pauly like that," Smith flared, " you bein' a stranger and all. Canty, who's this whore anyway? And, who's that in the back seat? Why he looks good enough to eat." Smith broke out into a gutteral laugh.

Diamond stiffened.

"Why if it isn't the Ponder boys," Canty lilted. "These are good friends of mine, boys. I just had to show them how pretty it is here in the mountains. Do you have any news for me about talking to Queen?"

"That's why we been trackin' your Jeep." Terrell came around to the driver's side and stuck his face up close to

Canty's. She glared back but did not move. "Queen said she'd see ya tomorrow. She'll see ya anytime before her TV crap comes on. You ever seen any of that shit she watches?"

"Not sure but I thank you all very much. Please tell Queen thank you and I'll be there about ten in the morning."

Smith leered. "You comin' alone?"

"No, I'm not comin' alone. Sheriff will be with me."

The three began flapping their arms like chicken wings. They jigged around the Jeep yelling "bawk, bawk, bawk."

Canty put the Jeep in gear and spun the tires sending dirt flying. "See ya, boys" she waved a hand and kept going.

"Jeezus, what in hell was that? Jeezus." Canty couldn't tell whether Max was asking her or talking to himself.

"That, my friends, is what I am dealing with in order to get the most beautiful land you have ever seen into the hands of Burke McGuire and Hearn Guilford Golf Designs, Inc. That is what I am dealing with so that you two can build and decorate and—"

"Say no more, Canty." Diamond spoke up her voice strained.

Diamond and Max spoke very little on the drive back to town which gave Canty room to point out landmarks of the area. "We have a lot of wonderful Cherokee history in this area. Over there," she gestured, "were the original trails and campgrounds of the Cherokee when the white man arrived. We sure made a mess of things, didn't we?"

Canty took the odd pair to many of the shops and businesses in Wynton. It was difficult to introduce Diamond. The men swallowed and postured, the women shied. Max commanded no attention at all. They took a short tour of the old Court House, which had dominated the square for nearly one-hundred years. Canty told them how proud the towns-people were of the old red brick building that was now on the Historical Register. An eighteen-foot tall palladian window, original wavy glass in tact, pulled in the outdoors and lit up the main courtroom, benches and judge's dais. Their feet clattered on the gleaming heart pine floors and turned the heads of the workmen painting the bead board walls.

"Hey there, Canty. Good to see ya, gal," greetings echoed from the tall ladders, reaching nearly to the top of the twenty-five foot ceiling. Appreciative whistles floated down around them. "Who're your friends?"

Canty laughed. "Better keep working guys. The tax payers of Wynton will be after you if they catch you socializing on the job."

Canty then offered to show them urban Wynton, which drew a chuckle from both. She drove the Jeep slowly through several streets off the square. The brick and stone homes echoed the old shot-gun style architecture of the forties. Deep porches graced the front elevations and carefully tended gardens were alive with spring flowers.

"Canty, these homes are the most perfect examples of the Craftsman style of architecture I've ever seen. Do you realize the jewels you have here in Wynton? Look at those windows, look at the porches and columns…"

Max became so animated he was ricocheting back and forth across the back seat. Canty expected he'd leap out of the Jeep and start running up to touch the houses. My God, she thought, Toby never acted so wired when he was two. This man is nuts.

"Canty, darling, who lives here?" Diamond talked through Max's staccato comments. "Please don't tell me Ponder-like things inhabit these delightful little homes."

Canty prickled. "No, Diamond. This whole urban area is filled with hard-working, and for the most part well-educated people. The homes were constructed when the paper mill was the dominant life support of Wynton. Most of the residents here are descendants of those people. Let's go take a look at our mansions."

Ignoring a protesting yelp from Max, Canty drove back through the square and slowly passed by several large antebellum and Victorian homes. Max, now seeing new architectural delights once again became so excited he bordered on irritating. Even Diamond began talking over Max about period decor and how exciting it was to research and authenticate a project.

Well, I can say one thing about these two, Canty thought, they do love what they do.

"Canty, darling, I don't quite understand something." Diamond's voice was heavy with disappointment. "All these mansions have signs. Antiques, law offices, Boutiques and Hardware. These are all shops. What happened to all the rich people in town?"

Canty heard genuine concern in Diamond's voice.

"I agree. Let me tell you a little more of our history. The government decided that the Wynton area of the Blue Ridge mountains would be designated a national forest, and a watershed lake and dam would be installed to compensate for the growing needs of the exploding population south of here. The big paper mill had to relocate. The government took a lot of land from my grandfather, too, although most of it was straight up and down. Most of the people of Wynton work in towns nearby that still have some industry or are growth oriented like Gainesville. My father started a small lumber mill when I was just a little girl and it not only survived the downturn in Wynton, but has grown. Pop is a very smart business man, and among his many talents, can build a house as close to square as you'll ever find."

"The O'Neil name means a lot here, right?" Diamond questioned. "Sounds like your father helped save this town from total annihilation."

Canty laughed. "Pretty close, but as I said, most of these people work elsewhere, but will never move. At least not my current generation. After that, I figure we're going to need more exciting opportunities to hold the young people here. If we can capture a serious resort—"

"Resort!" Max yelled. Canty swerved the Jeep in reaction to the sudden outburst. "Guilford Golf Designs, Inc. doesn't do resorts for God's sake. They do golf clubs. No game rooms, kiddy ponds and water slides for God's sake. We are talking golf clubs, as in for the rich and famous and dedicated-to-the-game, people."

"Max, quit being so damned anal." Diamond kept her voice low. "Canty, you must excuse the man. He thinks the world should all be tuned in to his brain, God forbid."

Canty let the latest Max and Diamond altercation slide. "Here's Toby's school." She pulled the Jeep into the parking lot as close to the ball field as allowed.

Max spoke quietly again. "Who, may I ask, is Toby?"

"My son. He's ten, he's smart, he's handsome, and a great ballplayer." Canty glanced at her watch. "Practice is nearly over. Thought you might like to add more atmosphere to your future plans."

"Ma, Ma!" Toby was hurtling toward the Jeep. "I made a double play!"

Canty watched as her son came close and saw Diamond. He slowed to an amble, staring at Diamond all the while. She nearly burst out laughing at the surprised and confused look on his face.

Diamond reached out her window. "Hello, Toby, I'm

Diamond. It's nice to meet you. Your mother has been driving us all around the territory of Wynton, today. You sure are one good-looking dude."

Toby's gaze slid toward Canty. She nodded slightly.

"How do you do, ma'am." He put his grimy hand in Diamond's. The hard, sophisticate look melted away.

"Oh, my," Diamond whispered, "aren't you something? I'd like to hear more about your double play, Toby." The huge brown eyes brimmed and dried. It was so quick, Canty wondered if she imagined it.

"Hi, son." Max stuck out his hand. "Your mother is a really nice lady, you know. Hope we'll see you play a little ball one day. I used to."

"Oh, Max." Diamond, the decorator, the business woman was back. "The boy doesn't want to hear what you used to do. Canty, dear, can we all find a Dairy Queen or something? I'll bet Toby would love a cone."

Toby was transfixed. He barely acknowledged Max because he could not tear his gaze away from Diamond. Canty would pay millions to catch what was going on in his brain right now.

"Hop in, Toby. There's a DQ on the way back to the motel. Toby, sit in back with Max." Toby came out of his trance, and scooted into the back. Canty watched his dear face in the rear view mirror. He was grinning and staring at the back of Diamond's head.

I believe my son has fallen in love, she thought, or he is just plain not believing his eyes. Or both. She giggled inside.

Toby and Max ordered cones for all and Diamond delivered each with a flourish. She slid closer to Canty and looked directly into her eyes, and Canty saw sadness that made her shiver. The smiling, bright red lips quivered. "You are so lucky, Canty O'Neil. What a beautiful young boy."

Canty took her cone, her heart swelling. "I know."

★   ★   ★

"Pop, her name is Diamond! She's as tall as you. She has white hair that puffs around her like there was a storm going on. She called me Toby."

"That's your name, isn't it, son?"

"Pop," Toby never took a breath, "you gotta see this Diamond. She had all white clothes on that were sparkly. Even her boots were shiny and slick looking. Her bracelets and stuff made clinkety noises like little bells ringing. And Pop, she smelled good. I mean really good."

Canty grabbed her water glass and took a big swallow before she choked on her food.

Pop chewed his dinner slowly. He finally stopped and put down his knife and fork "Sounds to me like you saw some kind of apparition, Toby."

"No, she's real, Pop. Ask Mom. Maybe she can come to dinner."

"Toby," Canty interrupted, "Diamond and Max will be flying back to Florida tomorrow. I'm sure we'll have a chance to invite her and Max for dinner sometime."

"I'll be really looking forward to meeting this Diamond, Toby." Pop grinned at the boy, then winked at Canty. "She sounds right interesting."

"Pop, Diamond is the decorator for Hearn Guilford Golf Designs, Inc., and the barely acknowledged Max is the architect. We had quite an afternoon together, including a quick meeting with the Ponder boys. I'm going to be seeing

Queen tomorrow morning."

Pop's grin dissolved. "Not alone."

"No. I've already contacted Tully. He'll pick me up at my office. I've also informed the Ponder boys that I'd be bringing Tully with me."

Pop reached to grasp Canty's nearest hand. His eyes were cold and his jaw was clenched. His face was furrowed with concern.

"Pop, it'll be all right. They won't fool with Tully."

"I can't abide those low scum creatures. They are sick, and totally untrustworthy." Pop's voice was a hoarse whisper. "They are animals, dangerous as hell, and you know it."

"Now, Pop, you said yourself that it wasn't going to be easy, but worth a shot." Canty took a deep breath. "No, I can read your mind, you can't come. It's going to be touchy enough bringing Tully. One more man and they might feel ganged up on. Then, God knows, I would be in trouble."

"Mom." A tremble in Toby's voice made Canty angry at herself for saying anything about danger with Toby within earshot.

"Gentlemen," she stood, "I declare this dinner over. We shall proceed to clear the table and wash the dishes."

"Pop, did I tell you about my double play, today? I hope Diamond saw it. Do you think she did, Mom?"

"We'll just have to ask her. Now quit stalling. You can tell Pop about your double play while you're washing dishes."

Canty watched as her son and father piled dishes and headed for the kitchen. Pop mouthed "I'm sorry" over his shoulder, and she blew him a kiss.

CHAPTER 12

"Burke, you are going to be lucky if Guilford ever gets its hands on that property. Max and I had a horrifying exposure to the Ponder boys and darling, they are murderous and disgusting. I wouldn't go near that property again, unless I knew those grotesque creatures were far, far away. As in Siberia." Diamond put a long black cigarette in her ivory holder and waited for Burke to light it. He did so, immediately.

Burke watched as she pulled on the cigarette holder and then blew out smoke in a thin, explosive line. Diamond had quit smoking six months ago. Diamond was not a woman easily intimidated. He glanced at Max. The man squirmed in his chair and would not meet his eyes.

The three sat in Burke's office and Burke was close to detonating with impatience at the total lack of information coming his way.

"What in hell happened up there? Was Canty O'Neil with you when you met the Ponders?"

"Darling Burke, Canty O'Neil saved our lives!" Diamond opened her large brown eyes wider and wider.

Max chimed in, his voice shrill. "She's right, Burke. I know what those reptiles wanted with me, too. They are scary as hell."

Burke snapped the pencil in his hand into several

pieces. "Will you please answer my question? What happened for God's sake?"

Diamond sat up, ram-rod straight, while Max puddled down further in his chair. Diamond cleared her throat and recrossed her elegant legs. Finally, she explained the brief encounter with the Ponders, as Max nodded and constantly wiped his palms along his trouser legs. Burke felt the apprehension tighten his own shoulders, their fear was palpable.

He tried to break the spell. "Okay. Other than all that, what did you think of Wynton and Canty O'Neil?"

Diamond removed the cigarette from her holder and tamped it out in the crystal ashtray beside her chair. "Canty O'Neil was unquestionably fabulous, refreshingly beautiful, and very smart. After meeting the Ponders, I assure you, you will absolutely need every ounce of that woman's knowledge to pull this off."

Max nodded and picked at invisible lint on his shirt.

"What did you think of what you saw? I'm not learning anything from you two. Did the Ponder boys have you take an oath of silence?"

Max squirmed more, and finally spoke. "Okay, okay, Burke. It's just that it takes awhile to get over the shock of those animals, not exactly what we're used to dealing with." Max sat back in his chair. "Burke that property is everything you thought, if anything you were conservative."

"And..."

"And, Burke McGuire," Diamond uncrossed her silk-sheathed legs, and put a hand on Max's arm. The brown eyes stared at Burke. "You are headed for a shit-load of trouble up there. I felt it, I smelled it, and I feel like I'm wearing it."

Max nodded and placed his hand over hers.

Diamond added, "And, you had better be checking with

Canty O'Neil, soon. Canty and the Sheriff will see Queen Ponder today. I'm sure they've already been there. I wouldn't put money on their chances of getting back."

Burke watched the pair leave his office, and hit the intercom button to Hearn Guilford's office. "Hearn, before you make any decisions, I want you to see the property."

Hearn laughed. "Burke, did Diamond and Max tell you they talked to me first?"

"No, but let's say I know how they think, and can pretty much predict their reactions."

Hearn's voice changed to firm. "Don't like what I heard. I don't want them going back there and I may put a period on the whole project. That means you, Burke."

Burke clenched his jaw. "Hearn, no decisions until you see the property." The silence on the other side of the wire was not reassuring. "I'm planning to get back up there in a few days. Would tomorrow be good?"

"Okay."

Burke clicked off the intercom before Hearn could say more.

His next call was to Jimmy, who as expected, objected to the request. "Not your decision, old buddy. If you have a problem, talk to Hearn Guilford. See you in the morning." Burke clicked off the phone before Jimmy could say more.

★   ★   ★

Hearn Guilford sat next to Jimmy in the co-pilot seat of the twin-engine Beechcraft, his knees up close to his chin, in an attempt to accommodate his lanky frame. Burke McGuire sat in the passenger seat behind Jimmy.

I wish I knew some kind of telekinetic magic, Burke thought. He stared hard at the back of Hearn Guilford's head.

I could beam my thoughts into that curly-headed man's brain. The man hasn't lost a hair but had a few turn gray. He brushed a hand over his red crew cut. Me next, he thought.

The plane passed over a high ridge, and then the valley opened up beneath. Burke instructed Jimmy to circle, then criss-cross the valley. Sweat popped out on the back of Jimmy's neck. He gave his friend a thump on the shoulder. "Relax, pardner. We're not even close to being as low as we were in the 'copter. I won't ask you to drop down any further.

"Be the first time you ever saw me disobey an order from you, man."

Burke was nearly as tense as Jimmy, but not for the same reason. When Hearn Guilford talked about ending the project, he had felt like the young boy who stood in front of this man, twenty years ago, portraying confidence with mush in his guts, praying he wouldn't wet his pants. Hearn was not one to vacillate, and no one knew that better than Burke McGuire.

"Is this one going to be worth the problems?" Hearn's sudden question caught Burke off guard. "Anyone tough in charge down there?"

"Yeah." Burke's mind raced. "Tully Jones, Sheriff Supremo, the living cross between Gargantua and John Wayne. He's the protection man. The guy was born and raised in the town, he's a college grad, and has five years of undercover police work in the deep metro slime of Atlanta under his belt. He has the influence, and power to help us. What I don't know is his attitude toward growth in Wynton. I've definitely made a bad impression on the man, which I hope Canty O'Neil can overcome for me because I sure as hell can't do it on my own."

Hearn chuckled. "Can't or won't."

"Both." Burke stared down at the valley. "One more

traverse, Jimmy. Follow the line of the creek. Man, that's a beautiful sight. See that big tree, Hearn? A driver and a five wood, over the creek, and for the good ones, a big wedge to an elevated green. See the way the valley runs, I can lay out most of the holes north and south. No tricky sunshine in the eyes of the wealthy who'll be out here."

Hearn spoke up. "Jimmy, that's enough. Let's go."

Jimmy sighed in relief and gained altitude.

Burke's throat felt so tight, he couldn't utter a sound.

Hearn spoke again. "Get your Canty O'Neil to do her homework. Hearn Guilford Golf Designs wants to see a legitimate, up-to-date survey within the next thirty days, after which I will put up option money, and make an offer."

Hearn turned and faced Burke. "I think I must be as whacko as those people you are dealing with, but we're going to pursue it. No investor money until we close. High risk for Guilford, but damn, that's some piece of property."

Hearn faced forward.

As the plane banked north and a breathtaking view of the Blue Ridge filled his eyes, Burke exhaled, grinned and mouthed a silent "thank you."

DAGMAR MARSHALL

CHAPTER 13

Canty watched through her office windows as Tully pulled up in the Sheriff's truck. He slammed the door and covered the distance to the front door in seconds. He entered her office, and was not smiling.

"Tully. Sit down. How about a cup of Willy's famous espresso? I'll tell her to make it extra sweet. You'll love it."

"No, thanks." He sat down hard in the chair opposite her desk.

She tried her best to look wide-eyed and contrite. "Burke McGuire loves Willy's espresso. The stuff earned her a ride in his Jag."

"This, Canty, is briefing time. I want to know exactly what you will say to Queen Ponder. I also want to know if you plan on discussing anything with Terrell or Smith."

Canty kept trying. "What about Pauly? He's the one I really need to get to—"

Tully came out of his chair so quickly, Canty gasped and held her palms out. "Dammit, woman. You get serious or you won't be going to see Queen Ponder today. I don't give a flying shit what Burke McGuire and Guilford what-evers want up here. I swear to God I'll lock you up and call your daddy."

"What are the charges?" Canty tried to remain calm but was beginning to seethe.

"Being a pain in the butt to the Sheriff." Tully folded his

large frame back into the chair.

"Now you listen up, Tully Jones. I am going to see Queen Ponder," she glanced at her watch, "with you or without you. Quit questioning me. We'll be running late if we don't leave here in exactly two minutes. You will, or you won't."

"You can't run me off, Canty. Let's go." Tully got out of his chair and glowered down at her. "I'll say this once. If we see one sign, one little bitty-eensie, sign, that those weirdo's are even thinking violent, we'll be outta there, bye-bye, and see ya."

Canty stood and fired gray ice. "Tully Jones, I'm not stupid."

★   ★   ★

Tully jerked the pickup off the main road and headed toward Ponder property. Canty grabbed the hand hold over her window. Her tongue still smarted from her last trip up the Ponder road. Tully's knuckles were turning white.

"Relax, Tully."

His gaze snapped to her face briefly. "Canty, I'd feel better driving into Jurassic Park than where we're going."

Canty sighed. Gradually, Tully slowed to a sensible speed. The road became more rutted and narrower. Tree branches reached out like ancient sentinels set to stop their progress. They were probably all ghosts of dead Ponders, she thought.

Suddenly, they pulled into the open. The ancient Ponder cabin stood about one-hundred yards in front of them. She could also see Terrell, Smith, and Pauly. The sun glinted off Terrell's shotgun barrel.

BLAM!

Canty yelled and ducked.

"Shit," Tully growled, but kept moving.

The sounds of Terrell's shotgun reverberated off the surrounding mountains followed by his high-pitched nasty laugh. Smith echoed his brother's laughter. Pauly snorted, snuffled, and swiped at his dripping nose with his grimy shirt sleeve.

Tully pulled up closer and closer until Canty thought he was going to park on the front steps of the cabin. He shut off the truck motor, the front bumper inches from the porch. Terrell and Smith backed up the broken wooden stairs and stood waiting.

"Very clever, Sheriff. One good intimidation deserves another." Canty's heart was pounding. "I hope you didn't make them crazier than usual."

"Stupid backass idiots."

"Stupid backass, dangerous idiots." Canty snapped.

"Hey, who's the one who had to come here? Sure as hell wasn't my idea. Let's get this over with."

"Hi there, Terrell, Smith, Pauly. Is Queen in there? Can we see her now?" Canty picked her way up the stairs to the porch and faced the Ponders.

Terrell once more had the shotgun barrel at rest on his left arm. He stuck out his hand and she shook it firmly. Canty was repulsed by the long knotty fingers and filth caked nails. She battled every one of her natural instincts not to rub her hand on her pants to rid it of anything Terrell may have left there.

Terrell opened his mouth and to Canty's disgust, smiled, showing a few orange-yellow teeth and black-spotted gums. Smith moved beside him and mirrored the grotesque expression. Pauly continued to snuffle and snort and wipe his dripping nose on any part of his shirt he could get to.

"She's expectin' you. She's not expectin' the Sheriff, there. She won't see him. He can just wait out here with us. We'd love the company, wouldn't we, Smith?"

Tully nodded briefly. Guess he figured it's smarter for him to be out here watching the boys than turning his back on them.

Canty heard Smith make obscene sucking sounds when she passed by him to the door. Her stomach flopped and tightened. She kept going.

The inside of the gloomy cabin reeked of old grease and stale smoke. Faded checkered curtains hung limp on the few small windows. The only discernible light flickered from a black and white TV on a stand beside the blackened stone fireplace.

"Get out. Go away. I hate you!" The sudden screech of the bird turned Canty's skin cold and bumpy.

"Hello, Queen. Nice bird."

Queen sat rocking in a huge chair. Her voice came hoarse and whispery. "Bird's name is Black. He's my best friend."

As Canty's eyes adjusted to the dimness, she could see the large bird on his perch, his eyes fixated on a smeary, yellowing mirror beside him. "Get out!" he yelled at his own image. His voice was eerily like Queen's, only a lot louder.

"Shut up, Black. Now, Canty, don't get too close. I don't look so good no more and my legs hurt so bad I haven't cleaned up for awhile." Queen looked swallowed up in the large old rocker. She was wrapped in a dirty washed out once-blue robe and her bony feet were bare. Long strands of whispy-gray hair spilled around her face and Canty could barely make out the hawk nose and beady black eyes she remembered from the past. Her skin looked the color of slate. If she hadn't spoken, Canty would have believed she was dead.

"Good to see you, Queen. Thanks for letting me visit."

Queen started pushing the rocker, back and forth, back

and forth. "Nice to see you, Canty. You are as pretty a thing as I knew you would be. I hadn't gotten up close to you in a long time. You're all grown and I hear you have a boy."

"Yes. His name is Toby and he's ten." Canty sat down in an old ladder back chair near the rocker.

Queen suddenly burst into a choking, shrieky voice. "If I'd quit shooting at'cha, maybe you'd come by and bring the boy sometime. That'd be nice." The shriek died.

"Well, yes, it would." A fat chance day in hell, it would.

"Get out! You stink. You're ugly!" Canty jerked as the bird cried out.

Queen jumped up from her rocker with a speed and agility that astounded Canty. The old woman took two strides toward the bird and draped a piece of black material over its head. It quieted.

"Damn, stupid bird," Queen mumbled and returned to her chair. She focused her half-hidden black eyes on Canty. "Damn piece of crap, that bird, but like I said, he's my best friend." Her voice crackled. "Fact is, my only friend. Now, what brings you here?"

Canty shifted her weight and the chair creaked loudly. She hoped it wouldn't crumple under her. She exhaled. The room was now silent except for the reh, reh rocking sound of Queen's chair.

Canty swallowed and moistened her dry lips. "Queen, I know you probably have a real good idea of why I'm here so I'll get right to the point. Your land is valuable and there is a very viable and wealthy purchaser out there who could set you up for the rest of your life. You could have pretty clothes, a nice home with heat and air-conditioning, and a new truck, just for starters. You and the boys could live high and maybe even get some help for Pauly."

Reh, reh. Silence. Canty wished she could get up and go to the bathroom.

"Don't that sound nice. 'Cept I ain't sharing with Terrell and Smith. Not a penny. Don't have to and won't. Only reason I would think twice about sellin' is to take away what they think they got."

"That's fine." What a stupid thing to say. Keep your wits about you. "The purchaser would like to know how much your land is worth to you, so he can make a reasonable offer."

Queen leaned forward, her black eyes glinting. "Tell Mr. Purchaser to tell you what he'll pay. Got 'bout eight hundred acres, give or take, in Jaw-gee, got 'bout two-hundred acres, give or take in North C'lina. And, you can tell Mr. Purchaser that I, Queen Ponder, am the sole owner of this land. It's all mine. I can decide how much Terrell and Smith and Pauly will get, if any, and nobody else. 'Course, if they find I'll sell and that they won't have a nickel, I could be dead and gone before you close the deal. Then you'd have to go to them." She flapped her bony hands and shrieked again.

Ah, she was trying to laugh when she made that sound. Canty's mind was spinning. She had not expected to only have to deal with Queen. That could be good and bad. If Queen refused to share the wealth, all hell could break lose and Queen could be a shotgun target, just like she said. Canty had no doubt that Terrell or Smith would kill her. If she could appeal to Queen's family instincts, she might convince her to share enough of the proceeds to keep Terrell and Smith happy. Poor Pauly would never know the difference one way or the other.

"Queen, I would like permission to bring you an offer for your land."

"Talk to me. Nothin' in writing. Don't like that."

"Queen, these people don't make verbal offers. They are professional business men with a lot of money to invest, and there is no way they'll do anything on a handshake."

Reh, reh. Reh, reh.

"What's this Mr. Purchaser person want with all my land? He may want to do something I can't abide."

"He has planned a beautiful golf course community. There'll be a huge clubhouse and a lot of big, expensive homes for very wealthy people."

"Ha! Now ain't that somethin'? Big-money folks shittin' on my land. Ain't that somethin'?"

Reh, reh. Reh, reh.

"Queen, how about I talk to the purchaser and get his offer? I'll come and present it verbally, just like you said. We can work out the final negotiations, and then put it on paper. Will that work for you?" Say yes, old woman.

Canty's question met with silence. Queen got out of her rocker and pulled the cloth from Black's head. "Get out. I hate you. Get out!" Black screeched.

Terrell and Smith came rocketing through the door. Canty jumped up and turned to face them. Thank God, Tully filled the door frame behind them, right hand poised over the butt of his gun.

"Queen, that damn bird o' yours is goin' to get someone killed, yellin out like that. We thought you was in trouble." Terrell pushed the words through his remaining teeth, slurring and spitting.

Queen resumed her seat in her rocking chair. She pointed at Canty. "You, Canty O'Neil, you come back here when you got somethin' to say." She turned her head to the TV.

Terrell and Smith burst into high pitched laughter that gave Canty chills.

"S'it for you, Canty darlin'. Queen ain't talkin' no more to you today. Why, she may never talk to you ever agin." Smith walked up close to her. "Now if you was to marry me, she'd damn well have to talk to you." He slid his slimy tongue out and slowly moved it over his lips.

Canty swallowed the bile that rose in her throat. She pushed past Smith and Terrell. She kept her eyes on Tully. "Thanks, Queen. We'll talk again soon."

Canty walked past Tully and got into the truck. Tully followed, cranked the engine and backed slowly away from the porch.

"Oh God, hurry, Tully. I don't need any of your one-upmanship ego trips right now!" Tully continued backing up at his own pace until they were nearly out of sight of the cabin. Canty wanted to scream, and stomp her foot on the gas pedal.

"Bring that whore in white, next time, Canty! We want a closer look," Smith yelled and waved.

"Yea, and bring the little fag man, too. We want ta get closer to him," Terrell screamed. He fired the shotgun, straight up. BLAM!

Tully spun the truck around and they headed to the main road.

"Well, I got my foot in the door, Tully. The next visit should be more productive. Let's get moving. I have to call Burke McGuire and get some numbers."

Tully glanced over at her. "Canty O'Neil, sometimes I think you are crazy as hell."

CHAPTER 14

"Burke McGuire, please. This is Canty O'Neil." Canty waited, foot jiggling.

"Canty. Are you all right?" Burke sounded genuinely concerned.

Canty stopped jiggling her foot. "Why wouldn't I be?"

His voice came through the phone, low and strong. "Diamond and Max were here earlier. They said you were going to see Queen Ponder, and were predicting headlines of your certain death. They were definitely impressed with the fearsome Ponder boys. They were literally in terror just talking about them."

So, he'd been worrying about her? Canty thought, grinned slightly and tucked a lock of hair behind her right ear. She felt damp under her arm pits. "They are just super darling, those boys. They could terrify a momma bear with cubs. Also, I'm having a big problem picturing Diamond terrified. Doesn't compute. She cussed them out."

Burke laughed. "I don't doubt she cussed them out, but in the telling, there was real fear. So much fear that Hearn Guilford was about to call it all off."

"Oh, my God." Canty stood and began pacing.

"Settle down. We flew over the property yesterday. Hearn couldn't resist it anymore that I could. No investor money, yet, but he's willing to carry on to closing."

Canty sat back down.

"However," Burke cleared his throat, "he wants an up-to-date survey in thirty days. What happened with Queen yesterday?"

She wanted to tell him to take a deep breath between demands. "Right now, we are one tiny step closer to making something happen. Queen did exactly what I thought she would. She wants numbers, verbally. Any paper work, if she even decides to make a deal, will come later."

"Damn it all, Canty, you know better. I've gotten some of the scum of the swamps down here to work with me on paper. Let me at those people."

"Burke, you have to do this my way, or no way. It will come together on paper after the negotiations, if we even get that far. Now, I suggest we look at offering fifteen-hundred an acre. I realize there are several hundred acres that will be unbuildable but their value lies in views."

"Send me a written report on how you arrived at that figure and I'll handle it from there."

Canty's voice tightened. "Burke, I'd be happy to send you a full market evaluation if I could. What would make that very difficult would be the fact that comparables don't exist. No one has bought or sold that much property up here, ever, except the United States government, and that was fifty years ago. North Carolina numbers are also non-existent."

"I can't tell Hearn Guilford that my broker in North Georgia has asked to spend over a million of his dollars—"

Canty grew impatient. "You will have to do just that. Tell him your broker will be glad to sit down with him and map it all out as to the why's and wherefore's, but there are no concrete comps." Canty was now more than just a little damp under the arm pits.

"Cool it my hot-tempered Irish beauty."

"I'm not your hot-tempered Irish beauty." He was laughing at her and Canty was livid.

"Perhaps you belong to the revered and respected Sheriff Tully Jones."

"I do not belong to anyone. Let me know what you and Hearn Guilford want to do."

"Canty," his voice softened. "I thought you had a sense of humor. If not, we're in big trouble."

"Your sense of humor is pretty hard to pick up on over the telephone. I've never seen anything funny in the ego-driven, domineering male personality."

"My next funny lines will be spoken in person. I can't afford to have you angry with me."

When are you coming back? Canty wanted to ask, but held her tongue.

"I'll be back in touch with you within a week. We'll meet with Queen at that time. By the way, Diamond and Max thought you were terrific. All personal feelings aside, they also told me the Sheriff would be with you today, and I was very glad to know that."

"Thanks." Her foot was jiggling again. A week? An eternity.

CHAPTER 15

Two days later, Burke McGuire stepped out of a red Explorer, and approached the office. Canty couldn't believe her eyes.

Willodene was horrified. She pointed a ruby-red finger nail at Burke and squinted hard. "You can't come in here driving something so common as an Explorer, Burke McGuire. You'll ruin your image!"

He smiled at her. "It's good to see you, too, Willodene. My espresso in the pot?"

Willodene settled. "I'm serious. I hope nothing happened to your Jag."

Burke assured her his Jaguar was fine. "I wanted to be a less conspicuous target around here." He stuck his hands in his pockets and swaggered close to Willodene. "A very well-known officer of the law in Wynton had no respect for the capabilities of a fine machine like my Jaguar. She was so insulted by your sheriff's total lack of appreciation of her beauty and speed, she begged me to leave her home until I educated the man."

Willodene burst out laughing. "Just for that, I'll put on the pot."

Canty willed herself to walk slowly toward Burke. "You're five days shy of a week, but only three if you just count business days. Welcome back."

When he turned and smiled at her, Canty wanted to hug his neck and kiss him hard. She tapped her nails on Willodene's desk to distract herself.

Burke's smile grew broader. He stepped closer and focused his clear, blue eyes on her face. "Great to be back. Couldn't wait another minute to meet the Ponders."

Canty took a deep breath. "I'm glad. The sooner, the better. Come have dinner with us tonight and we'll see Queen tomorrow."

"When's dinner?" He moved closer.

"About an hour from now. You can follow me home." Her breath was shallow. His whole body was inches away. She felt bathed in the heat of him.

"I'd follow you anywhere," his voice low and demanding.

"Coffee's ready," Willodene sounded abnormally loud. Burke backed away.

Damn, Canty thought. "Thanks, Willy. I've invited Burke to dinner tonight. It's time he met Pop."

"Yup, it is," Willy said under her breath.

Burke followed Canty to the ball field to pick up Toby. They stood at the fence and watched Toby's team practice bunting.

"That's your son." Burke announced as Toby stepped up to the plate. "He's his Mama made over. I'd know him anywhere."

Canty smiled. "Yes, that's the love of my life. Others have tried, but no one can steal my heart, it's taken."

Burke threw a casual arm over her shoulder, and gave her a light squeeze. "We'll discuss that some other time," he whispered.

Canty hoped he didn't feel her tremble.

"Looks like a good athlete, keeps his eye on the ball." Burke dropped his arm when Toby saw them and came running over.

116

"Hi, Mom. This Mr. Burke you talked about? Did you bring your Jaguar? Sir?"

"Toby O'Neil. Get your manners out of your pockets and shake hands. Yes, this is Burke McGuire and no, he didn't bring the Jaguar this time."

Burke reached for Toby's outstretched hand. "Sorry, Toby, we'll have a ride in that Jag next time. Nice bunting. Takes a special touch to be good."

Toby puffed up. "Thanks, sir," he grinned now, the gray eyes flashing.

"Let's go, Burke. Toby, ride with Burke in case we get separated."

Burke looked directly at Toby. "I'd appreciate that son. Don't want to get lost and don't want to run into the local sheriff on my own. You'll be my safe passage ticket."

The two car caravan pulled into the O'Neil drive as the sun was setting. Pop came out, and Toby introduced Burke and Pop. Canty saw the frown on Burke's face when he noticed Tully's truck in the drive.

"Tully brought Willodene," Pop said. "Dinner's about ready. Come on in, Burke and put your feet under our table."

Pop presided at the head of the table, Willodene at the foot. Toby and Burke sat across from each other. Canty looked directly at Tully. "Hi," she said.

"Hi," he grumbled.

Pop said the blessing, and Willodene started passing the cornbread. "Burke," Pop spoke, "I gotta say I'm pleased to meet you. Canty's been tellin' me about you, and your vision. Seems like you could be a very important part of Wynton, and in between tasting the best home cooking you'll ever savor, we'd all like to hear just what you're plannin' to do on the Ponder property. You don't mind, now, do ya?"

Canty looked up to meet Burke's eyes. His face smiled but his eyes were dead serious. "No, sir, I don't mind a bit, soon's I can take a breath from eating. And, you're right. This is the best home cooking I've ever had the good fortune to savor. Thank you for letting me join you at your table."

Tully nudged Canty's foot. She glared at him. He mouthed, "Bull," and glared back.

Willodene chimed in, and Canty could feel her panic about to boil over. "Clower, I believe you're going to be pleased with what Burke McGuire has to say. Of course, we all know what the big problem will be."

"Now, what's that, Willodene?" Burke asked between mouthfuls.

Tully leaned back in his chair. "Ponders, of course. MugWire, I can't see that you have an ice-cube's chance in July of makin' a deal with Queen and the boys."

Damn, Willy, you stirred the pot that time, Canty thought.

Burke continued to eat.

"We'll get to that, Tully," Pop commented. First, I want to hear all about this vision."

Tully kept on. "Pop, I know you're as scared of the danger to Canty as I am and I will not hesitate to inform Mr. MugWire here just how you feel about it." Tully reached for the platter of pork.

Canty wanted to stick his hand with a fork.

"All in good time, Tully." Pop grinned down the table at Willodene who was trying to stare Tully into looking at her. Pop shook his head and Willodene backed off.

Canty took a deep breath and stifled a grin. Guns were drawn, knives were sharpened. The boys were about to have at it. Should be interesting.

Burke focused on Canty and smirked. Tully belched.

Willodene passed the beans, her lower lip sucked deep under her overbite. Toby gulped down his milk and kept on eating.

"Okay," Burke announced. "But if I start talking, it'll stop me from eating." He winked at Willodene.

"Burke McGuire, you eat all you want, honey." Willodene's flamingo pink nails glimmered as she toasted Burke with her sweet tea.

Tully nudged Canty again under the table. She ignored him. "Damn," she heard him mutter. He cleared his throat and buttered more cornbread.

Burke threw his intensity over everyone like a cloak, and he cast a spell. As he described his plans for the development, he held everyone's total attention, and drew a breathtaking mind picture of the enormity and luxury of the finished product. Pop and Willy were totally absorbed and even Toby had stopped chewing. Tully tried to look bored, but his foot was tapping under the table. Canty knew he was listening hard.

All without a picture or a map, Canty thought. No wonder this man was so good at what he did.

"This development," he concluded, "will be the most important thing to happen to Wynton in its lifetime. The people of the town will be very proud of what they see, and, the economy of Wynton should experience considerable growth."

"Should?" Tully interrupted, his voice edged with steel.

"Sheriff Jones, you of all people should be able to visualize the vast potential of the development and impact on the town. You, along with the O'Neils, are the heartbeat of Wynton. I need your help. Can I count on you?"

Canty couldn't believe how swiftly Burke McGuire changed directions. The guns were holstered, the knives sheathed. She saw Tully flush. Anger or embarrassment, Tully? She wondered.

"Before Tully and Burke McGuire agree or disagree to anything, it's my turn." Pop put down his fork and sipped his tea. "Now, I've been listening to all this, and it's very entertaining but," his gaze shifted to Burke, "careful you don't put the cart before the horse, now. Careful you don't spend your money, until you got the land signed, sealed, and delivered, and most important, careful you don't let anything happen to Canty. I'd be right angry."

Canty heard a snort from Willodene. Pop went on. "Tully here's always thought he could protect her from anyone or anything, but I know my headstrong daughter. I'd say he's 'bout right, as long as he can see her." Pop narrowed his eyes at Tully. "She can slip away from you like quicksilver, Tully, and you know it. You got your hands full, son."

He looked back to Burke. "Burke McGuire, you'd better take me real serious. Those Ponder's'll chew you up, spit you out, and laugh while they's stomping you to death. You're a mighty smart man, I can tell that. I like your vision, just be careful how you go about gettin' it done. I know you've heard about the boys meeting up with your friends a few days ago. Heard your folks couldn't even talk for awhile after seeing them."

"Mr. O'Neil," Burke talked low, "I've dealt with swamp varmints for years and there's no one meaner. I figure I'll be meeting with the same kind of personalities in the Ponders. My friends have never had to come face to face with any of those folks before. I've always had the path cleared before they had to get started. The fact remains, it's my job to find and procure land for Guilford. I like my job, and the adversity that goes with it is part of making it all happen." He grinned. "It's also the part I like the best." He leaned back in his chair

120

and looked at Canty. "I also think your daughter can take care of herself just fine."

Pop smiled. "Enough said. Now, pass me that cornbread, will you, Toby."

"Pop," Canty spoke up, her voice tight, " Tully, Burke, and I are going to see Queen tomorrow. She's expecting us."

Pop looked square at his daughter. "Well, I wouldn't disappoint Queen Ponder if I was you."

CHAPTER 16

Canty was ready to punch Tully smack in the jaw. He was driving like a damn lunatic. She clenched her fist and held it in front of his face.

"Whoa, now. Don't mess with the driver. I could have an accident. Got your seat belt on, MugWire? Don't know if I can control this wild woman up here."

Canty turned to smile at Burke. "You look a little mussed."

"I'd rather be flying an airplane, which I don't know how to do, than be locked into the back seat of this damn vehicle with Jones at the wheel. I'd give myself a ticket if I were you, Sheriff. Reckless driving."

"You don't know what reckless driving is until you put your feet into Canty O'Neil's transportation. Whenever I need something constructive to do for the department, I go track Canty, if I can catch her, and write her up a big, fat, ticket. Richard Petty called just last week. Wants a backup driver and heard about our Canty. Thinks he can mold her into a first-class race car driver."

"Very funny." Canty tried to relax as Tully turned off the gravel road onto the rutted dirt drive leading to the Ponder cabin. She heard Burke groan as Tully careened around a sharp turn, the left rear sliding into a large hole

"Tully, slow down, damn it." Canty yelped. Tully slowed but not much. Canty could hear Burke mumbling in the back seat.

Tully spoke up. "That some kinda Irish curse you throwin' at me, MugWire? Back of my head's on fire. Careful you don't curse me bald."

Canty turned again and shook her head at Burke. "Shut up," she mouthed. Burke's face flushed. Thank God we're here, she thought. A few more minutes and I might have to protect these two from each other instead of Ponders.

Tully parked the truck the same few inches away from the porch steps. Terrell, Smith and Pauly were nowhere to be seen.

Tully chuckled. "I'd be wary, MugWire. Just 'cause those boys are out of sight doesn't mean they aren't close by."

"Scare tactics, Sheriff? Won't work." Burke hauled himself out of the back seat. Canty waited for him before she ascended the rickety wooden stairs to the porch. She turned to Tully.

"I'll just knock and see what happens."

Tully's right hand covered the butt of his gun. "Are you telling me Queen doesn't know we're coming?"

"Queen told me to come talk to her when I had something to say. She also wanted to meet Burke McGuire. All points accounted for, so here we are…Queen, you in there?"

"Go to hell. Go away you ugly thing. I hate you!"

Burke tensed. "Jeezus, what's that?"

"That's Black, Queen's mynah. He only says what he's been taught."

Queen's whispery voice sounded through the door. "Come on, Canty, and bring your friend in, too. Don't mind. I knew you was comin'."

Canty and Burke stepped into the dimness. Tully remained on the porch. Canty was surprised to see Pauly kneeling on the floor by Queen's rocker, his head buried in her lap. She could make out Queen's hands resting on his shoulders. She was patting him as though he were a baby.

Pauly looked up when Queen addressed them. His face was covered with snot and sweat and tears. God, he was so ugly, Canty thought. So pitiful, and so ugly.

"Pauly here feels bad cause Terrell and Smith went off without him. They's probably working on their still and they don't want Pauly to know exactly where it is." Queen looked down at Pauly. "Them boys is sometimes mean to you, poor boy, but Queen'll take care of you."

"Queen, I brought Mr. Burke McGuire to meet you. You can ask him anything you want about his plans for developing your property."

Queen suddenly shrieked and Canty could feel Burke jump. "That's her laugh," she whispered to him.

"Jeezus," he hissed through his teeth. "Glad to meet you Miss Ponder."

"Get out you fool. I hate you!" Black yelled. Queen pushed Pauly aside. He melted into a huge lump on the floor, still sobbing. She flipped the black cloth over the bird's head and returned to her rocker.

Burke stepped close to Queen's chair and hunkered down. He started speaking to Queen so quietly, Canty could barely hear him. Queen fixed her black eyes on his face and listened. She wanted to step closer but didn't dare make a sound. While Burke was talking, he pulled a huge handkerchief from his back pocket and handed it to the gulping, sobbing Pauly. To Canty's amazement, Pauly took it. He stopped crying and began wiping his face.

Queen shrieked. "You must be someone magic, Mr. McGuire. Pauly don't take anything from strangers. I'll be damblasted."

All Canty could hear was the reh, reh of the old rocker. Frustrated beyond belief, her whole being was so tense, she felt shooting pains in her head.

"Now, Mr. McGuire, small talk's over. I want to know everything you're planning for my land. This property's been Ponder for near on to a hundred years and it hasn't changed much." She pointed a bony finger at Burke, "I don't like what I'm hearing about developers getting ready to tear apart my mountains, not at all. I don't have much time left for breathing in this life and that," she glanced down at Pauly, "is all I care about helpin'. Now start telling me just what's on your mind."

Burke got up from his crouch and began pacing around the cabin. Queen never took her eyes off him.

"Miss Ponder, I plan on developing the most beautiful, private and very expensive golf course that's ever been done in the mountains or most likely, anywhere in the United States. It's what I do, and I'm good at it."

Canty swallowed. Not too hard, Burke, not too hard.

Queen snorted. "Is that so, young fella?"

Burke crouched in front of Queen's chair so the two were on eye level. "Yeah, that's so. I plan on developing this land so that no one driving by will even realize what's been carved out of these beautiful woods. Your valley will be shaped into a phenomenal golf course with very little earth moving. It's so perfect, it's scary."

Queen began asking questions. Burke began pacing again. Nearly an hour passed before the two stopped talking. Canty thought it the strangest scenario between two such different people she had ever seen. They seemed to have melded into a common thermal and swirled in a private tempo of communication.

Finally, Burke hunkered down once more. He placed one hand over Queen's clasped hands. "That's it. Sound right?"

"I gotta see some drawins of how this is all goin' to look first, and I wanta meet that Diamond woman, the boys' been talkin' about and that other feller, the architect. If all's like you say, then we got a deal." Queen focused her black eyes on Burke's blue ones and nodded.

"It will be, Miss Ponder. I'll have the drawings ready in a week or so and Canty here will get the contract ready for the closing, which will be for thirty days from today."

"I could change my mind in thirty days, Mr. McGuire. I right could."

"But, you won't. I know you. You won't."

Queen shrieked again and pointed a long bony finger at Canty. "You let me know when the drawins are ready and about time and place for the closin', Canty O'Neil. Wait, I got somethin' for you that'll save you a lot of trouble."

Burke moved back beside Canty. Canty touched his arm and he smiled down at her. "You are unbelievable," she whispered.

"Thanks. So are you." He grabbed her hand in a quick squeeze. They both watched as Queen made her way to an old chest by the fireplace. She raised the top and pulled out a sheaf of crinkled and spotted paper.

"This here is the only survey of this property you'll find. The recorded survey ain't worth jackshit." She shrieked again, sending chills up Canty's spine. "Fore I got such bad legs, I walked every inch of this property, measurin' and writin' Took me exactly a year and a month to cover it but I'd swear to anyone, it's true. You go get this recorded. You got all your fancy aerial stuff but this here will tell you all you'll ever need to know."

"Well, I'll be damned," Burke muttered. He took the

proffered sheets. "Thank you, Miss Ponder."

Queen sat back heavily in the old rocker. "Queen will do, Mr. McGuire."

"Burke, to you, Queen." He tipped her a two-finger salute.

"Canty, you and Burke go on, now. Terrell and Smith liable to show up and start a ruckus. I'm tired after all that talk. You set up a time for me to see them drawins and get all that money. Tully can let me know. Don't want you or Burke back this way until them things is ready. Understand?"

"Completely." Canty steered Burke toward the door, carefully avoiding the lumped form of the blank-faced Pauly. She turned to say goodbye to Queen, and saw that the old woman had fallen asleep.

As she got into the truck, Canty told Tully what had happened inside the cabin.

"You are kiddin' my butt! That old woman is no more going to show up at a closing than pigs can fly. And, this boy isn't going back up there with anybody's messages, either. You can't tell me you believe that old woman."

Burke reached into the front seat waving the survey papers in Tully's face. "Do you see this, Jones? This is the most complete survey of Ponder land ever made and Queen gave it to me. Now do you get it? This is a done deal, so quit being a pain in the ass whiner and let's get on with the show."

Canty turned around to face Burke. "He's turning red in the face. Enough," she whispered.

Tully drove back toward the main road in the same maniacal manner he had driven up the mountain. It was all Canty could do to hang on to the grip over the door. She didn't dare turn to see how Burke was doing. She saw Terrell and Smith coming through the woods in their direction. "Get down!"

BLAM!

"Get down!"

Tully's truck lurched but kept on going. "Damn idiots. They better not have damaged this truck." He stomped harder on the gas.

★ ★ ★

Queen jerked awake at the sound of the shotgun blast.

"Ugly, you're ugly. Go away!" Black screeched.

"Damn fools." She looked down at the misshapen flesh on the floor that was Pauly. She could see enough rise and fall in his body to know he was breathing. "You got one sorry family, Pauly boy. Shame you ever came into this world in this place."

After a few minutes, Queen pushed herself up from the rocker and grabbed her rifle. She opened the door and stood, looking.

"We're home, Queen. Your brothers is home. What's for supper?" Terrell staggered toward the porch with Smith following.

"No supper for you two drunks. You been drinkin' the only money you'll ever have. Go sleep it off."

Terrell stumbled up the rickety stairs and wrapped an arm around a post. He waved an empty fruit jar in her face. "You got that right. Smith and me makes the best. Woulda saved ya some but, it's so good, I drank it all up. Smith! You got a little drop of stuff for Queen, here. We need her to fix us somethin' and maybe just a little swaller will make her act nicer."

"Need more'n a little swaller to nicen her." Smith

grumbled and flopped down on the bottom step. "I drank it all anyway."

"You both go to hell. Go away." Queen backed herself to the doorway and raised the rifle.

"Shit almighty." Terrell lurched at her, dropping the jar and his shotgun. "You stupid bitch, gimme."

Queen slipped back into the cabin, and slammed the door.

"You lissen, Queen. Me and Smith got to find out somethin'. We saw that soft-ass Sheriff hightailin' it out of here just now. We know Canty O'Neil was with him, and somebody else. I know you didn't invite them for no picnic lunch. I'm gonna bust this door down, and you're gonna tell us what is going on."

"Just come on," Queen rasped, "door don't lock you know."

Terrell and Smith entered, grinning drooly grins. "Look at old Pauly," Terrell stood unsteadily over Pauly. "What you doin' lying on the floor like that? Get up Pauly!"

"Terrell, quit yellin' at Pauly. Look, you made him cry." Smith shuffled over to Pauly and grabbed his arm to help him get up. Pauly jerked his arm away and humped back down into himself, sobbing.

Terrell laughed. "See! Now, you made him worse."

Queen shook her finger at Terrell and Smith. "If you boys had taken him with you to your nasty still, he wouldn't be cryin'. You hurt his feelins bad."

"No, Pauly," Smith bent over and stuck his hairy face in Pauly's, "nobody ever gets to the still. They'd have to find it on their own, and nobody's gonna do it."

Pauly blubbered louder.

"Shut up!" Smith thumped his fist on Pauly's head. Pauly, shut up. "Now, Queen, fess up. We want to know what you're up to. We know somebody's wantin' to buy our land. You cain't make no deals to sell it without us, and we ain't sellin'."

Queen whooped. She kept on, holding her stomach, until tears rolled down her face. "You ain't tellin' me nothin'. I'll do as I please." She gasped and quieted, fixing her black eyes on Terrell. "But don't worry. You'll be taken care of. I'm the only one who can read and write, so you two are just goin' to have to trust me. You was right. We're lookin' at a contract for this place in about three weeks and if I like it, it's done."

"No!" Smith yelled.

"Yes!" Queen yelled back.

Black fluffed his feathers. "Yes!" he cried in Queen's voice.

Terrell grabbed his shotgun and aimed it at Black. Queen was out of her rocker, and back-handed him on his ears in a split second. "You do that one more time and I hope you know what kinda flowers you want on your gravesite."

Smith howled with laughter. "Queen, didn't know you had it in ya. You can still move quick. Terrell, put down that damn gun. We don't want to cook the goose, here. Okay, Queen, what kinda money we talkin?" He turned to Terrell. "We get enough money, we don't need no still. I'm gettin' tired a haulin my ass up there anyway."

Terrell broke the shotgun and let it hang over his left arm. He rubbed his right ear. "Woman, you's mean as a snake. Always was. Be lucky you's my sister or you'd be dead right now. You'd be shit on the walls. You'd be bloody dung."

Queen sat and rocked. Reh, reh. Reh, reh.

"Say somethin'." Terrell demanded.

"Soon's you put that gun down. Cain't you talk without it, you scairdy cat? Scaird of old Queen. Gotta threaten you own sister. Big man!" Queen screeched and rocked faster.

"What?" Terrell softened his voice.

Queen slowed the rocker, and fixed her black eyes on Terrell. "We got us a nice offer, and we'll be walking off this piece of mountain as rich folks. We gonna get us over a million dollars."

Terrell and Smith froze.

"I ain't kiddin' boys. I don't kid 'bout such. But, I got to go to the closin' and approve what they's written up in a contract. As soon as I see that architects drawins and settle my mind about what they plan to do with this land."

Smith jerked back. "No contracts, Queen. Them Florida boys will try to rape us for sure. I cain't read no contract. Just tell 'em to give us the money and we'll be long gone."

"Sorry boys, got to have one. They won't give us no money if we don't sign a contract, and have an official-like settling of it all with attorneys and everything. Jes won't get nothin'. I'll sign, you can do a x-mark. I'll read it to ya, or have Canty read it. Don't matter. If we don't like somethin' we can get it changed before we get our money from 'em. They's offering more than I would ask. Close, but more."

"Did you meet the man buyin'? What's he gonna do?" Smith edged closer, his boot heel crunched on Pauly's hand. Pauly howled.

Queen jabbed Smith in the stomach, hard, with the rifle barrel. "One more time, Smith. One more time you hurt that boy and you're a dead man."

Smith doubled over, and gagged. "Oh, shit, Queen." I didn' mean it. Pauly don't feel much of nothin' anyway. He's too stupid to feel anything."

Terrell stepped between Queen and Smith. "Hey, we're about to be rich. We all gotta read and sign and close. You don't want to miss it, do ya, Smith, you asshole? 'Cause if you do, I get your share."

"The hell you do. You know what havin' that money'll mean. Betcha it'll buy me a piece of that white whore and her fag friend. Oh, man, I'd like that. Betcha, Canty might even take a fancy to you, Terrell, if'n you got money."

Queen screeched her wild laugh. "You boys could have your pick of any pig in the sty, but that's as far as it goes. Money won't help you none." Queen stopped her rocking. She focused her black glittery eyes on her brothers.

"Let me tell you this," she jabbed her forefinger at each one, "that Sheriff's got to be comin' up here, maybe more than once in the next few weeks. He's my messenger. He's goin' to let us know when them drawins are ready and when to be at that closin'. I don't want no shootin' at him, understand."

Terrell howled and jigged around the room. "Just a few pops to keep him honest. Won't try to hit him."

Queen drew a bead on Terrell with the rifle. The sound of the hammer being cocked stopped Terrell's dancing. "Whoa, now Queen. I'm only kiddin'. I promise now."

"Me, too, Queen" Smith continued slobbering through his few teeth. Won't shoot at the candy-ass until after the closin'.

DAGMAR MARSHALL

CHAPTER 17

Tully left Canty and Burke at Canty's office, and drove off, still furious at Canty and her promises to Queen.

Willodene greeted Burke with a big smile, and a fresh, steaming cup of espresso.

Burke thanked her with a peck on the cheek. Canty controlled a big hoot of laughter as Willy's face turned as red as her newly crimsoned nails.

Burke took a big, slow swallow of her brew. "Tell you what, Willodene, after meeting Queen Ponder and getting shot at by the Ponder boys, this espresso was just what the doctor ordered."

Canty smiled at her friend. "You know, Willy, after that, Burke is right. Even I'll have some of your famous espresso."

Willodene feigned great shock, and poured a cup for Canty. She handed Burke a pink message slip. "I got this message for you from your Mr. Guilford."

Canty watched Burke frown as he read the note. "Bad news?"

He glanced at her. "No."

She was stiff, and furious at his indifference. "Let's go in my office, Burke. I need to sit down and relax after our Ponder episode."

He followed closely behind her, and shut the door. "You in love with Tully Jones, Sheriff Supremo?"

"Burke McGuire, that's none of your business." Her skin prickled.

He slapped his hand on her desk. "It is! I don't care to make a damn fool of myself pursuing you if that gorilla has extracted an undying promise of love from you."

Canty didn't know whether to laugh, or get angry with the enigmatic personality in front of her. "Scared to tangle with the gorilla, are you?"

He put his cup down, and pulled her to him.

She felt chilled, hot, and dizzy. Her groin ached. Her legs felt stringy and loose. He kissed her, hard, then softly. His hands stoked down her back and he gently pulled her close so she could feel his hardness. Suddenly, he put his hands on her shoulders and pushed her away. Gruff, but with a grin. "That's better."

"That's not good enough. It's my turn." I've got to sit down, she thought, before I fall down. My God, what this man did to her. "Tell me about your relationship with Diamond. She thinks you're wonderful."

Burke laughed. "Canty O'Neil, you never cease to amaze me. For such a small woman, you sure jump to big conclusions. Diamond has another name," he leaned toward her, and pointed at his lips, each word spoken like a bullet fired, "Mrs. Hearn Guilford. I don't mess with Mrs. Hearn Guilford."

"Oh." Canty sat down behind her desk, relieved to be protected from the spontaneous combustion of their closeness, relieved beyond belief at Burke's words.

"Oh, what?" Burke sat down in the chair opposite Canty's desk. He crossed his thick arms over his barrel chest and rocked back in the chair until Canty pictured him flat on the floor. "Let me tell you a little about Diamond. Beneath that highly polished knock-you-out exterior is a very serious, and talented person. She came from dirt poor, worked her way through some design school, and did the old scratch-and-claw routine to the top. She created herself, used her brains and talent, and married a very wealthy man who happens to be Hearn Guilford. She has helped him to become even wealthier. I will tell you, they're a good marriage. Where in the name of God she found Max, I'll never know, but they're attached at the hip when it comes to business. He's genius stuff. Gay as a duck in spring, but genius." He let the chair rock forward and land on all fours. "Okay?"

"Okay." Canty worked on a serious face, hoping her total joy at Burke's revelation, wasn't reflected in her expression. "Now, please tell me what you said to Queen, and what this contract will be about."

"You still haven't answered my question about the gorilla."

"Burke, let me say this, Tully Jones is the dearest friend I have, besides Pop and Toby. We grew up together. We're childhood buddies. There is no romance."

"Give me a break. He'd cheerfully make hog slop out of me, at the slightest provocation, and not just because he doesn't like me. He doesn't like you and me. There's something you're not telling me, and I don't believe your childhood buddies story."

"Believe it."

"Who is Toby's father?"

"It isn't Tully Jones."

"I didn't ask who it isn't."

"Damn you, Burke. Wait, please wait."

"I don't wait easily."

"You will have to this time. We've got contracts to write. We've got land to buy. We've got business to do."

He grinned. "Lighten up, Canty."

Most damn frustrating person, man or woman, that I have ever met, Canty thought.

Burke pulled her up from her chair, and wrapped his muscular arms around her. He bent his head, and whispered in her ear. "Push me away."

Canty's voice cracked. "Hell, no." She hugged him back, and offered her lips to his. Their tongues met and swam together, locking and pushing. She felt that he was sucking her insides into him, and her body felt melty and soft against him.

"I've got to go back to Orlando tonight." He mumbled. "That was the message. Hearn needs me to sign off on some big equipment we ordered."

"Mmm. That's a shame."

"Come with me."

Canty pulled away enough to look into the wonderful, blazing blue eyes. "You're crazy."

"Crazy for your sweet body."

"Help."

"Love me?"

"Working on it."

"Knowing your work ethic, I'll soon be loved by Canty O'Neil." He gave her a perfunctory kiss on the nose. "I have a great idea. I want you and Toby to come on down to Orlando, company plane, your own golf villa, and meet with Hearn Guilford. Something tells me, you'd be the bottom line in making him feel solid on this project. He's still spooked, and on edge and he isn't going to be too keen on letting Diamond and Max come back down here to meet Queen. He needs the O'Neil touch."

Canty looked hard into his eyes. "What if I screw it up?"

"You won't."

Canty laughed. "With that vote of confidence, I couldn't say no."

CHAPTER 18

"Pop, Burke wants me to fly to Orlando next week, and meet with Mr. Guilford. He wants me to bring Toby, too."

Pop rocked back in his chair. Willodene gulped her sweet tea. Tully frowned.

Toby went wild. "Mom, can we go? Please. Fly? Oh, man!"

Canty suppressed a smile. She was excited as Toby at the prospect of going to Florida, meeting Mr. Hearn Guilford, and discussing the terms and conditions of the contract, but the fact that Burke had personally invited her and Toby...

"Canty," Pop's voice broke into her thoughts, "you been over this contract with Burke McGuire. Don't see why you need to go gallavantin' down there. Doesn't Mr. Guilford trust McGuire without meeting you, too, and dragging Toby away?"

"Pop, it will only be for one night."

"Where'll you and Toby be stayin' that one night?" Willodene waggled her fingers at Canty, her nails gleaming cotton candy pink.

"In our own golf villa. Just Toby and me."

Tully folded his long arms over his wide chest. "Now, how do you know all that, already?"

"Just a damn minute!" Canty jumped up from her chair. "I'm a grown woman, and a very capable woman. I have a son who doesn't need to hear the nasty little innuendoes I'm hearing. I'm surprised at all of you. Toby and I will drive to Peachtree-Dekalb Airport Thursday morning, and we'll fly to Orlando aboard the Hearn Guilford private jet, and aboard the private jet will be a pilot, a co-pilot, and a flight attendant. Period."

"Canty, calm down. We're just hassling with you, honey." Willodene's voice was smooth and sweet. "Besides, we all like Burke McGuire," Willodene's elbow met with Tully's ribs.

"Well, I know you do Willodene." Canty watched Tully's face. He wouldn't meet her eyes.

"I do," Toby spoke, and cracked the tension in the air. "I think Mr. McGuire is really nice. I'd like him even if he didn't have a Jaguar." Toby wriggled and grinned. "While we was, were, coming home last night, he said he'd like to show me stuff about swinging a golf club. He said I look like a good athlete," Toby dropped his head. "Said I keep my eye on the ball. He liked that."

Pop cleared his throat. "Sounds to me like the whole thing is settled, so there's no need dragging out this conversation. Canty, it's a good thing for you to meet with this Mr. Guilford, I know. Your old Pop's gonna look out for you and my grandson, you know that."

"It's right from you Pop but I don't need my two dearest friends acting like I'm some kinda wild, brazen hussy, looking for trouble. This is business, pure and simple. You people!" Canty was seething. "Burke said Hearn Guilford was still edgy about this place, and he's sure I can calm him down, and make him believe it's okay here."

Willodene planted a kiss on Pop's cheek, hugged Toby, and started for the door. "Gotta go. Come on, Tully. Ride me home in that hot dog truck of yours." Tully followed without a word.

"Canty, you calm down. Toby, off to bed," Pop ordered.

Toby scooted. "Now, what was all that about, Canty O'Neil?"

"I just hate being hovered over and bossed and accused and..." Canty bit her lip.

"Your old pop sees a woman mighty attracted to a fella who is mighty attracted to her. I've seen you two together. You two nearly made the tablecloth catch fire with those looks of yours the other night. Thought old Tully'd lose his dinner, right then."

Canty tucked a hank of hair behind her ear. "I don't know why, but that conversation just now flew all over me. We've all worked so hard and I am so excited about the project. Pop, it really could happen. Tully and Willodene made me feel like some kind of cheap, scheming woman."

Pop took her hand and patted lightly. "They didn't mean to, honey. You know how you all love to put each other in the barrel, and start shootin'. That's all it was. Tully's hurtin'. He saw it all."

"I guess." Canty felt gnarly in her stomach. She plopped down in the rocker beside Pop. "Pop, do you really think Burke McGuire is attracted to me, or am I just a means to an end for him?"

He answered quickly. "I say 'yes' to both questions."

"Pop!"

He grinned at Canty. "Now don't you get all riled up with me. You asked. My first impressions of Mr. McGuire included smart, and determined enough to use any means or anyone to accomplish what he sets out to do. Smart enough, that whoever or whatever was standing in his way will either be part of the scheme of things, or will be eliminated from the picture."

"You make him sound heartless, and I don't agree. I see him as a very focused man, very intense. You should have seen him talking to Queen. It would have blown your britches. He had that old woman sucking up every word out of his mouth, and begging for more. She believed he was magic because Pauly took a handkerchief from him and Pauly never takes anything from people he doesn't know, ever. She asked him a million questions, and he answered every one without hesitation. She even dug into her private papers and gave Burke a survey of the property that she herself had done several years ago. She said it took her over a year to do it, what with her bad knees."

Pop chuckled. "What I wouldn't have given to see that scene. Old Queen gettin' mesmerized by a man. Hard to believe. Now, what about Tully Jones?"

"Tully was outside."

Pop stopped rocking and looked straight into Canty's eyes. "I mean what about Tully Jones? He's a fine man and he loves you."

Tears stung her eyes. She turned away and took a deep breath. "I know you would love to see Tully and me get serious. I believe most of Wynton would love that but it won't ever happen. We're just friends, deep, caring friends."

"He turn you down?"

Canty whirled. "Pop, promise me something. Don't ever ask about Tully Jones and me, again. Promise me."

"I don't know if I can. I care about the man, and I care about you. With him, there'd be no chance of you gettin' hurt again. Old Tully, now, he'd die by fire before he'd hurt you. Well, I'll be damned, Canty, you got big tears comin' down. I haven't seen you cry since you was little. What's goin' on?"

"Time you knew what happened." She pulled away from him and gestured for Pop to sit down with her. She related the story of Tully's marriage.

Pop took her hand and made her look at him. "Little girl, you been dealt some sorry cards." He wiped her tears with his old red handkerchief, and held her close again.

"Pop, it's all right. It'll be all right." She kissed his nose. "I love you, Pop."

"Love you too, Canty. Can't take no more of this. Can't take seein' my Canty cry."

She kissed his forehead and managed a wobbly smile. "I'm going to bed."

Sleep wouldn't come. The whole awful truckload of unhappy memories came roaring back. The details of the time twelve years ago were as clear as new ice.

Canty had only two more days before she had to return to UGA, and still Tully Jones hadn't come home from Atlanta for his promised time with her. Canty wanted so badly to be with him. He was tall, and strong and ruggedly handsome, and she had loved him since he stood up for her against the Ponders when she was just twelve. She was devastated when he left Wynton five years before to pursue a career in Criminal Psychology at Georgia State in Atlanta. After graduation, Tully decided to join the Atlanta Police Force, and rarely ever came back to Wynton. But he had promised to come home for just a few days just to see her, before he started his next assignment.

The phone! "It's me, Canty. Tully. I'm on my way. I'll see you in about an hour. Look pretty as always, please, ma'm."

Thank you, Lord, she thought. She postured in front of her mirror. Her cheeks were flushed, and her hair reflected crackling reds and golds from deep brown depths. Her gray eyes framed in heavy black lashes, sparkled. Her lithe frame was dressed in snug jeans and a blouse that she let stay open almost to her cleavage. "Yum, I feel pretty, yes I do."

She strode out to the porch and breathed a sigh of relief when she saw Tully's truck coming over the ridge. He stepped out, the rugged features split by a big smile. She knew she was smiling back so hard, she probably looked like a clown.

"Hey, you're lookin' mighty good." He held out his arms. Canty was enveloped by a huge hug, and she wrapped her arms around him.

"Tully Jones, you are so special, and I love you so much. I missed you until I hurt. I know once I get back to school, we'll hardly see each other again, and I can't stand knowing it. Tell me we have the next three days—"

"Canty, I only have a few hours until I have to report back."

"What? You can't mean it. This is our time. Dammit! I swear I'll call your boss and tell him how desperately I need to be with you. I'll tell him how long I have loved you. I swear, I'll do it, Tully."

"Whoa." He pushed her away and ran his finger down her nose and over her chattering lips. "If what I have to say wasn't so important, I'd listen to you do it, and get a good laugh. We've got a lot of talking to do, in a very short time, Canty."

"Talking. Poof. I want some loving, serious loving. I want you and I'm tired of waiting."

Tully put his big hands on her shoulders. "My headstrong, outspoken girl, I love you. I've cared about you since you were in the first grade and I was the bus monitor. You came on that bus like you owned it. You owned me from that day on."

"Yea, Mr. Big Shot fifth grader. I knew you were crazy about me when you kept yelling at me to find a seat, and quit talking so much." She ran a finger over his lips. "I especially knew you were crazy about me when you set those Ponders straight. I know one thing, that was the day I knew I loved you, and always would." She signed theatrically. "My hero."

They both laughed easily. Canty grabbed Tully's hand and pulled him to the porch. "Wish Pop would get these swing chains to be quiet. You can't swing and listen at the same time."

"Pop is the finest man I have ever met. He's deep courage, that man. He says what he believes and doesn't waver. You're like him."

Canty gazed into Tully's hazel eyes which reflected the blue in his shirt. He looked gorgeous. "That's the biggest compliment I could ever have, thank you. Now let's quit talking. I want more hugs and kisses. I want passion. I want you, and I won't give up. You can't deny me any longer. I'm damned grown-up now, and you know it."

"Canty, I've got something to tell you." His usual booming voice was whisper soft.

Alarm signals shot through her body at the tension in his voice. "Well, tell me."

He bent over as if in pain. His fists were so clenched, every knuckle glowed white. "You'll want me to go away."

"What are you talking about? We're in love. Canty's voice was cracking. "What in the name are you talking about? Tully." Canty bristled. "It can't be another woman! For God's sake, what?" Now, Canty's mind was dissolving in fear.

Tully went stone silent. He stood up and began pacing the length of the porch. Back and forth, back and forth. Canty felt faint from holding her breath.

He slammed his fist on the porch rail, and turned to face her. "Canty. I'm married. I've been married for nearly a year."

Canty yelled, and went at Tully with fists flying. "No! You're lying. No. You've never lied to me. You're being mean." Tully crossed his arms over his chest and let her flail.

Canty started laughing hysterically. "Oh, sure. Very funny. Hell of a way to get rid of me. Tully. I love you. Please, tell me you're joking. Tell me!"

"No joke." She saw tears glistening in his eyes.

Canty flopped back down into the porch swing. This isn't happening. I'm sleeping and it's a nightmare.

Tully's voice brought her back to reality. "Can you believe I fell for the oldest trick in the book? She told me she was pregnant by me, and I believed her. She wasn't pregnant, but she's my wife."

Canty's voice rasped. "Idiot. Why in hell did you screw her anyway? You can divorce her. She tricked you. Divorce her!"

Tully sat down beside her, and put an arm around her. They swung, the only sound was the creaking of the swing chains.

He took a deep breath, and began to speak. "There's more to it." Canty laid her head on his chest, her tears dripped on his shirt. As his voice seeped into her ears, she wanted to scream, anything to block the sound. Canty felt Tully's body tremble.

"She was a fragile woman when I met her. I'd taken her in on a drug bust and God, she was so pitiful. She begged me to help her. Said she had no family. Promised she'd go cold turkey, or whatever it took to get clean. I felt sorry for her."

"Idiot. Bitch." Canty snuffled into Tully's shirt, and hoped he hadn't heard her.

"So, I got her assigned to a rehab center, and found her a job. We just fell together, I guess. When she told me she was pregnant, that was it. She'd been clean, and was doing good on her job. So, I married her."

"Shit."

Tully ruffled her hair, and stretched out his long legs. Canty wanted to roll into a ball and hide under his armpit.

He rumbled on. "She slipped up, and got high one night, and told me she wasn't pregnant, and if she was, she wouldn't be sure who the father was anyway."

"Damn and shit."

"So, I put the word divorce on her. She OD'd that night on some bad cocaine, and when I came home, she'd been unconscious for hours. She's now in a mental institution, and the odds on her recovery are not good. Canty, I'm married until she recovers or dies. I love you, but I can't ask anything of you, understand?" He tipped her face to him and kissed her lightly on the lips.

Canty watched as he rose and walked to his truck. He didn't look back.

★   ★   ★

Canty went back to the University. For the first time in her life, she partied, and partied hard. She met the blonde god. He was physically flawless, and she was swept up in his aura and sophistication. He was from Long Island, New York, a place heard of, but never seen by Canty O'Neil. She had only read of the immense wealth of the people who lived there and when he described his home, and his string of polo ponies, Canty was mesmerized.

"Canty," he'd say, "you have two languages, University and Mountain. It's really cute." He'd cup her face in his hands and suck deep kisses from her mouth until she was weak kneed, and wet all over.

Still in disbelief and despair over her love for Tully, she clung to the god for reassurance of her desirability. He definitely thought her desirable, and after drinking several beers laced with tequila one night, he made her his little mountain woman and Toby's mother.

And now, Pop, dear wonderful Pop, had opened the wounds again. His asking about her relationship with Tully tonight nearly broke her heart.

Canty got out of bed, and walked to her window. The sky was putting on a spectacular show tonight. Barely a slice of the new moon was showing, and the stars and planets were so thick, the sky looked like solid, brilliant ice. Her thoughts tumbled, unorganized and painful. Memories she thought she had blocked out of her mind began slipping into place. The blur of her past focused clear again.

Tully had come home, unexpectedly, in between assignments, just before Toby was born. Canty hadn't told him anything, and she suddenly felt cheap and horrible when she saw the shocked look on his face. He grabbed for her and hugged her as close as he could. She could feel the huge body tremble, and a too quick thudding of his heart. "Who's the lucky father, damn it?"

Canty knew this conversation was going to be painful. She had begged Pop to be there, but he refused, saying he couldn't watch the unjustified demolition of Tully Jones. She took a deep breath. "No one you know, Tully."

His craggy face turned stone hard. "What does that mean?"

Canty shivered. "It just means that the baby's father was someone you don't know. You don't know everyone I've met in the past years at college. After all, you were gone, you got married and so-" Her voice was shaking so she couldn't go on.

Tully took her arm and helped her up the stairs to the porch. "Come on, fatso, get yourself up these stairs, and sit down."

She laughed, and it felt good. He propelled her toward her favorite rocker, which she gratefully plumped into. She watched him stride to the end of the porch and effortlessly pick up another rocker and set it down beside her. They both sat, staring out into the mountains. Canty couldn't speak.

"Look at those clouds coming over the ridge, Canty. Ever see anything prettier? I love these mountains. I miss 'em like hell."

Canty swallowed. Her voice was thin as paper. "How's your job going? You Chief, yet?"

"Nope, not yet."

"Do you want to be?"

"Nope, not yet."

Canty whacked the arm of her rocker. "That's what I love about you Jones, you're such a great conversationalist. Sometimes I just want to yell at you to shut-up, and let me get a word in."

Tully turned to her, his familiar lopsided grin inched across his face. "More like just the other way around, O'Neil." He placed a large hand on her small puffy one, and started her chair rocking. "Rock A-Bye Baby On The Treetop," he sang.

She snorted, "You are so off key, you'll make this baby sick. Quit."

Tully kept his hand on hers. She felt the intensity of his gaze, and tried not to meet it.

"Canty."

She turned and focused on his face, his weather lines had deepened and she could see just a stubble of beard poking through his skin. The sight of him tore at her heart. "Tully, I know who the father was, but this baby never will."

She saw Tully's body jerk as though he'd been slashed with a whip. "The hell you say. Where is he? Does he know you're pregnant? Do you love him? Who is he?"

Canty stopped rocking. "He lives far away. He knows I'm pregnant with his child, but he doesn't want me, or the baby. Oh, he pretended he was going to send for me, but he didn't, and I'm not going to do a damn thing about it." She saw Tully's jaw lock, and the veins in his neck pop out.

"The hell you aren't! The son-of-a-bitch." He slammed his fist on the arm of the chair so hard, it split. Canty yelped. He reached over, rough fingers held her chin. "Did this happen right after I told you about my sorry ass marriage from hell? Did it?"

She pulled away. "Don't flatter yourself, Tully Jones. You broke my heart, but it mended, by God."

Tully dropped his head down, and Canty could see his shoulders quivering. She pulled him by the ear. "If you're laughing at me, I swear to God, I'll slap you silly." He raised his head, and Canty saw tears streaking his face.

Canty felt goose bumps and chills all over her body. The baby tumbled and kicked inside her womb, and she gasped at the sharpness of the blow. Her throat constricted so tight she couldn't swallow. She let her head flop back on the chair. "It's a mess, I know," she squeezed the words out between her teeth, "but Pop will be here for us. We'll be fine. It's not your fault, Tully. I swear to God, I'm not blaming you. I chose to lose it, and I lost it big, didn't I? Funny, isn't it? You got married because you thought she was pregnant with your child and here I am, pregnant as hell and no marriage." Canty reached for Tully's hand. "Tully, if you weren't married, would you ask me to marry you, now?"

Tully got up and stretched his long frame, his hands brushed the porch ceiling. "Nope."

Canty prickled. "What do you mean, nope? You're my best buddy. Nope!"

He leaned over her chair and kissed her lips lightly. "You and I, were not to be. We'd each be marrying the other because we felt sorry for the other. And that doesn't work. I know. I got to go."

"Why?" A lump formed in Canty's throat.

"I have assignments to full-fill in the big city, girl. I want to hear from you and know you're okay with the baby and all. I'm really into some heavy stuff and won't be able to reply often, if at all. You send word through my office. Promise?"

The lump grew larger. "Yes."

He pulled her out of the rocker and held her swollen body close. He brushed a clumsy hand down her back. "I'm coming home one day, Canty. Probably in two or three years, but I'm coming home for good. I won't ask you to wait for me because she may still be in my life."

Canty tucked her head into his chest and inhaled his very being. "I'm going to miss you, big time."

Tully strode away, his long legs gobbling up the distance to his truck in a flash.

★   ★   ★

When Toby was three, Canty met the new principal of Wynton High School. He was single, and great with Toby. After six months in Wynton, he took a job with a private school in Ohio, and she never saw him again. The owner of the new Antiques Boutique store on the square briefly started fires in her body, and she enjoyed some moments of passion, but no fulfillment. Besides, he constantly hovered over Toby telling him "not to touch this and not to touch that" in his precious Antique Boutique. When Toby refused to go into the store one day, Canty shrugged, and never saw him again except for an occasional wave in the grocery store.

By the time Tully Jones came home to run for office of Sheriff of Morgan County, Canty had checked out every eligible bachelor within a hundred mile range and found them all wanting bed, but no breakfast, lunch and dinner. She banked her fires.

Canty remembered her joy when Tully came back home, and her despair when he told her he was still married, and no medical breakthroughs were in sight to cure his wife's poor mangled brain.

He had pulled her close. "Like I said awhile back, Canty, we're just not to be."

"Let me tell you something, Tully Jones. When you told me that three years ago, I refused to believe it, but by God, I believe it now. If you haven't done anything about getting shed of that trickster you married, nuts or not, I give up. It took me awhile, damn it, but I give up. I just haven't found anyone like you, and I've looked."

Canty felt a tremble in his body. "I'll always love you, Canty O'Neil. I'll be there for you if you need me," he grinned just a little, "and no man will have you unless I approve."

Canty hugged his waist. "I'll always love you, too. But, I'll choose my own man. Just remember, you turned me down."

"Damn it, Canty O'Neil. I'd like to turn you over my knee."

Canty looked up into Tully's deep brown eyes, and inside she wanted to cry. "Don't try it, Jones. Don't you dare ever try it."

CHAPTER 19

A man wearing an ear-to-ear grin emerged from the front cabin of the plane. He headed directly toward Toby.

"Hey, son, you don't look so good. Look a little green around the edges."

"I'm okay, mister. Who's flyin' this plane?" Toby's bravado was interrupted with gagging.

Canty grabbed Toby's hand and held up the bag labeled "TossIt."

"You must be Canty O'Neil and son, Toby."

"Yes, it's me, Canty O'Neil and son, Toby. You must be Jimmy. Burke told me about you. He really bragged about what a great helicopter pilot you are."

"You got that right," the ear-to-ear grin became just a tiny bit wider. "I'm also a hellava co-pilot on this jet."

Toby gagged again. Canty held the bag up to his face. He threw up, quickly. He sat back, his face pale. "Whew and double it," he gasped, chest still heaving. "Whew. Glad that's done."

Bridgette appeared, and gazed tenderly at Toby. "Here you go, Toby." She handed him a bubbly drink in an etched delicate tumbler. "That will settle your tummy so you can enjoy the rest of the flight."

Canty took the glass before it got to Toby's outstretched hand. "What's in there?"

Bridgette smiled a dazzling, white all-teeth-in-line-smile. "I'm sorry, Mrs. O'Neil. That was thoughtless. Just Alka-Seltzer. Should calm him. Would you like some champagne, Mrs. O'Neil? I can bring you and Toby some cheese and crackers. By the way," Bridgette bent over and her incredible cleavage threw Canty's head back, "Burke McGuire thinks you two are terrific. Glad to have you on board."

"Okay, Bridge, back with the cheese and crackers." Jimmy popped her behind lightly. She smiled again, and Canty found herself fascinated with the perfect application of her lip liner.

Canty felt dowdy and plain. Just like being around Diamond.

Jimmy looked down at Toby. "Now, the captain of this plane says you need to join him up front. How about it, son?"

"You're kiddin'." Color began returning to Toby's face. He gulped down the Alka-Seltzer and began unfastening his seat belt.

Jimmy led Toby up front. "Want to come, Mrs. O'Neil?"

"No thanks, I'll let you boys handle it." Canty leaned back in the plush suede seat. She let her gaze wander around the interior of the plane, and took in the incredible luxury of the appointments with awe. The buff and teal fabrics, and polished-brass accents were dramatic, but soothing. Her seat enveloped her softly. It turned and tilted. She had access to a telephone and a small TV. There was no sensation of flight. If she didn't know better, she would swear she was sitting in someone's living room. She laughed to herself. She felt the tension of the past week seeping out of her pores.

"Mom, fasten your seat belt, we're descending for a landing." Toby appeared, his gray eyes shooting sparks. "Oh, man, that Captain is a neat guy, Mom. You should see what's up there."

Canty was startled to realize she had fallen asleep. She fastened her seat belt and in spite of the impending excitement ahead, wished the flight were longer. The Captain's voice came through the sound system, pointing out highlights of the Florida landscape and to Toby's delight, he pinpointed Disney World, Sea World, and the Epcot monument. The landing was silky smooth.

A waiting limousine whisked them through Orlando, and headed northeast of the city. Jimmy announced, "Next stop, The Grove Golf and Country Club, a Hearn Guilford design, of course." He phoned Burke, and Canty felt herself tingle at the sound of his name.

"Burke says, 'Welcome to you both.' I'll get you to your villa and then I'll show you what I can of The Grove before dinner. Mrs. O'Neil, it really is nice to meet you and Toby. .Why, I was expecting coveralls and dirty bare feet from you mountain people. You look good. I mean really good."

Canty laughed. "Well, Toby and I scrubbed up and wore our Sunday best for this trip, so's we wouldn't embarrass anyone. We wanted to surprise Mr. McGuire. Toby, show Jimmy your shoes, son, and your socks."

Toby grinned and displayed his new Nike's. He pulled up his chino pant legs to reveal the whitest of sport socks.

Jimmy threw a hand over his eyes. "You keep those pant legs down, son. You could blind someone with those bright whites of yours."

Toby flushed red with laughter. "You're so funny Mr. Jimmy."

As they rode, Jimmy called their attention to the rolling hills covered with dark green, bushy trees in perfect rows. "You see there, the life blood of the area."

"Mr. Jim, are those real oranges on those trees? I mean,

I never have seen oranges growing on trees. That's really neat. Like the pictures in my geography book only real. Man." Toby's eyes were wide with amazement.

"They're a pretty sight, all right. Burke and I were raised among those pretty trees, and growing oranges is tough, and I mean tough work. Look over there, and over there." He swung his arm to areas on both sides of the highway. "See all those bare hills? That's trouble. That's who got hit by frost or inadequate watering systems. Couldn't recover. Working those groves can tear a man apart."

The limousine drove through a gated entrance, and rolled softly down a road lined with live oaks and Spanish moss. The driver stopped in front of a one-story cedar and stone house, so artfully sited, it never ruffled the scenery. Lush tropicals, ponds, and fountains wound through the surrounding property.

Inside, Toby gasped at the view from the twenty-foot high glass windows of the villa. Wide green swaths of grass rolled into stands of tall pines and oaks, and little carts with colorful tops scooted along paths rimming the thoroughfares of green.

"That, son, is a golf course fairway. Fairway number seventeen to be exact. The tee is to your left and the green is four-hundred and eighty yards to your right. Pretty, ain't it."

Toby remained at the windows. "Look, Mom, that man's going to swing at the ball." Toby hooted. "He missed! Shoot, it's right there in front of him, and he missed. There he goes, swinging again. Missed again! I could've hit the ball by now."

Jimmy chuckled. "He's just taking his practice swings, Toby. I agree, he's taking too much time. Whoop, there it goes."

Toby watched the ball going straight down the fairway. It suddenly turned left, and disappeared into the pines. "Wow!

What a neat trick. You see that, Mom?"

Canty laughed. "Whoa! I don't think that man thought it was a neat trick. He just slammed that club down hard."

"Your Mom's right, Toby." Jimmy interjected. "He wanted that ball to stay on the fairway, bet on that. Looks like we got some golf educatin' to do, here."

"I'm ready, Mr. Jimmy."

Canty and Toby met Burke for dinner at the sprawling glass and rock clubhouse. She saw the smile in his blue eyes before he even reached them. The tingle in her groin felt visible and she flushed. His stride was purposeful, as was everything about Burke McGuire. He stuck out a hand to Toby and brushed Canty's cheek lightly with his lips.

"Mmm, you smell good Canty," he whispered.

Canty hoped her goose bumps weren't showing.

They were escorted to a table overlooking a tropical paradise of trees and plants, surrounding a pool that curved and flowed in harmony with the vegetation. Ground lights twinkled throughout the landscape. Canty was so entranced, she let Toby do all the talking. Jimmy had taken them on a short tour before meeting Burke and Toby was ecstatic remembering every golf hole on the back nine, the perfect grass, the white sand traps, and the alligators sunning.

Burke jumped in on Toby's first inhale. "Now, how would you like to play some golf, Toby? Jimmy and I want to start you off right. We can have some fun while your mom is making big deals happen with Hearn Guilford."

Canty jerked back to reality. "Burke, aren't you going to meet him with me?"

Burke focused on her, and she wanted to reach out and trace his square jaw, and brush her hand over his crew cut. "No, Hearn wants to talk to you, alone. He knows exactly how I feel about the whole project. He wants no outside influences leaking in to the conversation. Don't look so terrorized. I guarantee, he's a lot easier to talk to than Queen Ponder." He laughed, "In fact, he's a lot easier to talk to than I am. Aren't you glad to hear that?"

The dinner was fabulous. Shrimp cocktail, filet mignon, vinaigrette salad, crusty, warm rolls and real butter. The asparagus was fresh and tender. Toby practically inhaled the wild rice, a dish, until today, unknown to his young palette.

After dinner, Burke took them to the pro shop, and picked out three putters and a handful of practice balls. Canty was impressed by the muffled elegance of the shop, filled with beautiful golf clothes, and shiny golf clubs. Now she knew what it meant when people said something just smelled like money. Her favorites were the golf hats, especially the ones with the name Michelle McGann inside. She tried one on, and postured in front of a mirror, tilting the glamorous bowed and beaded straw hat at different angles.

"The heck with golf, Canty," Burke appeared behind her, grinning, "You just model those hats. Anyone who looks that good doesn't need to play."

"No way. I still want to learn and," she turned and poked a finger in his chest, "when I get good, I'll treat myself to one of these hats."

Burke grabbed her hand and flattened it on his chest. "You are good. Canty—"

"Mom, look at this putter. Look at it, it's taller than I am."

Canty's heart was thudding and she had an almost uncontrollable urge to plant a big kiss on Burke's grinning lips.

Burke motioned them outside to the lighted practice

putting green. Canty was sure she would see little elves hopping around with nail scissors, trimming and trimming. No grass could possibly look that good cut by a lawn mower. They spent a half-hour stroking balls and listening to Burke on the importance of being able to putt well. "Yup, the big money is on the green. You watch. The pro's can all get off the tee, and for the most part make a good second shot. But, when it comes to being around the green, and having a touch," he looked at both of them and pulled out a pitching wedge, "this club, and a putter are where it's at." He declared they had had enough for their first lesson.

"To bed, my friends. It's almost ten, and this boy is ready. Got to get up early. Have a young man slated for his first lesson on the golf swing. Have a lady who has a very important meeting and she needs to be sharp." He pointed at Canty. "Breakfast in the lounge at eight. You'll be meeting with Hearn at nine. Hop in." He sat behind the wheel of a golf cart. She slid across the seat to make room for Toby and felt the hardness of Burke's body from her shoulder all the way down past her knee. She sighed and cleared her throat.

"Me, too, Canty O'Neil," he whispered.

Canty could not keep her eyes closed. Every time she slid her eyelids down, a new thought about the contract entered her mind and zap, wide open again. She finally got up and padded into the great room. The tile floor felt cool. Moonlight beamed into the huge glass expanse overlooking the golf course. Toby sat, chin resting on knees, gazing out into the black-green of the night.

"Toby, what in the world?"

"Whoa. You scared me, Mom."

"Sorry, honey, but you startled me just being there. I couldn't sleep either. Too much going on." She felt the familiar deep tug of love as she saw him get up, all gangly, tousled-haired and beautiful, back-lit by a moonbeam.

Toby turned his slender body back to the window. "I was just lookin' at the course. Isn't it something? I can't wait to play golf and be on that course. I wonder if I'll be any good. Mr. Burke and Mr. Jimmy might get annoyed with me if I'm not. I putted all right, Mr. Burke said. Wasn't that neat, Mom? You could practice all night on that lighted putting green. Mr. Burke said that when the pros play a tournament here, he's seen many of them out there until the sun's ready to come up. They practice, practice, practice."

Canty wrapped her arms around him from behind. She could feel the energy zinging through his body. He would never sleep tonight.

"Tell ya what, Tob, I'm going to check on hot chocolate. Neither one of us seems very sleepy."

Canty found hot chocolate mix, and in minutes, she and Toby stood sipping the thick, creamy liquid. The tension slid from her limbs. "Tob, here's to Instant Hot Chocolate and Microwave Ovens."

"Mom," Toby's gaze never wavered from his dark view of the fairway, "this sure is a different kinda place. It's like a whole different world. Awful flat, though. But I like it all right. The people are nice. Mr. Burke wants to build a golf course like this on the Ponder land? Sure can't figure it. Going to take a lot of dirt moving, I know that."

Canty hugged him.

CHAPTER 20

Hearn Guilford stood at the door, and Canty returned his firm handshake with her own. He smiled down at her from his lean six-foot three-inch frame. She liked the craggy, weathered face, and the profusion of salt and pepper curls that framed it.

Instead of seating Canty opposite him at his desk, Hearn led her to a small grouping of two fawn-colored leather chairs in front of a large bay window, overlooking the golf course. A glass-topped rattan table between the chairs was set with a silver coffeepot, and two silver-clad espresso cups. All the pieces were engraved with The Grove logo.

Canty was impressed with the beauty of the office, and the fine furniture, but surprised that it wasn't much more spacious. In Canty's mind, a man of Hearn Guilford's stature should have a ballroom-sized office. This room couldn't be any bigger than her office in Wynton.

"It certainly is good to meet you, Canty. Please, have a seat. Coffee?" Hearn Guilford's voice low timbered and even-toned, wrapped around her and made her comfortable immediately.

"Yes, thank you." She nearly chuckled thinking of Willodene and her famous espresso. Oh, she'd love to be here, right now. She took a sip. "Delicious."

Hearn lifted his cup in a toast. "Special espresso for a special guest. Welcome to The Grove."

She sipped again. Willodene's didn't taste like this. "My dear friend and secretary is heavy into the espresso, and I'll be honest, hers tastes like dirt to me. This is wonderful."

A smile flashed in his direct, light brown eyes. "I'll find out just how this is made, and the flavor so you can pass it on to her. Now, how about that view?"

They swiveled their chairs and faced the panorama outside. Perfect emerald green fairways stretched as far as the eye could see. The vegetation lining their boundaries was lavish and full of tropical color. "It's so perfect, it looks like a painting," she said. "I'll also tell you, I don't know a thing about golf courses, or how they are built, but I have learned how beautiful they can be."

"There's nothing Burke McGuire can't teach you about golf courses and their construction, Canty. The man is a genius at it. He seems to be quite taken with your innate knowledge of the mountains, and how to work with the people there." He paused and a smile flickered on his lips. "In fact, I can't say I've ever seen him so impressed with anyone he has chosen to work with before."

Canty felt a tingling run through her scalp. Chosen. Not exactly, McGuire. "I'm also impressed with Burke McGuire." Absolutely.

"Good. As a matter of fact, Diamond and Max also think you are something special and that, too, is a rare compliment." He grinned, "More rare than you can imagine. My beautiful wife was born with a perceptiveness about people that astounds me. I trust her judgement completely. Max, on the other hand, was left behind the door when that admirable trait was passed out, but fortunately, his type of genius doesn't require too many people skills. And, he believes totally in Diamond's reactions to people."

Canty smiled. "I really enjoyed Diamond and Max. The good people of Wynton were struck dumb when I introduced her. She absolutely blinds people with her sparkle and beauty. She really does." Canty hoped she didn't sound sloppy.

Hearn chuckled. "I've noticed that a few times, myself." He put his cup down and the brown eyes were serious. "Canty, we've got a problem. I've based my reputation as a businessman on honesty, and professionalism. My clients know that when I ask for investment money, I've left no stone unturned to ensure a successful project. I'm deeply trusted. I'll not tolerate losing the trust my clients have in Hearn Guilford Golf Designs. Bottom line, I can't ask for money based on a handshake."

Canty listened.

Hearn sat back in his chair, but stayed in direct eye contact with Canty. "I've seen the property, and in a few minutes, I want to know everything you know about the land, and the Ponders. Their instability comes down as dangerous from what I've heard."

He rose and crossed the room. One wall had drawn curtains, which he pulled open to reveal a wall-sized topography map of the Ponder property. "I've already invested a large sum of my own money in the project, and I realize that I'll take a loss if we can't close on the property. I've taken those risks before. The next move will be to bring in investors." Hearn sat back down, and once again looked straight into her eyes. "I'm not happy with the situation as I see it. I can't accept risking anyone else's monetary loss, loss of trust, and worse, anyone's loss of life."

Canty was still.

Hearn leaned back in his chair and turned to gaze out at

the view. "Thanks for listening. A rare trait, especially under the circumstances. You ready?"

"Yes." Canty put down her silver cup, and leaned back, ever so slightly, for just a moment. She was determined to look relaxed. Her insides were bubbling. She left the chair, and shifted her usual quick stride down to second gear. She reached the topography map, and began naming the ridges and peaks surrounding the Ponder valley. She named the varieties of trees and plants, and explained why they grew where they grew, plus their importance to the ecosystem of the valley. Canty described the flow of the land, the creeks, and how the winds prevailed through the valley at different times of the year.

"One of the problems you will have is here, along Secret Creek." Canty traced a thin blue line with her finger. "It's called Secret Creek because of two things. One, no one has ever found the source, and two, it is so delicate and narrow most of the time, you hardly notice it. It makes a wonderful, soft sound as it flows over and between the rocks of its bed, but a sudden mountain rain storm can cause it to explode over its banks and flood the area up to forty or fifty yards around it. You'll have to be careful not to build any important part of the course close to it. It will, though, be a real asset because of its beauty. Some bridges over it would be nice."

"Excuse me." Hearn's voice was in her ears. She gasped, and turned abruptly. She had been so absorbed she never noticed that he had stepped over to the topo and was directly behind her. "Do you realize you have been talking non-stop for twenty-five incredible minutes?"

Canty smiled. "Thanks for listening."

He backed off, smiling. "Canty, I could listen to you

164

for hours. You're like a damn poet describing the land. I've never known anyone to be as hands-on knowledgeable about a piece of property before, especially a piece I felt would be so difficult to work. I was worried about several aspects of designing this course among mountains and creeks, but I'll take your advice about Secret Creek under advisement. It was one of my stumbling blocks. Now, I want more of your mountain lore about the land. You've given me a lot of confidence in foreseeing the problems. Come, sit back down."

She walked with him back to the chairs. A cut glass pitcher and two cut glass tumblers, all engraved with The Grove logo, had replaced the coffee service.

"Orange juice?" He grinned and poured some in her glass.

"Perfect. I must admit to being thirsty after talking so much. It's not my style but that property—"

"You're terrific. You have the same passion and intensity about what you do as Burke McGuire. Never thought I'd meet a female Burke McGuire."

"I agree about Burke. I have never met someone who cared so much about what he does as Burke. He is focused, really focused. Has he always been like that?"

Hearn chuckled. "He sure has. Burke blew me away with that intensity of his when he was only twelve years old. It's in his genes. I wouldn't get in his way when he's convinced and determined."

Canty laughed. "You sound like my father describing Burke's personality. You make him sound a little ruthless, too."

"No, Canty. I said convinced and determined. There's a fine line between that and ruthless. I've never known Burke to cross it." He sat back and turned to the view again. "We do have one more serious obstacle," he rotated his chair back to face her, "those Ponders are obviously crazy and shotgun happy. You've convinced me that you're a necessary asset to building this golf course. I'm also convinced because of Burke, Diamond and Max, that you know how to deal with the people in Wynton. I'm not convinced that you can control those mountain boys, and I don't want to find out that neither you nor anyone can, at my or your expense." He leaned toward her, and she saw steel in the clear brown eyes. "I have a zero-tolerance level for violence, especially when my people are involved."

Canty's throat tightened. She deliberately turned her chair to the view, took a sip of orange juice, and hoped her voice would work. She swallowed, and swung back to face Hearn.

She held his eyes with hers. "Now, I've heard tell you have some rough encounters with your swamp boys around here. Anyone get shot at? Anyone ever get killed?"

Hearn's face broke into a smile. "You are quick, aren't you?" The smile disappeared. "No, no one has gotten killed, yet. Burke and most of his crew do carry, though. Those swamp boys would use a gun on another human if they were driven to it, but we've made sure that didn't happen. From what Diamond and Max tell me, the Ponders are mean, scary rough. According to them, those boys will fire without provocation."

"Here's the way it is." She relaxed slightly when his gaze had softened. "The family created and procreated itself years ago. They isolated themselves, refused education, and health care. They only socialized when one was looking for a mate. Eventually, they had enough men and women to keep their community alive. They probably had eighty to one-hundred self-surviving people up there for fifty or sixty years. They were totally independent and self-governing. They raised cattle, and grew their own crops. The terrible toll of incest, and lack of immunity to diseases, has all but destroyed them. Queen Ponder can read and write. God knows how she accomplished it. She is the last of the matriarchs, and is fast losing control over her brothers. Terrell and Smith are mean as snakes and stupid as cows. They have no sense of right or wrong. Pauly is so severely retarded, it would make you cry. I can make no guarantees about dealing with them, except I feel very strongly that they would kill each other before they killed an outsider." She saw Hearn's eyes squint slightly, questioning her statement, and went on.

"They've scared the fool out of some folks, and can be destructive when they've a mind to, but they have never killed an outsider." Canty took a deep breath. "Not too reassuring, I know," she added.

"No, not too reassuring."

Canty jumped back in before Hearn could question her further. "This has to be handled quickly. Burke, through his own brand of magic, had Queen seeing big dollar signs, and ready to make the deal, although I believe that Pauly is her real motivation. She's incredibly protective of him, and wants to get the money to make sure Pauly is taken care of for the rest of his pitiful life. She told me that Smith and Terrell have no right to any of the money, should she sell. The boys definitely know Queen is working on a sale but they have no idea that they are not part of the pie, and she doesn't intend that they know until it's too late. The Ponders play a dangerous game among themselves, and I'm counting on that to keep them from doing anything murderous to any of us."

"Still not reassuring, and very risky."

Positive, Canty. Be positive. "I have grown up in the Blue Ridge, Hearn. There's no other piece of dirt and mountain rock to compare to the Ponder property for sheer beauty, and relative ease of development for your project. It doesn't exist. I want this project to succeed. I'm the key to make it happen and I fully intend to make it happen. I won't let any of your people get hurt. I know I'm right about the Ponders killing themselves before anyone else. I need your vote of confidence, and I'll be on my way back to Wynton."

Hearn unfolded himself from the soft leather chair, and walked again to the topography map. Canty held her breath, and watched as he ran his fingers over the surface as though memorizing every mountain peak and valley. His mouth was a thin line and deep furrows showed between his eyes. Her thoughts were ricocheting around her brain. Was he going to give it up? Yes. She was too bold, too pushy.

Finally, he turned to look at her. The furrows had smoothed, the lips were full again. She tried a small smile, but her mouth refused to move.

He reached out his hand and she put her hand in his. "Canty O'Neil, I'm glad as hell to know you. You're a pro. I want you to know, I still consider this high risk, but people like you and Burke McGuire seem to thrive on challenges like this one. You believe in what you're doing, and that's what I am going on. But, I will not ask for any investor money until the property closes and becomes Hearn Guilford Golf Designs, Inc. I'm laying a lot on both you and Burke. He's been tested."

Canty smiled at him. No wonder this man didn't need a ballroom to impress anyone. "I'll pass."

Canty left Hearn's office, and found Burke glued to the wall outside the door. She gave him a big smile. "He said, 'yes', handshake, and all. I see why you think so much of the man. He's first class. I would've liked him even if he'd said no."

"He shook your hand, and smiled? Hearn? What'd you do to him, woman?" Burke was laughing and shaking his head in disbelief. "Hearn doesn't do business with—"

"A handshake, I know. How about a handshake and a nod?" Canty put her hand over her mouth to keep from bursting with laughter at Burke's expense. She had never seen him so puzzled, and excited.

He grabbed her in his arms and planted a hard kiss on her lips. "You're brilliant!"

"No, Hearn said you're the brilliant one. I think he sees me as a manipulator, a professional, but a manipulator."

"He's right, you are. The best!" He planted another kiss on her lips.

She pushed him away, her knees already wobbly. "The best what? Professional or manipulator? And, what did you do with Toby?"

Burke grinned, the blue eyes dancing, "Why, both but maybe a little heavier on the manipulator side." He stepped behind her and pointed toward the driving range. "Look out there."

Canty spotted Toby, the familiar thick mop of hair blowing in the breeze, golf club in hand, his gaze intent on whatever Jimmy was telling him. She saw him nod and place the club behind the ball.

Burke put his hands on her shoulders and she could feel him tense, his touch was burning. "Look at the little squirt. Turn sideways, he almost disappears. Don't you feed that kid?"

"Why do you think I have to work so hard and deal with people like the Ponders, and Burke McGuire's of the world?

That boy can eat up a storm. He's just- -"

"I know, a growing boy. And, I tell you, looking at those hands and feet, he's got some growing to do to catch up to those body parts. Got broad shoulders, but sloping, just enough."

"Sloping just enough for what?"

"Just the way a good golfer is put together. He's got all the right stuff and the kid is coordinated as hell. His daddy must have been an athlete. Shows."

Canty's heart started to pound. She gasped.

Burke turned her to face him, almost roughly. "Listen, damn it. I don't care who his daddy is just so he's far away from you."

"Who his daddy was."

The square hard planes of Burke's face softened, just a little.

"Toby's daddy was killed shortly after I gave birth. We weren't married. He never knew him, so I never gave him his name."

The hard planes became rigid again. "Son of a bitch left ya, right? Did he know you were pregnant?"

"Yes." Tears burned in her eyes. Pain recalled, hurts, she knew. She turned back to the window, and watched Toby swing. She saw the ball leave the club in a high arc, and quickly lost sight of it in her tears.

Burke took Canty and Toby to the airport later that day. Canty's joy at gaining Hearn Guilford's okay to get on with the project was tempered at leaving Burke behind. He gave her a perfunctory peck on the cheek, and blew in her ear. She wanted to return the gesture, badly.

"Stinker," she whispered.

The blue eyes flashed. "I'll be back in Wynton tomorrow night. The drawings are ready and Diamond and Max have reluctantly agreed to a meeting with Queen. I've already called Tully and he's setting it up with Queen."

Canty looked out of the plane window until Burke was just a speck. She leaned back in the plush leather seat and sighed. The man is scary, he's so damn sexy. God!

Toby talked of nothing but golf on the flight back. He began speaking a foreign language, and she had to keep interrupting him for definitions.

Toby tried very hard to explain par, bogey, eagle, and the importance of knowing yardage to the pin, and on and on. So far, it boggled Canty's mind. But she loved Toby's enthusiasm. Canty couldn't ask more questions, she didn't know what questions to ask.

"Toby, the only yardage to the pin I've ever learned about was cutting and sewing curtains."

He smiled his big, wide smile. "Mr. Jimmy and Mr. Burke both said I have a real natural swing and maybe I could be good some day. But you know what else they said, you gotta practice all the time, every day. The real pros are always practicing. Maybe Pop can rig me up a place to hit balls. We could go to the driving range. I really like those guys, Mom."

"Me, too."

CHAPTER 21

Burke pulled the Explorer into Wynton after dark. Bypassing Taco Bell, he chose Hardees. The parking lot was practically empty, and he noted, no Sheriff's car.

Sheriff must be mighty busy, he thought. No tail coming up the mountain, no parking lot welcoming committee. Damn, was he with Canty? Old Tully Jones covered her like a blanket. That just friends stuff was pure shit.

There were three men at one table, and one massively obese man sat alone. His tray was filled with orders of fries, two shakes, and three burgers. Burke's stomach felt queasy watching him stuffing his bloated face with greasy hands.

"Can I hep you?" A tiny little voice emanated from a corpulent female behind the counter.

"Yeah, you can hep me." Jeezuz. Wynton was too small to have so many fat slobs like this taking up space. "One burger, an order of corn on the cob, and a large shake, to go." You're gonna look just like 'em, Burke. Gotta quit these fast-food, deep-fat fryers for nourishment.

He caught the three men looking at him. He acknowledged them with a quick grin and a nod. They looked away and continued eating.

This was supposed to be a friendly town. Bullshit.

Burke picked up his order. The tiny voice squeaked a "Thank you, and come back now."

He walked to the Explorer and cursed. There, on the windshield was a piece of paper, stuck on with bubble gum, and a note in red crayon, "Go back to Florida."

Burke rolled the paper around the gum and stuck it in his jacket pocket. Well, at least he felt at home. Why, these folks were beginning to recognize him even without the Jag. Made a man feel mighty good.

At the Best Western, he checked into the same room as before, and was glad, as before, that he could park the Explorer under the security light outside his door. He called Hearn Guilford.

"I'm back in the Land of Oz, Hearn. There're a lot of very strange creatures lurking around this town. I think I just saw some of the Wicked Witch's best fat friends at Hardees. Not friendly folks at all. The welcome sign isn't out for a good old Florida boy trying to make a living."

"Keep your gun ready, and lock your doors," Hearn ordered.

"Right, big Daddy." Burke grinned. A loud crash outside stopped the smile from going any further. "Got to check something, Hearn. Call you back in a few minutes."

He hung up hearing Hearn Guilford yelling at him for information.

Burke opened the door, and stepped outside. "I'll be damned." The windshield of the Explorer now blanketed the hood in millions of colorful, shiny pieces of glass. He heard a gurgle and a spit.

He yelled into the darkness. "Come on out, you chicken-shit. Come on out!"

The muzzle of a shotgun slid onto the fender of the Explorer, followed by two of the ugliest faces he'd ever seen.

The revolting heads rose higher, supported by skinny bodies in tattered plaid shirts and bib overalls

"How do, Mr. MugWire. I'm Terrell. This here's my brother, Smith. We're Ponders. We don't like being called chicken-shit."

"Only chicken-shits bust out windshields, and so you are chicken-shits. You do notes in red crayon?"

They looked puzzled.

"Can either of you chicken-shits read or write? And, what the hell do you want?"

The two glanced at each other and communicated with no words. They stepped out from the Explorer their boots crunching in the broken glass, and stood under the light.

Terrell spoke first. "Sonny, I bet you got one nice ass but you ain't gettin' anywhere around here with us. We own the property you want. We don't know if we want you to have it." He raised the shotgun.

Burke's heart thudded. "If you boys are really Ponders, you must want some of that money, now, don't you? You blow me away, it's gone."

Smith gurgled and spit brown gunk on the sidewalk. "We ain't blowin' nobody away." He put his hand on the barrel of Terrell's shotgun and pushed it down. Terrell spit more brown gunk. "We're deliverin' a message from Queen. She wants to talk with you a bit tomorrow."

Burke kept his voice low, and strained to hold his temper. "I'd already planned on going to see her. Canty O'Neil will be with me."

Terrell spoke up. "Aw, we was hopin' the white haired whore and her tight-assed friend was comin'. We got some words for them. Whooee, we do. Tully Jones comin'? I sure would like a piece of that boy." Terrell wiped snot from his nose with a grimy hand. Smith scratched at his crotch.

Nausea crawled up his throat. His gun was resting, unloaded, in his golf bag, in the Explorer. These ugly bastards were scary. Burke took a step toward them. The shotgun came up level again. Burke stood.

"Terrell, put that damn thing to rest." Smith pushed the muzzle down. "He ain't gonna hurt us. He don't have no guts. But, Queen likes him. Queen's right purty, ain't she?" Smith smiled a black, slimy smile and ran a deep liver-colored tongue around his lips. "You can have a piece of Queen. Trade ya for the white-haired whore."

Burke took another step closer. Their eyes were pale ice blue and red rimmed. They stared, unblinking. Burke spit on Terrell's boot. Terrell stood his ground. Burke watched his eyes, and saw just the tiny flicker of uncertainty he wanted. He took one more step closer. He could smell rotten breath and damp filth. The nausea rose higher.

"I'd like you two chicken-shits to get out of my face. Go home and tell Queen I'll be there tomorrow just like we planned. She knows I'm coming. You boys just wanted to have some fun now, didn't you?"

BLAM! Terrell fired, straight up. Smoke from the blast winnowed slowly up, and away.

Burke stayed nose to nose with Terrell. The filthy man's foul breath made his eyes sting. He put one hand on the gun barrel, holding it steady, still straight up. "God, you chicken-shits stink. Now, get the hell out of my sight. By the way, where can I get my windshield replaced?" Burke watched the hideous faces carefully. They turned toward each other slightly, mouths open and slobbering with more brown gunk. Neither spoke.

"Fun's over, Ponders." The deep voice of Tully Jones reached Burke's ears.

Burke stayed still, hand on the shotgun barrel. "Where you been, Sheriff? These Ponders, or whatever they are, should be in jail for destroying property, disturbing the peace, and air pollution. They sure as hell shouldn't be allowed to carry firearms. You ever smelled these boys, Sheriff or are you too smart to get that close?"

"You got that right." Tully laughed. "Terrell, Smith. Git. I'll see you tomorrow. I'll just have to tell Queen what bad boys you've been tonight." Tully stepped behind the Ponders and pulled them back by their overall straps. They both snapped to life at once. Burke let go of the shotgun as Terrell yanked at it, and both of the men took off running into the darkness.

Burke faced Tully Jones. Anger rose up from his feet, through his groin, darted around his intestines, and slid up his throat. He clenched his teeth to keep from bursting into a yell. He tightened his fists to keep from swinging.

"Tell me something, Sheriff, you write with a red crayon?"

Tully raised his eyebrows. "Don't understand the question, MugWire."

"Don't play dumb with me, Sheriff. You protecting those slimy idiots? What about the damn busted windshield? What's with this town, anyway?"

"I'm not protecting the Ponders." Tully leaned back against the truck. "I'm trying to protect you, MugWire. Those boys would have loved to do a lot more damage than they did. They would have liked to have had your face look like that windshield. You're either really tough, or really stupid to face them down like that."

Burke unclenched his jaw and took a deep breath. "I

want to know why you let them run off, and who in hell is going to fix this windshield?" Burke stepped up close to Tully's face. "You wouldn't be just a mite scared of them now would you, Sheriff?

Tully crossed his long arms over his chest and inhaled. He let his breath out slowly. "You want that property?"

"Or what? Don't tell me you're going to try to follow up their intimidation act? I don't intimidate, Sheriff."

Tully grinned, and Burke knew smoke had to be coming out of his ears. Smug son-of-a- bitch, he thought.

"Mr. MugWire." Tully's voice remained soft and even. It made Burke furious.

Last time you pull that MugWire stuff, Sheriff. Last damn time. Burke fought to hold his voice calm. "Yes, I want that property. Yes, I intend to have that property."

"Why? Why in hell is that property so important to you?"

"Because, Sheriff, that is the most beautiful opportunity for a golf course I have seen in all my years of designing and building golf courses. That property is me. That property is what I do."

Tully scuffed aside some diamonds of glass with a huge boot. "I admire your determination. You know, you can't do it without Canty and me, and arresting Terrell and Smith right now might ruin the stew. I don't want anyone getting hurt."

The anger started again at Burke's toes. He cut it off at his groin and managed a slight lift at the corners of his mouth, hoping the sheriff would notice how calm and affable he could be. "Nobody's going to get hurt. I promise you."

Tully shifted his weight to the other foot and scuffed more glass. "You can't promise anything around here, boy."

"Sheriff, it's time we settle whatever it is you are always

sitting on my butt about. Is it the property, the development, or is it Canty O'Neil? Scared you're going to lose there?"

Tully's eyes took on a fixed glare. "There will be no Canty O'Neil problems here. She knows who she is, and what she wants. We're just friends."

Burke felt his jaw lock tight, the attempt at calm and affable disappeared.

"MugWire, I just don't care for bulldozing strangers trying to ram something down Wynton's throat. You strike me as a man who gets what he goes after, so I'm just being here, doing my job, and making sure I approve of what you're goin' after. You're going to have to accept the fact that you can't do it alone."

What or who? "Fair enough. Stick close, Sheriff. I plan to share everything with you, and Wynton. No secrets and no lies."

"Fair enough."

Burke focused hard on Tully Jones' face. "Before we say goodnight, Sheriff, I want to make something real clear. Like I said, no secrets and no lies, and I'll expect the same from you. I know Canty will be honest with me, but you, I don't think so. I only hope you're being square with me about your relationship with Canty because she's one hell of a woman, and I swear to God, I'll fight you for her." He saw Tully's jaw tighten.

Burke returned the glare in Tully's eyes. "Got your attention, Sheriff?"

Tully Jones stepped to the motel manager's door. It opened immediately without so much as a knock. The manager came out armed with a large broom, and slowly began sweeping up the glass.

"Joey here will have your Explorer towed to our auto

shop in town. It'll be ready, and outside your door in the morning. Right, Joey?" Burke heard Joey snort and spit.

The sheriff turned and melted into the darkness. Then a powerful engine roared, and tires crunched on the gravel drive.

CHAPTER 22

Canty sipped Willodene's espresso, trying desperately to enjoy it. She vowed she would find out how Hearn Guilford had his espresso brewed. If the woman insists on making this stuff she had to get her a decent recipe. Where was Burke?

The incoming call light blinked on her phone, followed closely by Willodene's announcement that Burke was on the line for her.

"Hey. Where are you?"

His voice rumbled with discontent. "I'm still at the undistinguished Best Western waiting for my Explorer to show up. Had a visit from the Ponder boys last night. Little bastards busted my front windshield."

Canty felt off balance. What was going on? "Call Tully!"

"No need." The timbre of his voice was pitched at low controlled anger. "Seems your Tully Jones showed up at the scene just as I was about to get my head blown off. God, I'd hate to die at the hands of shit like that. I had the dog dirt under control, but your hero stepped in anyway, and saved the day. What a guy."

Canty winced. "Burke." Her voice came out choked and in whispers.

"Don't be nice. I can't handle nice right now. Here comes the truck all duded out with a new windshield. I'll say one thing, your hero works fast." The phone clicked.

Those damn Ponders. Damn. She bet Burke stood them down, though. Canty pictured a very cool, but angry Burke, giving no quarter, standing square as a block· of stone. Bastards, chicken-shit, dog dirt. The man had a way with words.

Willodene announced that Diamond and Max were about an hour away. Well, they should all have a very entertaining lunch hour. Off to see the Queen. Hope she didn't decide to lop off their heads.

The gathering of Burke, Diamond, Max, and Canty was scheduled for twelve noon. They would then proceed to the Ponder cabin, and hopefully, finalize negotiations with Queen.

Canty walked to her office windows, and as always, her eyes targeted the mountains. The sun reflected off bare granite on the top of the nearest ridge. Canty thought it looked like some heavenly light bursting from inside the mountain. Hot tears stung her eyes. Her chest felt as though someone wrapped a hot towel around it. I feel your quiet strength, old rocks. Goosebumps raised on her arms. I'm terrified of what might happen to you, good friends. I promise, I won't let any scars change your face. I won't let you down. Please God, let this place Burke wants to create be a good thing.

"Hey, quit day dreaming and say hello."

Canty jumped in surprise, and felt her whole body throb as Burke pulled her close in a hard hug. "Ooof! You old bear. You're going to break my ribs." She laughed at the joy of seeing his face, his red hair, his blue eyes and inhaling the delicious woodsy smell of his after-shave.

Burke pushed her away and frowned. "You're a mountain woman witch, an enchantress, born in a secret place in the forests of the mountains, probably behind a Ponder still somewhere.

"Burke McGuire, you never cease to surprise me. Where did that come from?"

He took her face in his hands. She tried hard to memorize every weathered line that sprayed around his blue eyes, every crevice parenthesizing his strong, wide mouth. He traced her lips with a finger tip.

"You could make any man into a poet." He laughed. "You could make any man into a blithering idiot with one flash of those gray eyes." He traced her arrow straight brows and she felt senseless.

"Burke," she barely breathed his name. Canty pulled his face close and touched his lips with a feathery kiss. She heard him moan. She pulled at his lower lip with her teeth.

"Quit, before I take you right here." He drew back. "You're something else, and you're beginning to scare the hell out of me. I'm a love 'em and leave 'em guy, but I could make an exception."

Canty put her hands on his shoulders. "Really?"

"Yeah, really." He put his hands on her buttocks and pulled her to him.

"That all you want?" Canty covered his mouth with hers.

"For now," he mumbled.

Canty turned away from him. "McGuire, you can be a real pain in the butt, you know."

He grinned. "I know."

Canty took a deep breath, and felt her brain clicking back on go. "Tell me more about the Ponder thing before Diamond and Max show up. You know, I never thought of those boys as anything but stupid, mean children. Now, I am thinking they are ugly, smart, big boys. Pop was right, they can be dangerous."

Burke related the Ponder incident, and how nearly by magic, the sheriff appeared and made everything all right. The sarcasm in his voice splashed like acid all over Canty.

"You don't like my friend Tully, do you?" She narrowed her eyes at Burke.

"Don't try to intimidate the intimidator, O'Neil."

"I can't deal with you, Tully Jones, and the Ponders all at once. I know I can't trust the Ponders, but if I can't be in the same room with you and Tully, nothing about this project will work. I need him, and you need him, like it or not."

Burke just looked at her, a slight quirky smile sneaking across his face. "I respect your friend the sheriff, for trying to protect Wynton from rape and pillage, as well as trying to protect Canty O'Neil from the same. I believe the first part can be settled painlessly." The quirky smile grew wider. "The second part can't."

Canty bristled. "Listen here, Burke McGuire, I don't call consensual sex rape and pillage."

"I will get along with your friend as long as..."

Canty tilted her face enough to lock her eyes with his. "No conditions on my friendship with Tully. Never. Until you trust him, and me, nothing will work. Back off. Just let us mountain people guide you, and quit thinking you have to be the big macho, boss man all the time."

"But, I am the big, macho boss-man all the time." He kissed her nose. Canty, what is it with you and Tully Jones? Why can't I figure it out?"

Canty looked into the blue eyes, and wanted to melt into the surprising softness she saw there. She felt awkward and vulnerable.

The intercom startled both of them, and they pulled

apart. Willodene's voice came through the phone announcing the arrival of Diamond and Max. "Wait until you see…" she breathed into the phone, and then cut herself off.

Diamond and Max swept into the office, and Canty greeted them in-between sneezes. Max offered her his hand-kerchief, a silk square, which she would never use to blow her nose. She smiled at Max, her eyes streaming with tears, and tucked the handkerchief into his shirt pocket. She turned, and snatched up some Kleenex from the box on her desk.

Diamond spoke, laughter bubbling in her throat. "Darling, isn't Max wonderful, and so gracious? I am so sorry. Obviously, my perfume continues to tickle your nose. However, it weakens the knees of men. Now, dear girl, wipe your eyes, and tell me how I look."

Canty blinked. Diamond wore a white leather jacket, over white silk pants and blouse. The jacket was heavily strewn with tiny, twinkling gold stars. Lush ribbons of fringe lined the jacket sleeves from shoulder to wrist, and edged the hem of the jacket. It was the most incredible piece of clothing she'd ever seen. Instead of her usual sandal-style high heels, Diamond's spectacular long legs were dressed in thigh-high soft white leather boots, the three-inch heels studded with gold stars. Her earrings, flickering and sparkling with gold stars, dangled nearly to her shoulders.

"Canty, do I look all right? I wouldn't want to offend this Queen person by not dressing for the occasion."

Willodene bustled into the office holding a tray of steam-ing cups of espresso. Her eyes were fixed on Diamond. Her hands, the fingers accented with fire engine red nails, barely maintained the balance of the tray. Canty had visions of espresso-splashed white leather and a screaming Diamond.

"Let me, Willodene." She took the tray and set it on

her desk. She noted Burke's face, flushed, and set in a tight lipped smile.

Max, looking drab and bored as always, removed a cup from the tray and sat down. "As you can see, Canty darling, I didn't do anything special to dress for the Queen, But then, upstaging Diamond is impossible. I don't know why this Queen person wants to meet us anyway. Is she as ugly as her brothers? God forbid." He sniffed and sipped again.

Diamond smiled her huge red-lipstick smile. "Max, you are such a frump. Really, Canty. Am I all right?"

"Diamond," Canty chose her words carefully, "I guarantee you that Queen Ponder has never seen anything like you, or your outfit. She will be mesmerized." Among other better unknown reactions, she thought.

"Well, I didn't want to insult her. I absolutely adore this jacket and my nearly-up-to-my-twat boots. Aren't they fabulous?" Diamond whirled in model fashion, fringe spraying out like a water sprinkler around her. Canty heard Willodene make a choked little noise. She couldn't look at her.

"Drink up, people," Canty ordered. "We are off to see the Queen."

They all brushed by the still wide-eyed Willodene and headed for Canty's Jeep.

"Where's Fido?" Max's whiny tone reached Canty's ears. She was too busy negotiating the steep, twisty, gravel road to the Ponder cabin to reply.

Diamond saved her the trouble. "What's Fido, darling Max?"

"For your information, Fido is a dog, in this instance, a watch dog. It's my special name for Sheriff Jones. I thought he followed you everywhere, Canty dear."

Canty made a deliberate sharp cut of the wheels

around a corner. Diamond and Max rocked around in the back, protesting loudly.

Burke glanced at her briefly, smiling. "I, too, would like to know where your guardian angel is hiding."

"He had an emergency on the other side of the county." Canty swallowed hard. Tully had told her to wait for him. She had promised she would and he would be furious. She lifted her chin. "I thought we could handle this ourselves."

Canty pulled her Jeep up close to the front porch as Tully had done. Burke nodded.

Max spoke up. "Canty, dear, are you parking on the porch? Don't tell me someone lives here. I mean this is something out of Tobacco Road. You don't expect Diamond and me to go in there, do you?"

Canty sighed. "Queen wants to meet both of you, today. She's expecting all of us. It's not so bad inside. Don't worry about the bird. He's on a tether. Can't hurt you."

Diamond and Max sat frozen in the back seat. Burke got out and opened the door next to Diamond. "Out, ma'am." He held out his hand and Canty was thankful that Diamond took it and, emerged from the Jeep.

Max's voice came out as a whimper. "You can't mean it." Canty almost felt sorry for him

"Come on, where's your sense of adventure, Max?" Diamond grabbed Max's hand, and dragged him out behind her.

Canty wanted to shake him out of his panic. "Max. Please, you have no idea how important this meeting is. Nothing will happen with this project until Queen meets with you, and approves of your drawings. Max, I mean it. It'll be all right." Canty stepped close Max. She put her hands on his bony shoulders. "It'll be all right." Max stiffened, nodded, and pulled his drawings out of the Jeep.

The four mounted the steps, and entered the cabin. Queen sat in her rocking chair watching the TV. Black's shiny black eyes were fixed on them. He flapped his large wings, and Diamond squealed.

Queen stopped her rocker dead. Her voice rasped like sandpaper on a rock. "Best you don't holler at Black, young lady. He don't take to it, 'cept from me. Why he might fly right in your face, and snatch out your eyes for that."

Burke grabbed Diamond's arm as she headed for the door. "Diamond," Burke commanded her quietly. Canty moved close to Diamond, and took her hand. Max had positioned himself behind the two women and Burke, facing toward the door. Canty reached in back of herself and grabbed Max's pant belt with her free hand, and held on tight.

Queen ignored the scuffling. "You must be Diamond. Step up. I got to see you up close. "With all that white on, you show up good in this dark place. That cowboy jacket you're wearin' is nice. I believe you are the most purty thing I ever laid eyes on. You must be the one Terrell and Smith call the white-headed whore. Honey, they's just crazy 'bout you." She rasped out a short laugh.

"Get out! I hate you!" Black crackled and Canty was sure she saw at least two inches of daylight between Diamond's boots and the floor. She kept a tight grip on Max's belt.

Queen stood, using her rifle as a cane, and dropped a dirty rag over Black's head.

"Canty, Mr. Burke, bring them two over here. I got to see them up close and I got to touch that jacket. Just touch mind you, won't hurt it none."

Canty watched Diamond take several measured steps toward Queen. Max didn't move.

"Come on, you first." Queen reached out her hand. Diamond

took it, and moved closer. Canty breathed a sigh of relief. Good old Diamond. Tough Diamond. You're doing great.

"I'm proud to meet you, Miss Queen." Her voice was soft. Then Diamond pulled the white jacket from around her shoulders, and placed it in Queen's lap. Queen gasped. The old woman's hands shook as she stroked the soft leather. A tear ran down Queen's cheek. She rocked, and stroked the jacket for an interminable time. No one spoke.

Diamond walked over to a dim corner of the cabin. Her voice, still soft, floated through the dim light. "What's this? Isn't this a loom? And, look, beside it. Isn't that a spinning wheel? So dark in here, it's hard to tell."

Queen jerked her head in Diamond's direction. The spell was broken. "What you doin' there, girl? That's my loom. That loom was handed to me from my momma, from her momma, from her momma. Other words, that loom was my great-granny Ponders. Lord, you wouldn't believe the purty things that she wove on that loom. No'n was as good as she was. I got close, they say, but I couldn't do what she did with that loom or that spinner wheel."

Diamond strode back to Queen. "Tell you what I'd like to do, Miss Queen. I'd like to trade you that loom and that spinning wheel for my jacket. What do you say?"

Queen cackled, then coughed, a deep bubbly sound. "Not in my lifetime. What you want with my loom and spinner, anyhow? They ain't worth nothin' like this jacket. "I 'preciate you lettin' me hold it awhile. I ain't got no place to wear such a thing no how. You are a crazy whore." She handed the jacket back to Diamond.

Diamond turned to Canty. The wide red-lipsticked mouth was drawn into a tight line and the huge brown eyes were slits. Canty whispered to her, "Every woman that sets foot in this cabin is called a crazy whore, and what in the hell are you doing, anyway? Calm down."

Diamond shut her eyes for a second. "I'll be okay," she muttered.

Queen pointed in the general direction of Max. "Now, bring that feller with the hair over here. You say he's the architect? Now, ain't that somethin'?"

Burke grabbed Max's arm, and force marched him to Queen's chair. Canty was close to laughing. Max, clutching tightly to his large roll of blueprints, seemed to have developed lockjaw. He looked pathetic.

Queen uttered a scratchy chuckle, and waved him closer. "You're a skinny one, now ain't ya? You scared of old Queen? It's Terrell and Smith you need to be scared of, not Queen. Them boys say they like your skinny ass."

Max was still speechless. Canty was amazed. Old Queen was playing with these folks, having fun. *Bless your old bones, Queen.*

"Speak up, Max. Show Queen your stuff." Burke's voice was light, but his fist was clenched.

Canty added, "Yes, Max, show Queen your drawings."

The atmosphere changed as Max unrolled his plans for the lodge. He put each page of work on her lap, one at a time, and answered her croaked-out questions about every rendering. Even Max couldn't resist the power of his own work, and began to deliver detailed explanations. Queen nodded and rocked, nodded and rocked, nodded and rocked.

An earsplitting scream jerked everyone to attention. The door flew open, and Pauly hurtled through it, howling in pain. He was followed closely by Terrell and Smith. Their liquored breath permeated the air.

Max grabbed for his papers.

Oh, god. These lunatics. Before Terrell and Smith could take in who was in the cabin, Canty grabbed Diamond and Max by a free arm, led them straight through the two men, and out the door.

"'Hits her. Right here, Smith. The white-headed whore and her skinny-assed friend." He made kissing noises. "Come to me, pulease. Aw, don't leave. I'm seein' 'em, by goddamn. You seein' 'em?"

"Yup, I do. Must be like one of them ellushunations. Who is the big man over there by Queen? I b'leeve it's that sonbitch MugWire. Don't see the sheriff here, this time." Terrell cocked the shotgun. "You tryin' to get Queen to sign somethin?"

Pauly started crawling to Queen. Smith went to the cowering man, and grabbed him by his hair. "You tell Queen anythin' and you will be wishin' you was dead, you stupid dummy. You hear? You keep your mouth shut." He flung Pauly back down by the chair, and kicked him hard in the stomach. Pauly screamed again.

Burke started forward. Queen jumped out of her rocking chair. She whacked Smith across the back of the head with the rifle butt. He dropped like a stone at Burke's feet.

Canty came back through the door. Burke was beside her, a vise grip on her arm. "We better go, Canty."

"My God, what have you crazy fools done?" Canty heard herself shouting at the boys, but couldn't stop. "Terrell and Smith, there's blood on the porch where you dragged poor Pauly up the stairs, and threw him in the door." Canty rushed to the slobbering hulk. Queen had resumed her place in the rocker, and Smith was out cold. Terrell lay passed out against the door, brown gunk sliding in small rivers from his half-open mouth.

Queen banged the rifle butt on the floor. "Canty," her

words were forced and painful sounding, "they been hurtin'
Pauly and I know it. I know what they're doin' to him. He
like as tried to tell me awhile back. They've been makin'
him do sex things. Look, there's blood on his butt. Oh, those
stinkin' boys."

Canty took a deep breath and fought back stabbing
tears of anger. "Queen, we can get them put in jail, I
know we can."

"No, ma'am. I got my own justice for them. They's mine
to deal with. They's my kin."

She reached over and stroked Pauly's shoulder. "It's all
right, baby. You'll see. I'll make it all right. Just wait until that
closing, Pauly. You'll see. Burke McGuire and Canty O'Neil,
I want that closing to be in the next few days or you won't
have no closing."

"We'll get it set up." Canty put a hand under Queen's
chin and made her look directly into her eyes. "Queen, come
down to town with us right now. I don't like you to be up here
with your brothers anymore."

Queen brushed her hand aside. "They's got to be a
closin' by Friday. This here is Tuesday. I can't hold out any
longer than that. Terrell and Smith are smellin' somethin'
bad in the air. Thank God they's too stupid to figure it out,
at least for now. Everthing's got to be settled." She pointed
at Burke. "We got the price right, and I trust Canty to
make the contract and closing statement read like it should.
They's only one attorney in Wynton, and he's not worth
anything, but that attorney has got to be there officially. He
don't have to say nothin' or do nothin', but he's got to be
there. Terrell and Smith won't believe nothin' unless he's
there." Queen's voice dropped so low Canty and Burke had
to lean toward her to hear her words. "They'll be no cash

money showin' up at the closing, you understand?" Queen stopped and took a deep breath.

Canty felt surrounded by the sound of the gasping rattle. She hoped Queen would quit talking. Soon.

"I want one thing special in that contract. I want it to say that something on this property'll be named after Pauly. Don't care if it's a rock. Just so's his name's on it."

"No problem, Queen." Canty grabbed Burke's hand, and squeezed it. He returned the pressure.

Queen held up one bony, trembling hand. "Wait, now. Only other thing to be said in that contract is that there will always be enough money to take care of Pauly. Canty, you got to figure how to do that, and figure where he can live. I don't see me bein' around too much longer, and I got to know he is taken care of. I got to know." Canty saw a tear trickle down Queen's yellowed cheek.

"Consider it done, Queen."

"I'm tired now. Been jumpin' around a bit today. Hope Smith has the dad-blamdest headache ever. Is he breathin'?"

Reluctantly, Canty bent over the supine Smith. His breath expelled in a vapor of liquor and rotten gums odor. The back of her throat closed up. "Oh, yes, he's breathing."

Pauly lay sleeping in his own slobber, still holding on to his stomach where Smith had kicked him.

Burke put an arm around Canty's shoulders. "Let's go."

The four were silent as Canty maneuvered the Jeep back down the road. As soon as she turned onto the main road, Diamond spoke. "You're all damned lucky that I'm not given to hysterics, or I would have turned that cabin into a demolition site."

Diamond's anger hit the back of Canty's head like a rock. Her perfume hit Canty's nose nearly as hard. Canty sneezed so violently, she felt Burke put a steadying had on the wheel. He put his handkerchief on her hand. She snatched it, and blew her nose as loud as she could. Damn that stuff.

"Canty O'Neil, you assured Hearn that those boys would do us no harm and no one would get hurt. I didn't believe it then, and I was right. Those animals will kill us all if they can, and not care either. Don't take me anywhere near that place ever again as long as those pigs live there. You all right, Max? You look dead pale. Canty, stop. Max is going to be sick."

Canty pulled over, and Max slid out of the Jeep, just in time. He threw up, over and over again, until Burke went out to steady him. Finally, he climbed back into the Jeep, his face streaked with tears. He didn't speak to anyone.

Burke broke the silence. "Canty, I still can't believe Queen can move that fast and be that strong."

Canty relaxed a little at the sound of Burke's quiet, strong voice. "Yessiree, bob, we mountain folks'll fool ya ever time. We're quick, we're smart and," she turned her head very slightly toward the back seat, "we know what we're doing."

Diamond's tone was sharp. "I have reasonable doubts. Canty, you're the mother of a beautiful son. You don't need to risk yourself like that. That's not smart."

Burke gave her knee a slight squeeze. She inhaled and exhaled slowly. "Diamond, don't go treading on my personal life." Canty echoed Diamond's tone. "I told Hearn that those people would kill each other, but not anyone else. They talk ugly, and I wouldn't put it past them to do some nasty things to a person, but they aren't killers. All they really want is to be left alone, and we're steppin' on their toes right now, big time." Canty tucked a lock of hair behind her ear. "By the way, Diamond, what was the big thing about Queen's loom and spinning wheel?"

194

Diamond waited a few minutes before replying. She carefully wiped Max's soaking wet brow. She murmured to pitiful Max that he was going to live.

"Diamond." Burke sounded rough and impatient.

"Okay. I'll quit for a minute. Now, listen carefully because I have discovered the main theme for the project, and decorating the lodge. I can't believe I found it in that gloomy, smelly old cabin." Diamond became more animated by the second. "Burke, you're not paying attention, darling."

"I'm listening, Diamond." He squeezed Canty's knee a little more. She flashed him a quick grin.

"Picture this whole project as steeped in artless elegance. The pure simplicity of looms and spinning wheels will envelop everyone. There will be a chic ambiance that will invite jeans, and diamonds alike. I'll build all the logos, the colors, everything around that beautiful old loom and spinning wheel. Max! Don't you love it, dear? It gives you a real starting place, love."

"We'll talk about it." Max whispered.

Canty noted the blue lights of the Sheriff's car were close behind her Jeep. She pulled over. Tully Jones loomed beside her. Burke left his hand on her knee. She didn't remove it.

"Shit, Fido, where've you been?" Max's raspy voice could barely be heard, but Tully's eyes narrowed in acknowledgement.

Tully crouched down and peered in at Diamond and Max in the back seat. "Canty, you been up to Ponder's without me." It was not a question.

"That's right, Sheriff." Diamond blurted. "We had to meet with Queen, just us. Those gutter litter were drunk, and unruly. They beat on poor Pauly. The boy was howling in pain. Max got sick, it was so disgusting. Can't you do something?"

"Mr. MugWire, what do you think?"

Burke leaned forward in front of Canty, keeping his hand on her knee. He put on his tight-lipped trouble-is-coming grin. Canty said a little prayer for peace.

"The Ponder boys were shit-faced, all right, but they didn't harm us, by golly. Old Queen, now, she knocked Smith cold with her rifle butt. Never saw anythin' lak it, Sheriff. You might want to get up thar, see if he's breathin'. I'd say you got good reason to tawk to them boys 'bout how they's treatin' ol' Pauly. Why, I'd call that an ex-treme case of child abuse."

Tully tipped his hat. "I'll see to it." He returned to his truck, and drove off.

Canty sat for a moment until the sheriff's car was out of sight. "Burke, putting down mountain talk was insulting, and beneath you. Tully didn't deserve that. Tully didn't tawk like tha-ut." She dragged her words. "I don't believe the Ponder's tawk like tha-ut. You got your southern drawl screwed up tryin' to be a smart ass."

Burke sat back and fired his blue eyes into her like a laser beam. "Your so-called friend gives me that MugWire crap one more time, and I'll decide what he deserves."

Canty continued on to the office. She remarked how classy her place looked with Diamond and Max's rented white Lincoln parked in front. "Now, park Burke's Jag next to that Lincoln and we'd have totally changed the image of Wynton and O'Neil Properties." Canty glanced at her watch. "How about we all meet for dinner at the house in about an hour." Pop would love to see all of you."

"Canty, darling." Diamond's voice was low and breathy, "if you don't mind, we'll be on our way back to Orlando. We've got plane reservations. Come on, Max."

Canty turned to ice. "But it'll be dark before you even get to Atlanta. I thought you'd be staying tonight. I wanted to talk over Burke's plans, and your new ideas for a few hours tomorrow. We'll be closing in a few days and," Canty sneezed. "Oh, damn." She watched as Burke escorted Diamond and Max to their car.

Burke walked to her. "Canty, I'm going to drive down the mountain in front of them. They're not used to these roads, especially at night. Apologies to Pop. I can grab a place to stay in Dahlonega. They'll be all right after we get that far. I'll be back tomorrow morning. Tell the Best Western to hold on to my room. I'll need it again." He gave her a light kiss on the cheek.

She watched them all disappear around the square, dust and leaves blowing up behind them. Canty felt very uneasy. This had not been a good day.

Dagmar Marshall

CHAPTER 23

Canty circled her desk, over and over again. Her stomach felt gnarled and twisted, like an old tree. She felt as though every muscle in her body was pulling and snapping like a rubber band. She held her hands out in front of her, and was surprised to see they weren't shaking.

It's all over. The minute Diamond and Max get back to Hearn Guilford, this time, it's done. Damn Diamond and her flash, and her big red-lipsticked mouth. She gets those Ponders all worked up just by being there. Stupid Max threw up all over the damn road. Poor sad fool. When Queen told Max to be scared of Terrell and Smith, it gave me shivers. I guess I'd be scared if I was him, too. What a damn crazy world. Here we go again. Hearn Guilford will hear Diamond and Max, and this time, he'll toss it all out.

Canty paced around her desk, again and again. She broke stride to face the map, the outline of the Ponder property lined in neon yellow mocked her. Any minute, that phone would ring, she thought, and wham, it would be over. Sorry, Pop and Toby. Sorry, Queen. Sorry, Wynton. Dear God, she prayed, I do not want to give up, or be told I have to give up.

Canty could not sit still. She went out to the reception area, and saw Willodene was on the phone. She was grinning so big her cheeks pushed her glasses up a notch. Canty heard her say goodbye to Clower. She hung up, and casually inspected her now poppy-red nails.

"Clower just invited me for dinner tonight, on the condition that I do the creamed corn." She pursed her lips, "Lord, how that man loves my creamed corn."

"Pop loves more than your creamed corn, Willy. I saw the handholding and whispering the other night. If ever two people looked in love, it was you and Pop."

Willodene turned away, and put her fist up to her lips. She took a deep breath, let all the air out, and took another deep breath. "Canty, sugar, I believe he's close to not being able to live without me, and my creamed corn."

Canty wrapped her friend in hug. "Suits me. When's the wedding?"

"Don't know for sure. Soon as you get out of all this mess."

Canty locked up all over. "Excuse me, what mess?"

"Now, Canty, you have to know Clower and Toby, and Tully, and me, are worried sick over this Ponder thing. Clower found out what happened up there yesterday, and he wasn't happy. Scared me, too. He's afraid that Burke McGuire will get you killed by pushing this sale. You gotta stop. You both gotta stop."

Canty glared at Willodene. She felt rockets going off in her head. "If Pop was unhappy he would've told me himself." She heard her voice, shrill and screechy, and willed herself to calm down. Willodene just stared at her.

Canty's jaw ached from the effort to stop herself from screaming. "This sale is going through. Don't you realize what's at stake here? I'm not backing out, and neither is Burke McGuire. I wouldn't ask him to. And, if Clower O'Neil wanted to marry you, he'd never let me stand in the way."

Willodene sagged like a punctured balloon. "Well, you'd be wrong about that. And, Clower and I both agreed neither of us would feel comfortable about a wedding right now. This isn't a happy time." Canty was horrified to see a tear slip from Willy's eye.

"Oh, Willy. I'm sorry. That sounded ugly, and I didn't mean it that way. This thing is eating me up, but I know I'm right. Wynton needs this project."

Willodene examined her freshly manicured poppy red nails as though she'd never seen them before.

"What's the matter now, Willy?"

"Truth be known, Canty, not everyone thinks Wynton needs this project."

"You going to back up what you're saying or just leave me hanging?"

Willodene shuffled papers on her desk.

Canty didn't move.

Willodene finally looked at her. "Canty, honey," she sighed hugely, "you know I'm at Linda's beauty parlor at least once a week, and you know I go grocery shopping at least once a week, and you know I'm forever in and out of Sally Jo's Dress Shop," she stopped and took a deep breath.

Canty stayed still.

"Truth be known, there's a lot of folks here in Wynton who don't want Mr. Hearn Guilford's development to happen. They're real upset about upsetting the Ponders, too. That spells big trouble. I've told a lot of them all the good that place could bring here, but I don't think I convinced anyone."

Canty's nerves tingled. "What's the point of this now, when we're so close?"

Willodene looked away. "I just couldn't keep it inside anymore. Everybody sees you and Burke and Diamond and Max and acts real nice, but inside there's some don't like it at all."

Canty saw tears in her friend's eyes and sagged. "Willy, please hang in there with me. I need your support so much. Wynton will see how good this will be. I'm convinced, and believe me, I wasn't at first. I promise, it'll be settled real soon. God forgive me, I'd never want to make you and Pop unhappy or anyone else in Wynton. You know that."

Willodene dabbed at her eyes, and tried a small smile.

Canty gave Willy a hug. "Burke's coming in a little while. He's determined to show me all there is to know about golf-course development."

Willy's small smile grew. "Good, I'll make some espresso."

Canty laughed. "Okay. I'll pass. By the way, have you ever made your espresso for Pop?"

"No."

"Don't."

Willodene flashed her a pained expression, and retreated to the coffee room.

By the time Burke arrived, a pot of Willy's espresso stood steaming beside Canty's own large drink of sweet tea. Canty unwrapped two chicken-salad sandwiches fresh from the only deli in Wynton.

"Hey, good looking." Burke's powerful voice rolled through the room. She tucked a lock of hair behind one ear, and smiled at him.

"You're not so bad, yourself." She gave him a perfunctory kiss on the cheek and slipped away quickly from his reactive grasp.

Burke growled. "What's the matter?"

"Nothing. Let's eat. I really do want to know about golf course development, and if you distract me too much, I won't learn anything."

Burke poured a cup of espresso and held it up for a

toast. "Well, here's to you, and learning."

"Your sarcasm is wasted on me today." She held up her drink of tea, and gave him an air kiss.

"What makes you so ornery today, O'Neil?" He put the espresso down and began munching on the sandwich.

"Let's just say its been an irritating day so far. Willy told me that Pop, Toby, Tully, and herself, of course, were scared-to-death for me dealing with the Ponders. Pop was sure you'd get me killed before this was over, and he found out about yesterday which only made it worse. That could only have been from Tully Jones. I could strangle him. Then Willy told me about half the town not wanting the project and scared to death of riling up the Ponders. Willy also added that she and Pop were close to setting a wedding date, but wouldn't do anything until this mess was over."

"Jeezus! Would you really strangle Tully Jones? What a great idea."

"Not funny, McGuire."

Burke pulled her face close to his. "O'Neil, I'm jealous as hell of your feelings for Tully Jones. You've made me think real serious about wanting you on a long-term basis. Tell me about it."

Canty found her gray eyes locked into the ice blue ones of Burke McGuire. She could feel her whole body tremble. "You are a pompous egomaniac. Just because you think you want me, I'm supposed to drop everything and be yours. I'll be damned if I'm going to jump into the sack with you anytime soon, if anytime at all."

"I haven't asked you."

Canty pushed him away. "You've asked me. Don't you think I feel you when we're close? Don't you think your vibrations fly right through me, and make me a puddle? Don't tell me you haven't asked me. And, don't think I haven't said yes. Stay off the Tully Jones thing, okay?"

"Okay," he said quietly, " let's talk golf. I'll catch up on the Jones story later."

They sat at the conference table for hours, and Canty was alternately thrilled and dismayed at the knowledge that poured from Burke McGuire. Could she ever learn a tiny bit of what he knew? If Max was right, she'd better. She gazed at the hewn profile and the square, hard jaw line. The backs of his hands were scattered with soft red, curly hairs. She wanted desperately to stroke those hands.

Burke went into detail about the land needed to construct a really special layout for a golf course. One hundred and fifty acres was the minimum, which all depended on the land itself. The mountain land would require at least two-hundred and fifty acres because of the steep areas that would have to be circumvented, but melded into the course layout. He explained that the drainage and irrigation systems would require more space than on flat acreage, again because of having to circumvent so many rocks and trees.

Burke turned and faced her. "You with me? This is pretty dry stuff."

"Absolutely." I'm with you all the way.

He stood up and stretched. "Canty, I'm going to preserve every stone and every piece of wood growing on that land that I possibly can, so I hope you won't get upset when you see areas being cleared for fairways and cart paths. We'll be moving a lot of dirt, but I won't change the basic layout of the valley or the hills. Look what I have here."

He rolled out a paper that nearly covered the table. It was a golf course layout, done in colorful acrylics, and it had the name "Secret Creek Golf Club, Wynton, GA" lettered on the border. "Still needs work, but there it is."

Canty was totally amazed. "How did you get this done so fast? It's incredible. It's beautiful. How do you know how many fairways, and how long each hole should be and ..."

He stopped her and made a sweeping gesture over the drawing. "A golf course consists of eighteen golf holes, a front nine and a back nine. Check the numbers." He jabbed a square finger on the green areas. "Each nine characteristically has two par fives, two par threes and five par fours. The length and shape of each fairway is determined by the lay of the land if possible."

"Simple enough."

He grinned at her. "Simple enough."

"Don't you laugh at me."

He stepped close, and she shivered despite herself. "Canty, I don't give a damn what you know about golf courses, right now. Your job is to procure that land for Hearn Guilford Golf Designs, Inc., and that is all." He reached for her and pulled her close. She felt his hardness, and she was on fire.

Canty swallowed, and hoped her voice would work. "But I care about the land and what it will look like. I care about Wynton and its future. I need to learn everything I can about the what and why of the whole project."

He nuzzled her neck. She wanted to bite him. She licked his ear.

"Do you care about me?" he rumbled.

"Yes."

He pushed her away. "You are the damndest woman I've ever met. Hell, I'm going to marry you, but I think I need to know you better before I take you to bed."

"What a great idea."

CHAPTER 24

Canty drove away from the office, still tingling. Burke spent another hour discussing the intricacies of building greens, and shaping fairways. He promised he would take her with him anytime while the course was being constructed.

"By God, I plan to be there."

Canty pulled into O'Dell Meyer's Shell station on the square, and began pumping gas. O'Dell appeared, his size sixteen boots shoveling a dusty path to the gas pumps.

Canty grinned at the tall, bone-skinny man with the basset hound face. "Damn, O'Dell," Canty coughed, "I've told you to pave this drive, at least by the gas tanks. The dust around here is awful and when it rains, it's a mudhole. I'm surprised anyone would come here." O'Dell Meyer's Shell station was the only gas station within ten miles of Wynton, and Canty wondered why he didn't laugh at her usual joke. "So, how's it going?"

O'Dell hawked and spit. "Everything was fine until the Ponders hit town about two hours ago. I'll tell you what, they's the sorriest excuses for men I've ever seen. Lordy, they was drunk. Them boys smashed my place up pretty bad inside. Just for pure meanness. I won't be paving no drives for awhile."

Canty turned off the pump. "Let me see."

The inside of O'Dell's station was in ruins. The contents

of the shelves and the cooler were strewn on the floor. All the candy, cigarettes, and cigars were mashed into the cooler mess. Even the yellowed shades at the windows had been jerked down, and torn apart.

Canty wanted to weep at the beaten look on O'Dell's face. "I don't believe this. Have you called Tully?"

O'Dell scratched his head. "Yes, ma'am. He ain't been here, yet. He's over in Gainesville. He'll be by. Told me not to touch anything 'til he sees it. Meantime, I got to round up some folks to help clean up.

Canty kicked at an empty soda can. "Why did they do this?"

"Canty, I'm gonna tell you something. I'm saying those boys came in here telling that I was the reason Queen got to talking to you about selling the property. Said if I hadn't of told them that you wanted to speak to Queen, would've been all right. They was madder than hornets. Said they's gonna get Queen, you and that red-headed man, too. They busted everything, and laughed doing it." O'Dell swallowed.

Canty gave O'Dell a quick hug. "I'm sorry I caused this mess. I'll get Willy and Pop and Toby to come over here, and we'll all help you clean up." Canty looked at the rumpled face. O'Dell was blushing scarlet. She pecked him on the cheek, and headed for the Jeep.

Canty drove up the teeth-rattling, bone-breaking, zap-your-tongue, gravel road in record time. She turned the Jeep around, and backed up as close as possible to the porch.

No sign of Terrell and Smith so far. Thank God. She'd smell them before she saw them. Gross, so gross.

Canty picked her way up the cracked, and tilted boards of the stairs. She knocked, and called to the old woman. She could hear nothing but TV voices. Canty pushed on the door. It swung open, and she could see Queen, slumped in her rocker, dimly visible by the light of the TV.

"Queen, it's me, Canty. Are you okay?"

"Get out. I hate you. Go away!"

Canty muffled a scream with her hand. Black! Damn bird scared her to death. He was flapping his wings wildly, but his close tether didn't allow him to leave the perch. Queen still hadn't moved.

Oh, Lord, please be all right. Canty moved quickly to the chair. Her throat tightened. Queen's face was black and blue with bruises, and her eyes were swollen shut. Canty leaned close and felt Queen's breath on her cheek. Thank you, Lord.

"Queen, it's me. Can you talk?" Canty grabbed the old woman's hand. It was icy. She rubbed and patted it. "Queen, it's Canty. Canty O'Neil. I'm here. It's all right. It's Canty." A lone tear seeped from a swollen-shut eye.

"Get out! I hate you!" Black was screeching, and he sounded panicky. It was Queen's voice. God knows, he saw whatever happened. She went to the bird, and dropped the old rag over his head. He made growling noises, and was quiet.

Canty sat with Queen for a long time, talking constantly. She rubbed the cold bony hands and arms, and finally felt some warmth. She went to the rusted old sink, found a grimy plastic cup on the edge, and pumped the well handle until icy-cold clear water filled the cup. She lifted Queen's head so she could swallow. Queen sucked in her mouth.

"Please Queen, try." She let a few drops of water fall on

Queen's cracked and bloodied lips. "Try, Queen."

Queen shuddered deeply, and moved her lips, her tongue reached for the moisture. She shuddered again, and sighed.

"Oh, Queen, I knew I should have gotten you out of here. Your brothers are horrible, sick men." Canty put her arms around the scrawny shoulders, and hugged the old woman. She held her cheek to hers and gritted her teeth in anger at the feel of the rough, beaten skin. "Queen, I'm so sorry. I'll get you out of here, right now. I'll even bring Black if you want."

Queen's voice was whispery but clear. "You git outta here, Canty O'Neil."

"What happened?" She gave Queen another sip of water which she took more easily.

"They said they was goin' to kill Black." Every word was strained painfully through her swollen mouth. "They know he's the only friend I got, and they was goin' to kill him." Another tear slithered through the cracks on Queen's cheek. "We got to close."

"We can close Friday like we said. That's two days from now. I'm taking you home with me until then. I'll bring Black."

"If I ever could have had a daughter, you'd be the one Canty O'Neil. Remember the time I saved your ass from them boys?" Queen tried to sit up, and sucked her breath in loudly.

"What? Your back? Broken ribs, maybe." They had beaten the living fool out her.

"Don't know. I can't go with you. I can't leave Pauly. You set that closing up for Friday morning at ten, and I'll be there. I'll be there half hour early so's you can pin up my hair a little. I can't do it no more."

"Queen, Terrell and Smith were in town and smashed up O'Dell's gas station pretty bad. O'Dell told me they had threatened to get me and Burke after they took care of you. They were very drunk."

Queen spoke with effort, her voice wheezed on every word. "Yup, they got to me first. They knew I'd pitch a fit if they threatened Black, and honey, I started swinging. They busted me up pretty good didn' they?"

"They're out of control, Queen. They need to be arrested before they hurt anyone else."

Queen tried a snorty laugh that made her cracked lips bleed. Canty brought more water and dabbed her mouth with an old cloth towel. "You arrest them and I won't close. Tully was up here wantin' to take them in earlier today. You'd never get them behind bars. Tully'd have to kill them and that would ruin everything. I won't close unless they're there. Got my reasons. Pauly got to come, too. Don't worry, they's done worse to me than this in the past. I heal up fast. We'll all be there. It ain't gonna happen unless they're there."

"I will, Queen. I just don't want to leave you." Hot stinging tears sprung from behind her eyes "And, I've never forgotten you saving me, never."

Queen's lips trembled in a feeble attempt at a smile. "Yup, you was in deep shit with those boys. Shoulda shot 'em that day. Saved everyone a lot of grief." She reached for Canty's hand. "Out of here. Can't talk no more. When it's over, you won't have to see us no more. We'll all be finished with Wynton. I care a lot for you Canty O'Neil. Don't let me down." Her head fell back on the chair and she slept. Canty could hear a slight rattle deep in her chest.

She lifted the rag from Black's head. "Get out, go away, I hate you!" he squawked.

★　★　★

Canty's headlights picked up the porch. It was lined with men. Pop, Tully, and Burke were on the top step, Toby was on the bottom step. They looked straight mouthed, and tight in the jaw.

Canty hopped out of the Jeep. "Havin' a party?"

"We've been havin' a bad time waiting for you," Pop rumbled.

"I'm fine. What's going on? You all look mad or upset or what?"

Tully came down the stairs toward her, but Toby beat him. "Ma, we were scared. We knew you'd been up to Ponders. Tully'd been by O'Dell's and saw the wreck. O'Dell told him what they'd said about getting you, and Mr. Burke, after they took care of Queen. Tully just figured you'd go there."

Tully loomed over her. "Canty O'Neil, what in hell were you doing all this time? Where have you been?"

Burke was in her face. "Scared us all. We drove up to the cabin, and the bird was screeching inside. We poked our heads in, and Queen just cackled at us and told us you were long gone. She wouldn't let us in, and she wouldn't tell us anything"

Canty disengaged herself from the group, and went to Pop. He was ashen. She threw her arms around his neck. A big hot tear trickled down her cheek, and landed on Pop's head.

"Canty, honey. This isn't like you. You all right?" Pop pulled her into a big hug.

"I'm okay, Pop. I'm sick with myself for worrying you so bad." Another tear hit Pop's head.

"A cryin' Canty isn't okay, but go on if it suits you."

Canty snuffled, broke away, and blew her nose. She faced the men. "Just let me say this. We've got to close on Friday. Those brothers of hers beat the hell out of Queen, and tore up O'Dell's station all in the name of stopping me, and Burke."

"Well, MugWire, you have stirred up a hornet's nest for sure." Tully said.

Burke snapped him a blazing look. "Sheriff, that family has been doing that stuff for over a hundred years. I sure didn't start anything. And, I'd be obliged if you would call me McGuire. The MugWire crap is old. You know, maybe it is you with the red crayon, and the bubble gum. And, why in hell don't you slap those animals in jail? What'n hell kind of sheriff let's chicken-shit like that run his town?"

"MugWire, lissen up." Tully stood so he could look down at Burke. "I told you, you can't...."

Canty stood between the two. "Burke, I know this will be hard for you to believe, but Tully can't arrest Smith and Terrell. He and I both know, likely as not, he'd have to kill them. Queen told both of us that Smith and Terrell had to be at the closing or the deal's off. She has her reasons, she said. Tully's having to go against the law waiting to try and put those boys behind bars, but he wants the deal to go through, too."

Tully stared at Burke. "Told you once, MugWire, you can't do it without Canty and me. I'm sticking my neck out, but only for Canty and Wynton's sake."

Canty said a quick prayer that the two wouldn't get into a fight. "Okay, we don't have time for attitudes. I'm fine, no one touched me. I was upset when I left Queen. I drove to a part of Secret Creek that I love and just sat awhile to calm down. I'm sorry I worried you, I really am."

Burke came close again. She looked into his fighting blue eyes and winked. He hugged her. Toby joined in, Pop grinned, and Tully sat down on the porch steps and shook his head.

"Friday it is!" Burke twirled her around the yard, and planted a kiss on her mouth. She returned it firmly. "Crazy mountain woman, I do love you," he mumbled against her lips.

"Me, too," she managed softly. "Now, I'm tired, men. I need a bath and I want to check on Toby's homework, and then it's goodnight for me."

★   ★   ★

Canty sat on the end of Toby's bed gazing at the thick dark hair splashed on the pillow. She could even see the dark lashes like pencil marks on his fresh skin.

"Dear son," she whispered, "I'm so sorry I scared you. I love you so much."

Toby stirred, and she saw a little grin spreading on his lips.

"Hey, you awake, you rascal?"

Toby popped up in the bed. "Mom, I love you, too."

Canty moved toward Toby and they hugged hard. She felt the growing tensile strength in his arms. She felt the planes of his face more clearly. "You're losing your baby fat, son."

Toby smiled and struck a strong man pose. "Been doing some extra weights. Coach and Mr. Burke said it's good for my baseball and my golf to develop the long muscles in my arms and I need a lot of shoulder strength and flexibility for a good swing."

"You love anything that has to do with a stick and a ball, Toby O'Neil." She hugged him close again.

"Will that Diamond lady be back?"

"We won't see Diamond or Max again until the Ponders leave. They are terrified of them."

"Bet Mr. Burke ain't. Isn't. I know Sheriff and Pop aren't. I know you aren't either. You need me to go with you on any Ponder business, I'll be there. I'm not scared of them."

Canty took a deep breath. Spoken like a true O'Neil, she thought.

CHAPTER 25

Burke drove back to Canty's office to work on the legal description of the Ponder land. He had hugged her and kissed her in front of everyone at the O'Neil's, but he was still angry about her lone trip to Queen's.

Like you could have stopped her, he thought. He just wished he'd been with her. She had more heart, and guts, than any woman he'd ever met. Add to that, brains. We're a match. Who else could live with us?

His train of thought was broken by headlights coming at the building. Sheriff Tully Jones emerged from his truck, and strode into Canty's office.

Burke remained seated. "Evenin' Sheriff. What brings you out so late?"

Tully sat in the nearest chair, and stretched his long legs out in front of him. "Lights. Canty doesn't leave inside lights on all night. It's three o'clock in the morning, MugWire. What the hell you doing?"

"I'll be damned. Does Wynton know what a conscientious law-man they have? You always stay up all night guarding the folks of this fair town?"

Tully's tone remained even. "I asked you, what the hell you doing here?"

Burke held up a sheaf of papers. "Finishing the legal description, as will be required for the impending closing of the Ponder property on Friday, as in day after tomorrow."

"Canty been here?"

"Sheriff, you hover over her like you were her legally appointed guardian, or more probably, her lover. Which one?"

"After the stunt she pulled today, don't you think she needs watching? That headstrong, bull-dog stubborn woman would worry any man. Fact is, she's gotten worse ever since you been around." Tully looked up at the ceiling. "Looks like in this case, likes attract."

Burke's blood was starting to sizzle. "Like I asked. Which one?"

Tully lowered his gaze, looked directly at Burke, and laughed. "Guess, MugWire."

Burke leaned back in his chair, and balanced on the back legs. "I sure would have hated it if you'd said lover." He let his chair slam back to four legs. "And I know you would have, if it was so. I don't have to tell you, I want that woman. She wants me, too. So exactly where do you fit in, Sheriff?"

Tully crossed his long, muscular arms over his chest, his gaze drifted back to the ceiling. "You might want to ask her?"

Burke jumped up, and slammed his hand on the table. "Damn it to hell, I have asked her, and all she did was smile, and say you two are lifelong friends. Bullshit!" He sat back down, hard.

"Leave it at that, MugWire. If she wanted you, she'd have you." He stood and looked down at Burke. He leaned forward, locking eyes with Burke. "I'm going to ease your pain, MugWire. I'm a married man. I'm locked into a union that only God could resolve."

"Bullshit."

Tully glowered at Burke. "I'd rather have walked

through fire than tell you that, but I've seen the way she looks at you. If I could be divorced tomorrow, it'd be too late. She's had enough bad times. You can bet I'm not telling you for your sake."

"Why'n hell hasn't she told me?"

"Don't really know. I knew I'd lost her years ago, but she pretended, and played the waiting game, until she met you. I know she wanted me to tell you. She's not one to reveal anyone's private thoughts, or lives, except her own. She's a hell of a woman. My jury's still out on you, MugWire." Tully rose to leave. "I don't know what's going to happen with your closing, but I'd keep my back against the wall until it's over."

Burke watched as Tully left the office, heard the slam of a door and the nearly simultaneous start of an engine.

"Advantage McGuire. Thanks."

After Canty dropped Toby at school, she drove to her office. When she rounded the corner of the square, she heard gun fire. Her eyes picked up Terrell and Smith standing just outside her office. Terrell's shotgun was smoking.

Canty stomped on the accelerator, and drove straight at them, horn blaring. They took off running. She saw them jump into their truck, and spin wheels.

"You bastards!" She yelled out her window as they passed her Jeep. Smith was grinning. He spat a glob of juice at the Jeep. Terrell leaned out his door and fired again, straight up. BLAM! They were gone.

Canty was shaking as she looked at the front of her office. The huge plate glass window with O'Neil Properties painted in black and gold, was gone. Shards of glass surrounded the window frame like giant bear teeth. People were running toward the building from all around the square. To her horror, she saw Willy's car, and Burke's truck parked beside the building.

"Willy! My God, where are you? Burke!" Canty picked her way through glass and rubble. She peered into her office, and felt an icy clawing in her stomach.

Willy was yelling and crying. She pulled frantically at a huge slab of ceiling that lay across Burke McGuire's head and back. "Canty, help me! I'm scared he's dead."

Burke moaned as the two women removed the chunk of sheetrock. He raised his head and stared at them. "What in hell?"

Willodene covered her face with her hands to block out the sight of Burke McGuire's glass-blasted features. Canty wobbled, but held.

Burke stood, and immediately crashed back into the chair. "Canty. I can't see anything but blood." He swiped at his eyes and yelled in pain.

Canty held his shoulders. "Stay still. You're absolutely a glass pin cushion. There's glass coming out of you everywhere. Don't touch your eyes! I'm getting you to the hospital. Willy, call the ambulance. Call Tully. Do something."

Willodene grabbed the phone.

"It was the Ponders wasn't it?" Burke mumbled through bloody lips. "Where in hell's that excuse for a sheriff?"

"I called him. He's coming." Willodene's voice went from alto to soprano and back to alto in earsplitting seconds. "It was Ponders all right, and they're gone."

"I'm going to twist those dog-dirt chicken-shits into the ground and stomp on their ugly heads. Canty, get me out of here."

"Oh, no you don't. You're going to the hospital. You've had most of a plate glass window blown into your body in trillions of pieces. You were also wearing a huge piece of my ceiling on your head. You could have some shot buried in you. You could have a concussion. You're going to need antibiotics, and stitches, right here." Canty brushed her finger lightly over a deep cut on Burke's chin. She touched his lips lightly with hers. "By the way, what were you doing here in the first place?"

Burke shook his head and grimaced in pain. "I was here most of the night working on the legal description so that we can be sure to make that Friday deadline, and quit trying to con me with that sweet stuff. Hurts like hell. Just give me a few minutes, and I'll be out of here."

Canty's gray eyes turned steely. "Wrong. Here comes the sheriff, and a deputy. I won't embarrass you by having the ambulance haul you out on a stretcher, but you will let the deputy take you to the hospital. I've heard they will admit flatlanders now."

Burke groaned. "Ha, O'Neil."

Canty swallowed hard, and turned away so he wouldn't see how upset she was. He looked double-awful.

Canty waited with Burke until the deputy came in and helped him walk out to his car. She saw Tully say something to Burke as he got into the deputy's car. They both looked at Canty, framed by the broken window. Burke nodded.

The sheriff strode toward her office, calling her name. She rushed past a ghost-white Willodene, and went out the back door to her Jeep. "Tell Tully I'm going for a clean-up crew. I'll be right back!"

As she drove, Canty dialed the hospital and was told by Marylou, the receptionist, that Burke would be fine as soon as they finished removing glass from his punctured body. She also learned that, other than a slight lump and a large headache, Burke had not suffered any serious head injury.

Fortified with the knowledge that Burke would be well tended until she finished what she felt she had to do now, Canty drove up the rutted road to the Ponder property faster than she'd ever dared before. The Jeep hit a large pot hole, and she cracked her head hard, on the side window. Canty stopped. She could feel a lump coming up just over her left ear. Darts of pain zinged through her brain.

"I'm tearing up one good Jeep for those Ponders. My frame must be twisted like cooked spaghetti. Damn this road, damn everything.

Canty slid down in her seat so her head could rest on the back. She sat until the lightning bolts zipping around her skull settled down.

Won't do any good for me to wind up in the hospital like Burke. That poor man looked like something out of a medieval nail torture box. She shivered.

Canty reached the old cabin, and backed up to the front porch. Her head throbbed in time with her knocking on the door.

"Queen. It's me, Canty. You all right? I need to talk to you."

"Go away. I hate you!"

Well, the doggone bird was okay, anyway. Canty pushed the door open, and peered into the gloom. The old woman sat, rocking gently, rifle by her side.

Queen's voice came scratchy and without expression. "I hear ya. Come on."

"Come on, come on," echoed Black and then shrieked.

"Shut up, Black, or I'll blow your stupid head off." Queen's screeching rasp sent new shafts of pain through Canty's head. Thankfully, Queen lowered her voice. "What you want, girl? It ain't Friday yet. You'd better set. You look right pale."

Canty walked over to the old woman, and looked closely. Queen's face was still a mass of bruises and her lips were puffy, but she was talking, loud and clear, and her eyes were open.

"Queen, I don't need to sit. I had to see you. Terrell and Smith shot up my office this morning. They blew out the glass window, and Burke McGuire was cut up badly."

"He's gonna be all right, ain't he? Don't want nothin' to happen to that boy or the closing. That'd be a damnable shame. That'd ruin everything. Where's those boys?"

"I was hoping you could tell me. You know Tully's going to be up here soon looking for them. They damn near killed a man, aside from wrecking my office. You don't just turn lunatics like that loose. You can't ask Tully to ignore them any longer and neither can I, deal or no deal."

Queen, using her rifle as a crutch, pushed up out of her rocker. She stood facing Canty and even in the gloom, Canty could see the black diamond brightness in her eyes. "Even Tully Jones won't find them if they don't want to be found. They got Pauly hid somewhere to worry me. They know I won't go to closing without Pauly. They's got to bring him home. They's got to bring me and Pauly to the closing. You tell Tully Jones that Queen will take care of them, both of them. Ponders take care of their own. Ponders serve their own justice. Been that way forever." Canty heard a strangly raspy sound coming from her throat. Canty recognized it as Queen's attempt at laughter. "What those stinkin' boys don't know gonna hurt 'em, bad. I got a surprise for them."

The old woman leaned herself back down. "Canty," it was a whisper, "if Pauly ain't home by now, it's cause they told him not to come home. They've done meanness like that to my Pauly all the time. He won't come home until they tell him. You and Tully Jones stay out of this."

Queen grabbed the barrel of the rifle and banged the stock down hard on the floor. Her voice rose to hysteria pitch. She nearly choked on her deep phlegmy cough. "Do you hear me! Promise me. Promise me." She dropped the rifle from her shaking hand and it clattered to the floor. "Get it Canty. Give it here."

"Get out! Go away!" Black screeched, and flapped his huge wings. Blue-black inky feathers drifted in the dim light around Canty.

She picked up the rifle, and put it back in the old hands. Queen's breathing rattled like knives in her chest.

"Queen." Canty heard her own voice crack.

"Promise, Canty O'Neil. Promise. I got to have Pauly. Tully can see to them boys after the closing. Tell him I'm deliverin' their sorry hides right to him after the closing. Promise me, now."

Canty looked directly into Queen's black eyes. "I don't know if it'll change things, but I promise."

She was half-way down the mountain when the Ponders' truck loomed in front of her. She slammed on the brakes. The Jeep slid on the gravel and nicked the front fender of the truck as she passed. Canty could see the truck, back and turn.

Those pigs are coming after me. Dear God! She glanced into the rear view mirror. The rusted grill of the old truck was inches from her rear bumper. The truck slammed into her, again and again. Canty's head snapped cruelly every time it hit. She couldn't hold on to the wheel any longer. She heard the squeal of metal as the Jeep slid sideways into a big pine on the side of the road.

"Tell you what," Terrell reached into the Jeep, grabbed Canty's arm, and yanked her out. "Now, what you doin' talking to Queen? You two bitches cooking up ways to get our money? Bet that's it, don't you think, Smith? Terrell grabbed at her breasts and pinched. "Well, damn, you grew some titties after all, bitch-whore. Not much to brag about, though."

Smith pushed Terrell aside. "Let me have some." He grabbed a breast, and pulled her to him. He covered her mouth with his rank, slobbering lips. Canty felt faint.

Terrell was now in back of her, his hands ran over her buttocks, and in between her legs. "Been a long time. When you gonna marry me, bitch-whore? Whoee, we'd make pretty babies. Shoot, gonna have lots of money. Shoot, we can have lotsa babies."

Canty turned her head away from Smith's gooey lips. "You leave me alone, or there won't be a closing. No closing, no money. Do you get it?"

Smith spat. "See what happened at O'Dell's? See what happened to your office today, bitch-whore? Could've been you. Understand your red-headed friend's in the hospital. You want to be there?" He yanked her head back by her hair. "You got pretty gray eyes. Wanna keep them? Wanna breath? You mess with our money, you're a dead woman, purty as you are, you're a dead woman." He pulled his lips back into a grotesque smile, black-yellow gums shining. "Be a shame I didn't have you first. Be a damn shame."

Terrell stopped his groping. He jerked Smith aside. "Let her go. She can stop everything."

"Shit no, she can't."

Terrell backhanded Smith. He yelped, came after him, and tackled Terrell into a stand of bushes. The brothers swung wildly at each other, yelling curses.

Canty jumped into the Jeep. She said a small prayer that the boys would keep fighting, and forget about her. She skidded and screeched to the main road, and hit the gas pedal hard. She prayed Tully Jones would not be in sight.

She looked into the rear view mirror just in time to see the Ponder's truck closing in on her. They hit her back bumper hard, and she had to use every bit of her strength to keep the Jeep from going into a spin. They leaned on their horn, and struck again. The jolt threw her into the wheel. The pain was excruciating. The Jeep was sliding side-ways. Canty drove into the slide, and felt the Jeep respond and straighten.

"No! You aren't going to stop me," she yelled. She floored the Jeep again, and pulled away. Another look behind her revealed nothing. She slowed at the City of Wynton sign, and drove into town.

Canty pulled into a parking place in front of the old brick building on the square that boasted a sign reading "John Milton, Attorney-at-Law. Wills, Trusts, Probates, Real Estate." She smoothed her hair with shaking hands. Her whole body felt beaten and violated. She sat a few moments until her stomach settled down. Her breasts still ached from Smith and Terrell's mauling, and her whole chest felt mashed from her contact with the steering wheel. She rinsed her mouth from her water jug and spit. She wanted to take a long, hot shower to feel clean again. Canty O'Neil, you were wrong. Those Ponder's are a danger to everyone.

Canty got out of the Jeep. She straightened her blouse and tucked it into her jeans. She walked around to the passenger side. The pine tree that stopped her had left its imprint on the door. Damn it. She walked around the back and noted faded blue scuff marks punched on her back bumper. Blue, Ponder-truck blue.

She took a deep breath, and dialed her office. "Willodene, I'm at John Milton's office. I'm about to scare him silly with what I am setting up here and I want you to come over and check all the forms. Please."

"I'll be there, honey."

"Have you talked to Burke or Tully?"

"Burke called from the hospital. If I thought he sounded like a bear eatin' briars before, I hadn't heard anything yet. He's hurtin', and furious. They're still pickin' glass out of his skin. Got a crew working on the clean-up, here." Willodene lowered her voice. "Where've you been? I've been worried sick. Tully was a basket case when you took off and he couldn't follow you. Crime scene and all that. Canty?"

"Working." She rushed on. "If you see Tully, tell him I'll be at the hospital in about an hour. Please, call and get a message to Burke. Tell him I'm getting the closing set up, and get Hearn Guilford to wire the money today. Please, check the hospital in Gainesville to see what we have to do to get Pauly admitted somewhere for care. I'll worry about getting Queen a place as soon as we know where Pauly will be. And, please come here as soon as possible."

"Yes, ma'am".

The attorney's office was done in dark, fake paneling, worn brown shag carpet and faded orange café curtains. The one couch, and one chair were upholstered in green, orange, and brown plaid, the pattern barely discernible. One table lamp illuminated very little, except its own cobwebs. Not a magazine in sight. Yesterday's Wynton Crier lay untouched on a dusty, off kilter, end table.

Great place, John. Canty walked down a short hall-way to an open door. There sat the corpulent John Milton,

227

Attorney, feet on desk, phone in ear. He waved her to a cracked leather chair in front of his desk. His conversation was dotted with comments about deer hunting and trout fishing. She didn't care to wonder to whom he was talking. He finally hung up.

"Why, Canty O'Neil. Long time, no see." He stood and stretched out his pudgy arm and shook her hand. "Bringing me some business, I hope." His smile opened up his round face, and pushed out his nostrils. His squinty pale eyes nearly disappeared into the folds of skin hanging on his forehead.

"John, we are closing on the Ponder property Friday at ten a.m. I'm going to need your conference room, and all the forms necessary. Willodene will fill them in. I'll send over a copy of the contract later today, so that you will know exactly what is taking place. Of course, you'll be there. Queen Ponder is looking forward to seeing you."

The smiling Buddha changed to a scowling, questioning Buddha. "You're kidding."

"I'm not kidding."

"But, that's a big land deal. I've been hearin' rumors about it, but didn't believe a one. Heard some high-rolling developer wants to make a golf course out of that land. How did you get the Ponder's to agree to sell that property? How much did it sell for? Don't tell me Terrell and Smith, and that gross, stupid Pauly will be here. I will assure you, I won't be in the room with those boys, and their shotgun. I will assure you, I won't. And, the fact remains, today being Wednesday, there would be no way to get that closing together between now and Friday. No way." His jowls wobbled in time with his tongue speed. Canty said a little prayer for her self-control. She had to

228

mash her lips together so the bubbles of laughter sitting in her throat would not get out and explode.

"John. Sit and relax. Just please go over the forms with Willodene." Canty waved in a dramatic welcoming gesture as Willodene entered. "Here she is now."

Willodene strode into the room, legal pad and pencil in hand. She squinted her round eyes and pursed her small mouth. "Canty, the hospital in Gainesville will fax us the papers for Queen to sign so we can admit Pauly. They'll have to do extensive testing and evaluation, of course." She turned to the attorney. "Where're your forms, John?"

Speechless, John Milton, Attorney, walked the thigh-rubbing mincing walk of a fat man to the files and began pulling forms. "Canty, I've never closed a big land deal like that. You got the survey?"

"I have the survey, John. I haven't asked you to close it."

"You know how to work up the Settlement Statement and the Deed? I don't know any of the details. I couldn't do it in time."

"John, I haven't asked you to close it. I know how and so does the Purchaser's representative. You'll have a copy of the contract later today, as I said. I only asked that you check it over. You don't have to do anything."

John minced back to his desk, holding a sheaf of documents. He showed them to Willodene.

Willodene used one long Poppy Red fingernail to flip through the forms. "Nothing here I haven't seen before."

"John, this closing will be a very touchy situation. Queen wants you there. She didn't think it right not to have an attorney at the closing, and I agreed. All her wishes regarding the money she'll receive are in the contract stipulations. The Purchaser's representative, Burke

McGuire will also be present. Queen likes Burke McGuire and trusts him as much as she could ever trust anyone, me included. It's the only reason this closing will happen. So, you must be there."

The Buddha plopped back into his beat up desk chair, and pulled himself close to his desk. The wheels on the old chair scritched and whined. John folded his pudgy arms and looked at Canty. "I tell you, Canty O'Neil, if those Ponder boys come in here with a shotgun, this attorney will not be present."

"Tully Jones will be there." Canty could feel her lips tightening and her mouth going dry.

"I wouldn't give a hoot and damnation if Tully Jones was here with six armed guards, I will not be present. Terrell and Smith are scary enough but if that poor creepy, idiot Pauly comes in, slobberin' and cryin', well, it's like I said, I will not—"

Canty jumped from her chair. All of her skin felt tight and dry. "Listen, John there's going to be a closing Friday and you will be there. Closing on this property will mean a whole new future for Wynton, new jobs, money, and a new life for the people. I don't think the people of Wynton would like me to tell them their own John Milton, Attorney, was the reason their lives were still stuck on hold."

John tried to rise abruptly. His large backside carried the chair just long enough so that it came off the floor nearly a foot. The chair crashed to the floor with a huge splintering of fractured wood. Willodene hooted with laughter. Canty sat back down slowly and gazed up at John Milton's moon face, red and splotched with anger.

"Are you threatening me, Canty O'Neil? How in the hell dare you to threaten me!"

"No, John, I'm not threatening you. I'm just telling you how important it is that you be at the closing. You can stand at the door of the conference room and run like hell if anything starts with Terrell and Smith. Okay? The town of Wynton needs you to be there. Queen Ponder needs you to be there. Guilford Golf Designs, Inc. needs you to be there. Don't you get it?"

The flustered man stood quietly. "All right, I'll be there. If that many people are depending on me, I won't let them down. You will need a notary. I can do that."

Canty stood again and held out her hand. John Milton, Attorney, shook it lightly.

CHAPTER 26

Tully Jones's truck was parked directly in front of the Wynton Hospital double-door entry. No one in Wynton ever parked in front of the doors unless there was big trouble.

Canty pulled into the nearest space and hit the ground in a fast jog. Dear God. Please. Burke, Toby, Pop.

The receptionist was calmly chewing gum and flipping through a magazine when Canty burst through the doors.

"Marylou, what's going on? Where's McGuire? Where's the Sheriff?"

The girl jerked up in surprise. "Hey, Canty."

"What's going on? Marylou, where are they?"

Marylou quit chewing, then began again. "Room Eight, last one on the right." She nodded to herself.

Canty ran down the hall. The scratched and torn face of Burke McGuire, surrounded by the stern, fixed expression of Pop, the tight-lipped look of Tully Jones, and the wide-eyed face of Toby, watched her enter the room.

Burke spoke first. "Come on over here, Canty." He patted a straight metal chair that sat beside his hospital bed.

Canty sat down and touched Burke's face and arms gently. She could still feel bits of glass under his tortured skin.

Burke spoke through damaged lips. "Seems I'm in conference with the VIP's of Wynton and I have been voted out of town. Glad they don't tar and feather anymore. That'd hurt double with all this glass still stickin' in me."

Canty sat as still as she could and hoped her shaking insides were not giving her away. "Okay, who's first?"

Pop finally spoke, and she could tell he was as unhappy a man as he'd ever been. His voice dragged over his words so slowly it was painful and hard to concentrate on what he was saying. "Canty, Tully and I, and Toby think all this has gone far enough. I know you've seen what those Ponders did to O'Dell's place, and he didn't do anything but send a message. There's gonna be a killin' before this is done. Burke here, he's lucky to be alive. Do you understand that it could have been you sitting in that chair in your office? We don't know if them Ponders was looking for a serious killin' or just breakin' glass for the hell of it to scare you. The fact remains, it's 'cause of what's goin' on that they been flushed out. You don't want to mess with scared or mad Ponders."

Toby walked around to Canty's chair and hugged her neck. "Ma, it coulda been you sitting there. I'm sorry it was Mr. Burke, but Ma, it coulda been you."

Tully spoke. His rumbling voice was edged with anger. "It's over, Canty. We have convinced Mr. MugWire, here, that it's too risky to go on with this game. He doesn't want to see anybody hurt, especially you. We have convinced Mr. MugWire that it's time for him to pack up his golf clubs, his plans, and be history around here."

Canty's head was spinning. She had her fists clenched so tight in her lap, her nails dug into her palms like razor blades. She waited. She waited until the silence was unbearable. She waited longer. Four sets of eyes were focused on her face. She matched each set with her own gray-ice gaze. Three sets were stony, colorless and expressionless. One set was fighting blue and dancing. She knew

Burke McGuire hadn't been convinced of anything. She wanted to hug him. He'd probably go straight through the ceiling, screaming in pain.

Canty cleared her throat. "Things haven't gone exactly the way I'd thought, but the Ponders want that closing to happen. They want that money. Tully, Queen said she wanted you to leave Terrell and Smith alone until it's over. She wants both the boys to be at the closing. Then she said, you can have their sorry hides."

Tully spoke up. "This is assault, Canty. I'm stretched to the limit on letting those boys stay loose any longer. The law about assault is clear and I've yet to read anything that says I have to recognize orders from Queen Ponder."

Canty sighed. "Not an order, a request. It's one day. One day. You won't find them before then anyway."

"Canty," Pop interrupted, "if those boys want this closing so bad, why are they raising so much dust?"

"Because they don't trust Queen. They don't trust anyone. So, intimidation is the only way they can feel in control."

Burke mumbled. "Damn fools nearly killed me. What good would that do?"

Canty took Burke's hand. "They could have killed you ten times by now. They could have killed any one of us, anytime."

"Point taken." Burke laughed and then yelped in pain.

Tully snorted. "So what happens after the closing? Those sweet boys gonna blow us a kiss and leave?"

"That's the way we'd like it but no, that won't happen." Canty took a deep breath. "Queen will announce that those boys aren't getting a penny except enough to carry them out of the county."

"Canty!" Pop yelled. "Terrell will blow the place apart."

"Gonna need Batman and Superman to be there." Toby chimed in.

"Gonna need General Patton and all the United States Army." Burke added.

"Like I said," Tully interrupted, "that damned closing won't happen."

Canty kept her voice level. "Burke, did you get my message from Willodene about asking Guilford Golf Designs to wire the money to the Wynton post office immediately?"

Burke gestured toward the phone beside the bed with a bandaged hand. "Done."

"Good. I spoke to Queen this morning and she is ready to close."

Tully exploded. "You were up there! Damn it, Canty. You promised you wouldn't go near that place until after the closing. Kee-rap. I thought I could trust you."

It took all Canty could muster to ignore Tully's outburst. She clenched her jaw and took a deep breath, her voice was slow and controlled. "The boys hid Pauly somewhere to keep Queen from slipping away. They'll bring her down tomorrow morning." Canty stood. "I have also spoken with John Milton, Attorney, and he will be presiding, maybe from an Exit door, but he will be there. Tully, Queen has requested that you please be there. She also said she's got a big surprise for those boys."

Tully jammed his big fists in his pockets, and scowled at Canty. "I can't imagine a bigger surprise than Queen telling them they're only getting traveling money. Don't like it, Canty."

Canty glared at Tully. "I still don't believe they'll try to hurt anyone but each other." She still felt the bruises on her breasts and denied them. "Burke, will you be there? Do you want to go on with this project, or should we drop it?"

Burke swept his gaze to include everyone. "Hey, living on the edge was always my style. But, I do believe Canty, and I do value your lives as well as mine. I've seen enough of Queen and those brain deprived brothers to know they're dangerous as hell. But, as Canty said, they could have killed anyone of us, anytime, by now." He turned to look only at Canty. "I've never let a broken plate glass window or a ceiling dumped on my head stop me from being at a closing."

Canty stood. "Now, if you'll excuse me, gentlemen, I've got work to do at the bank. That big jelly donut of an attorney will screw things up somehow unless I give him explicit instructions. Why don't you all call it a day, and let Burke get some beauty sleep? God knows, the man needs it."

Canty gave a grinning Burke a quick kiss on the forehead and left the room. Knowing Tully was busy, she made it to the Wynton Bank in record time.

When Canty entered the building, she knew immediately that the funds for the closing had arrived. John Milton, Attorney, was striding around issuing orders to the bank manager who sat nodding at his every word, a frozen smile etched on his lips. The two tellers, mouths open, were staring wide-eyed at the pacing attorney.

"Hello, John."

He whirled at the sign of her voice, his jowls wobbling. "Canty, so glad you arrived. I was just about to call you to tell you I need Mr. McGuire's signature on this deposit slip."

"I suggest you go to the hospital, Room Eight, and get Burke McGuire's signature on that deposit slip, all by yourself. I'm sure you can handle that. We plan to close at ten tomorrow morning, remember?"

He slapped his forehead. "Of course, I remember, dear

Canty." He lowered his voice. "The sheriff will be there?"

"Yes, John." Canty nodded at the manager, and handed him a piece of paper. "These are the instructions for the disbursement of the funds. We'll need the checks before ten in the morning." The manager took the paper. His hands trembled and the frozen smile showed signs of cracking.

John Milton put his clammy, fat hand on Canty's arm. His flabby face was chalky. "I understand Mr. McGuire was brutally injured after Terrell shot up your office. Is he all right? I mean will he be there?"

Canty turned away for a second and took a deep breath. "Mr. McGuire will be fine and will be at the closing." She leaned close to one puffy ear. "He will also be carrying a loaded gun. Not to worry."

John Milton, Attorney froze, immobilized.

CHAPTER 27

Canty started trembling as she crossed the ridge. By the time she parked the Jeep, she was sweating and shaking. She ran into the house and barely made it to the bathroom before she threw up.

Oh, God, what a day, she thought. She stripped off her clothes, and when she saw the bruises on her breasts, and between her legs where Terrell had pinched and prodded, she threw up again. Exhausted, Canty stood in the hottest shower she could bear. She washed and rinsed her hair three times, and scrubbed her skin until it throbbed. She didn't step out of the shower until it turned cold, and she was shivering.

She donned a warm sweat suit, and filled a glass with Pop's sweet tea. Destination, porch, she thought, and my favorite rocker.

Canty stared at the mountains. Her head hurt and her hands were clammy. "Mountains, I wish I were you right now. No thoughts, no worries, no doubts about anything. I'm so scared. Not the kind of scared that Tully and Pop were acting foolish about, not just drop-everything-and-forget-it, scared. Maybe I should give it up, but honestly, I knew the danger would be Ponder against Ponder, and I still believe it. I'm just scared I can't pull it off."

She sighed and rocked, watching tatters of clouds undulate and pulse through the mountain ridges as far as she could see. The sun tossed splinters of light into the sky as it began its ritual setting. Canty felt her beaten body go limp.

A wave of uneasiness snuck through her mind as she thought of tomorrow. Would those crazies show up drunk, and with Terrell's shot gun loaded? No doubt they would. Would Queen be able to control them? Would Queen have her rifle loaded? No doubt she would. Tully will be armed, and so will Burke.

She let her head drop, and an uncontrolled sob shook her body. What in the name of God have you done, Canty O'Neil? In the past few weeks, you have stirred up a pot of hope and excitement flavored with discontent and fear, in Wynton. You led the people of this town down a path that could either turn Wynton into a mega-rich pocket of the Blue Ridge or smash what little pride it has left. You prodded the anger of two very dangerous men. You scared Pop, Toby, and Willodene half out of their minds. Your best friend, Tully, would cheerfully lock you up for life. The most exciting and wonderful man in the world looks like he just put his face into a meat grinder because of you. What have you created? This town is your life's blood. You breath this place and your mountains. Your dream of helping Wynton and Pop and everyone has turned into a night-mare. What a big, damn mess.

She raised her head and focused on the sunset again. Burke McGuire popped into my life and every-thing changed. He's why I've tried so hard. I had to prove to him how terrific and smart I am. I love that bear of a man. Damn near got him killed. Still could get several folks killed. I can call it off. I can stop the whole thing, just like that!

Canty looked up to see the headlights of Tully's truck pulling into the drive.

Tully rolled down his window. "Well, I'll be damned, Pop, if old Canty doesn't look just like Queen Ponder on her porch. All she needs is a gun and a black bird. Better send Toby out first. She wouldn't hurt Toby."

Canty quit rocking. "I'm not going to hurt anybody, and you aren't funny, Tully Jones. I can't believe you and Pop coerced my Toby into acting with you to run Burke off and blow up the closing. The two men I trust most in the world. Well, you didn't succeed. Do you hear me?"

Pop got out of the truck and came to the porch. "Think I'll take a chance and sit down by my daughter. Come on, Toby. Need you to be here, close by. Tully, you'd better keep your distance, boy."

Canty began rocking again. "You are all welcome on this porch. Just quit messing with my mind."

Pop leaned over and put his face in hers. "Girl, we haven't run off your Burke MugWire. He's still in that hospital bed, but probably not for long."

"It's McGuire, and you know it. Quit acting like Tully. It's childish."

Pop straightened up, and sat down in the rocker next to Canty. "Like I said, we haven't run off Burke McGuire. But, we want to stop this before there's blood. Can't you see that? I told you once you only did one really stupid thing in your life. Well, this could be the second."

"Seems to me the one stupid thing turned out to be a beautiful thing." Canty blew a kiss to Toby.

"Not the same thing," Tully grumbled.

Canty stared straight at Tully. "Maybe not, but at least this decision was made rationally."

Tully met her look. "I don't think so, Canty. I think you have been blinded by Burke MugWire. The man doesn't give a damn about the Ponders, and the fact that their family has lived on the property for nearly one-hundred years. Burke is no mountain man, never will be. Mountain folks don't run people off their land just 'cause they're kinda crazy. They're going to die off soon, anyway. Leave it alone. Wynton can manage a few more years without a high-toned golf course. No closing."

Tully turned his back to Canty and spoke loudly to the night. "They will die off soon. Leave it alone."

"He's right, Canty," Pop pleaded.

Canty stood up. "No, Pop, he's not right. Queen needs help, and she wants this closing to happen. She knows she's in serious danger from Terrell and Smith. They're not going to kill me, or Burke, or you, Tully. They see only Queen as someone who can hurt them. But, Tully, you have to lock them up after the closing so Queen and Pauly can get away from here. Just be there, and they will be delivered to you."

Tully stepped close and put his hands on Canty's shoulders. "Canty, stay out of the middle of the Ponders. Let them resolve their own problems like they've always done."

"You scared of them, Tully?"

Tully's expression dissolved into a disbelieving stare. Canty wished she could cut out her tongue. Toby walked by her and she could see tears in his eyes. He went in the house and let the screen door slam.

"Pop, Tully, help me. I know I'm right. This will be a good thing for everyone here. The papers will be done tomorrow. The Ponders will be there. There will be a closing Friday at ten in the morning. It'll be all right."

Canty got up from the rocker and headed indoors. Looks like it's you and me, Burke. She let the screen door slam behind her.

"Toby, where are you?"

He appeared carrying a glass of tea. "Here, Ma. Thought you could use something to drink."

"Oh, honey, I thought you were mad at me for all times."

Toby tilted his face up to Canty and she could see the twinkle in his eyes. "I was mad at Pop and Tully for not believin' in you and Mr. Burke."

Canty took the glass. On second thought, looks like it's you and me, Burke, plus one. "Thank you, son."

Canty tossed and turned most of the night. She called Burke. When he answered, he was growly and impatient and she couldn't blame him

"I feel helpless, Canty. Not a good thing for me. And to make matters worse, a fat slob by the name of John Milton, Attorney came by for my signature on the deposit slip. Are you telling me that was our closing attorney? The man is a complete idiot. He asked me if my gun would be loaded tomorrow? Are you believing that? I asked him if his gun would be loaded and I thought he would shit in his pants right then."

She smiled to herself. "Yup, that was John Milton, Attorney all right. I wanted you to know that I have started working on getting Pauly admitted to proper care. Once that's done, I'll find a place for Queen. I'll bet she would love to watch that golf course develop. We can take her there."

"Okay, Miss Fixit. Will you be able to keep me out of jail after I go after those pieces of dog-dirt? Glad you got an in with the sheriff. I'm going to need it. Justifiable homicide, don't you think? How about that judge? Got any influence with him? Won't be *we* if you don't."

"How are you feeling?"

"Like hell. Like a thumbtack board. The only reason I haven't just quit and died is because I want those boys. They're mine."

"Burke."

"Canty. I love you, damn it. You should be here helping me pick the glass out of my body. I would do it for you."

"It is three o'clock in the morning, Burke. Go to sleep."

"Had a nice talk with old Tully. Did he tell you?"

Canty groaned. "No, he didn't. What did you two talk about?"

She could hear Burke mutter an obscenity. "You. What in hell else would I talk to that man about. Said if you wanted me, I would get you. Jeez He said we're both trouble-makers and we belong together."

"I don't believe you." Canty felt weak and puddly.

"I said I love you. I've never told a woman I loved her before because I don't lie about such important matters. You make me crazy."

"Same to you."

"You're worth waiting for." Burke's tone hardened. "By the way, sheriff told me he's a married man. Why hadn't you told me?"

Canty hesitated. "It was up to Tully to tell you."

"What exactly does that mean? Canty, sometimes you make me madder than this glass sticking in me."

Canty smiled. "Well, I love you, too. Goodnight."

"Thank you, Lord and thank you, Tully."

THE CLOSING

Burke was waiting at the office of John Milton when Canty walked into the shabby reception area. He looked terrible, but managed an expression Canty guessed was a smile. It made his cracked-glazed face look even crazier.

"Hey, this isn't a Halloween Party. Take off the mask." She stifled a chuckle.

"Very funny, O'Neil. Your Irish wit is nasty. Remember, Scots are tough. We do our best when we look our worst."

"Then you'll be incredible today." Before he could respond, Canty planted a light kiss on his lips. "I've got all the paperwork and the checks. Let the show begin."

John Milton, Attorney, appeared at the door, wide-eyed and pasty and announced the arrival of the Ponders. They had come in the back door, he said, and were in the conference room where the closing would take place.

"Queen says she needs you to fix her hair a little, Canty." His sweaty jowls shook with his voice. "Terrell's got that shotgun and Queen brought her rifle. Dear God."

Canty whispered back , "It'll be all right. Tully will keep everyone in line." She walked quickly to the conference room.

"Canty," Queen hacked and coughed her greeting. The depth of her misery made Canty shiver. "Can you fix me a little?" Queen sat in a straight-backed office chair, one of a dozen surrounding the table. Pauly sat beside her, his obesity hanging around him He looked at Canty with glazed eyes. His fleshy lips tried a smile. Drool slid down his pink, fat chin.

Terrell spluttered a laugh. "Gonna take all day to fix Queen. Gonna take more'n day, if ever. We'll never git this here closing done."

Queen pulled herself up very straight in the chair, her hand on the rifle barrel. "You two pigs hush, or I'll have the sheriff lock you up, and you won't see no closing."

Smith hopped from one foot to the other. "I ain't scairt of you Queen, you old woman. And I ain't scairt of the sheriff, neither. Terrell ain't neither."

Queen slammed the butt of the rifle on the floor, hard. "You had better be scairt of me." Her eyes glowed black as oil.

Canty's stomach flipped and tightened. This might be very interesting. Might be more interesting than she bargained for. Where was Tully? She walked around to the back of Queen's chair and pulled a small brush and comb from her handbag along with a card of hairpins which she placed in front of Queen. Pauly grabbed at the card and stuck it in his mouth in a flash. Queen snatched the card from him and he began to cry, a whimpering, sucking sound. Terrell and Smith broke into laughter.

"It's all right Pauly, baby. Queen loves you. You can have this back when we're done. Now, Canty, fix me."

Canty sighed and hesitantly touched Queen's hair. It felt clean and smelled soapy. She deftly brushed and combed and twisted the shoulder-length gray black hair into a granny knot on the top of her head. A few tendrils fell around her face. Queen swiped at them.

"Oh, no, Queen. That's the fashion. Makes you look young and a little wild."

246

Tully strode into the room. "It does, Queen. That's nice."

"Glad to see you, Tully." Canty smiled. You don't know how glad. "You look real nice this morning. I love the way you wear your guns."

"Well, if one gun is good, two is better. Wanted to equalize the room, here. Two for two." He spoke slowly and locked his gaze on Terrell. He then turned to Queen. "You and Terrell ain't loaded now, are you?"

"What good's a gun if it ain't loaded?" Terrell spit on the floor.

Queen tried to laugh and began coughing, a deep chest-searing cough. No one said a word until she stopped. A pitcher and glasses appeared, placed quickly on the table by John. Finally, she took a breath and drank.

As John walked by Canty, he remarked that Queen looked like someone beat the shit out of her.

"Two someone's, John," Canty said. The attorney did a full body, slow wave shudder and stood in the doorway.

Canty handed the contract to Queen. She was making frightening rattling noises with each breath. She drank more water. Her breathing quieted. "Where's that Burke McGuire?"

"Right here, Queen." Burke entered the room and zeroed in on Terrell and Smith. They did a double take when they saw his face and arms.

"Well, I'll be damnnationed, Smith. Old MugWire here looks like he tangled with a glass window."

"Terrell, it looks like he lost." They both whooped, turned their heads and spit on the floor.

Burke went up close. Tully's hands twitched over his guns.

"Tell ya something, scum dirt," Burke's voice was a snarl, "I'm carryin' and I know how to use it."

Smith started his hoppy dance again. "Whoooeee, I

scared. I might pee right now. You gonna pee Terrell, or blow his haid off."

Terrell held the shotgun on a level with Burke's face, a nearly toothless, slimy gummed smile on his face.

BLAM!

Queen shot a hole straight up in the ceiling. Rifle smoke hung on the air. A chunk of shattered ceiling plaster showered the table. Pauly sobbed loudly. Terrell put down the shotgun. Smith peed down his leg.

"One more show like that boys, just one more." Tully shouted. Both Glock 10's came out of his holsters.

"Set boys," Queen rasped. "We got a closing to do." Terrell and Smith sat.

Queen Ponder spent nearly half an hour reading through the contract that Canty had written, and Burke had approved. She nodded and mumbled. She coughed hard and drank more water. Pauly ritched around in his chair, and chewed on the card of hairpins. Terrell and Smith nodded off and snored.

Queen looked up at Burke. "Let's have a look at what you come up with on that legal, McGuire." Burke spread his survey on the table. He began going over every measurement of every section in detail.

Queen nodded again and again. "Wake up, Terrell. Wake up Smith. You disgusting pigs!"

Terrell woke up and looked at the survey. "I cain't read, neither can Smith, here. Wake up, stupid!" Smith woke up. "But I can see, and some of your ridge lines is way off. You gonna make it look less so we don't get as much money. I ain't signing anything. Smith ain't either."

Burke turned to face the brothers. "Here's the way it is, boys. This survey's been done by aerial, that's me, and by foot, that's Queen. It's completely accurate, and won't be changed. To make you feel better, that ridge you're talkin' about was quite a problem. Seems some folks who live on the other side proved that they owned the top of that ridge by recent survey."

Smith scratched at his crotch. "You're crazy as hell, MugWire. Who says they own it? Why that ridge has been Ponder property since way before I was born. It's a fact."

"The fact is," Burke's forced calm made Canty nervous, "that ridge is owned by the United States Government, Forestry Department, and they aren't in the mood for any trades with Ponders or Guilford Golf Designs, believe me." As Burke spoke, he continuously brushed drifting plaster fragments off the survey. He moved a whole pile of it to the end of the table and left it in front of Terrell and Smith. "John Milton, Attorney, can verify everything I have just said, right John?"

All eyes shifted to the door where John Milton stood, the EXIT sign glowing over his head. He simply nodded.

Burke spoke again. "Now John, if you can tear yourself out of that doorframe, I would like to see the Deed and your Notary Seal and," he focused directly, one at a time, on Terrell and Smith and then, Queen, "the money." Burke sat down.

Damn good actor, McGuire. Canty was caught between admiration at Burke's total control of the Ponders, and the urge to burst out in nervous laughter.

"Whooee, the money. Whooeee. Terrell and Smith splurted out words between their gums and chaws. "How much we get, Queen?"

Canty took a deep breath. She locked eyes with Burke. His body remained still but his eyes moved quickly to the boys, and then to Tully Jones who flexed his fingers on the gun triggers. All Canty could hear was the muffled snuffles and snorts of Pauly and the slushy chewing of Terrell and Smith.

Queen finally spoke. "Got a surprise for you boys. You don't get nothin' less I say so, and I don't know if I'm gonna say so."

Terrell spit on the floor. Smith spit on Terrell's spit.

"Pigs." Queen pushed herself up from her chair. "I'm the sole heir to the land. As the eldest, I was made the sole heir by our daddy long time ago, and I got the paper to prove it. I put it in the Wynton bank years ago, safe and sound. Now, you better act nicer or you're leavin' here with empty pockets."

Canty watched Terrell and Smith. They both focused glittery stares at Queen. Terrell backed away from the table and raised the shotgun to Queen's head. Tully's fingers went still on the triggers.

"Now, I'm tellin' you what whore-bitch sister, there ain't no such thing, and you better git us our rightful share or nobody's getting' nothin." He swung the shotgun on Burke, then on Tully, then back to Queen. "I'm gonna make this room turn red."

Queen stood straighter. Canty rolled her eyes to Burke, then Tully. They were both rock still and focused on Terrell.

"I want ya'll to hear me." Queen pointed a long bony finger at Terrell, and then Smith. "You ain't got the right to nothin'. I am the sole heir, and when I die, it all goes to Pauly, my son. One of you pigs is the daddy of this poor boy. Do you understand what I'm sayin'?" Queen lowered her voice to a hiss. "Remember that night long ago when you couldn't find nobody to mess with so you messed with me, your own sister. You'd been drinkin' your own nasty white likker, and you were stinkin' drunk. I screamed and fought but you raped the hell out of me, both of you. And, look what you did." Queen put her hand on Pauly's shoulder and touched her lips to his sweaty forehead. He pushed his mouth into a small smile.

"You're crazy, Queen. You remember doin' Queen, Smith?"

"Hell, no. I wouldn't wanna remember nothin' like that, anyway." Smith laughed a juicy tobacco mouth laugh. He spit. "Pauly don't know you're his momma. Don't know if I believe you, anyway."

"You believe it. I was bleedin' a lot after you two raped me. Momma saw what happened but she was too sick to help me." Queen took a deep honking breath. "If you boys had come home more and not be dead stinkin' drunk, you woulda noticed. Our momma died right after Pauly was born so I said he was your new brother. I was scairt you might hurt him and me if you knew the truth. Before Momma died, she told Daddy what you'd done and that's when he got the paper drawed up and signed. I went with him to the bank. Only time he ever talked nice to me."

Smith jigged and hollered. "Shoulda killed ya both, you and that piece of ugly crap. Then Daddy'd just have us. Woulda been the hewmane thing to do."

Canty moved to stand in front of Queen. Canty caught Tully's eyes, no expression at all. She then focused on Burke, the blue eyes shot lightning bolts. Canty spoke with all the control she could muster.

"We're not getting anywhere." She glanced toward the door as John Milton walked through, armed with papers and his notary seal. "Wait, John. We're not ready for you after all."

John stopped dead in his tracks. Canty hoped he wouldn't turn and run.

Canty eased Queen back into her chair. "You just sit, Queen. I'd like you and Terrell and Smith to talk together for awhile. Queen, you need to convince them about the survey, and let them know they will be getting lots of your money to help them find another place. The rest of us, including Pauly, will leave the room until you get it all straightened out, and we can go on."

Queen let out a shriek of laughter that startled all of them. "Canty, if you leave this room, it will turn red, I guarantee. You set. We'll act better. Terrell, put down that shotgun." Queen stood, raised her rifle and cocked it. The sound cracked through the room. The barrel was steady on Terrell.

"My God!" John Milton, Attorney, was frozen in the doorway, his round doughy face reflected terror.

"Sheriff, why'n hell don't you do something?" Burke growled.

Tully spoke loud and clear. "Stay still, MugWire."

"Everythin's under control, Burke McGuire," Queen cackled. "Put it down, Terrell. Far as I'm concerned, you're a dead man in about one second."

Terrell walked around the table, still holding the shotgun, only now he had it aimed at Canty's head. "Queen, you sign those papers and we'll be pickin' up pieces of Canty O'Neil. Weren't for her, we wouldn't be here right now." He strode closer. "I truly don't like you no more, Canty O'Neil, whore-bitch."

Canty froze. She saw a flash of Burke McGuire, headed straight for her. She tried to scream but nothing came out. Burke had knocked the wind out of her with a hard push away from Terrell. She saw the looming figure of Tully Jones behind Terrell, holding a hunting knife at his throat. Terrell put down the shotgun. Tully released him, and walked to a corner with the shotgun.

Smith started giggling and doing his hoppy dance. "Chicken-shit, Terrell. You must be the daddy of Pauly 'cause you're a scairty cat just like him."

"Shut up." Terrell moved to Smith and backhanded him across his face. Smith sat down hard in his chair.

Pauly burst into loud, sobbing tears, snot ran down his face. Queen took dead aim on Terrell again. He sat down. She placed the rifle beside her chair.

Burke sat Canty down in the nearest chair. He carefully rolled up the blueprints and the survey. He sat down. Canty caught his gaze. She tucked a tendril of hair behind her ear and rolled her eyes.

"You okay, Canty?" Burke asked.

"Yes," she gasped, her wind returned. "You're rough, McGuire, but thanks."

"Canty, pass me them papers now. I'm signin'."

Queen's voice snapped Canty back to reality. She spread the contract, the deed, and the survey in front of Queen. She pointed to the places for Queen to sign and initial. She put the papers in front of Burke, and he signed. She had John Milton, Attorney, notarize the signatures, his fleshy hands shaking so he could barely apply the seal.

Burke went to Queen. He put out his hand and Queen shook it. "Thank you, Queen Ponder. You're a real lady, and I'm proud to know you."

"You've done me a good thing, Burke McGuire, and I thank ya. Canty, girl, you'd better pay attention to this boy. He's a good'n." Queen chuckled. "Now we got to get back. I want ya'll to come by tomorrow. I got a surprise to show ya." Queen went to Tully. She reached up and pulled him down by an ear. "Honor me," she rasped.

"Yes, ma'am." Tully whispered, his face white marble, his guns holstered.

"Now, come on boys. I'll tell you how much money I'm getting' ya after we get back."

Terrell walked to the corner where his shotgun stood propped against the wall. "Ain't goin' without my gun." He picked it up. John Milton did a quick turn and was gone from the room, his large backside just skimming the door frame.

Smith spat one more time, and followed Terrell out the back door. Pauly got up and he and Queen shuffled out. As she passed Canty, she turned and looked at her. "I'm one of them rich bitches now, ain't I, Canty O'Neil? Gonna get me one of them white jackets with the fringe, by golly. I might let that Diamond lady have my weaver and spinner. She's okay." The deep burning cough shook her bony frame.

Minutes later, Canty, Burke and Tully stood and watched as Terrell and Smith got up into the cab of their abused, fenderless truck. Queen and Pauly struggled to get into the back bed. Smith started driving off almost before Pauly got his legs off the ground. He spun the wheels and flung gravel.

Canty felt frozen inside. My God. Pauly was Queen's son. How sick. Pauly was her son by one of those miserable, mean, monster bastards. The pigs raped her. Canty's stomach heaved remembering her own moments of terror at the hands of Terrell and Smith.

Canty grabbed Tully's arm. "Let me be the one to cut their balls off and you can hang their disgusting bodies from a tree. But first, we'll put them in cages and leave them on the square to be stoned. Then, I'll cut them.

Then, you can hang them. There is nothing too evil or awful that can be done to them."

"Hey, remind me not to get you all riled at me." Burke pulled her close and ruffled her hair. "I got a better idea, though. Let me haul their sorry asses to the nearest swamp. The 'gators love rotten meat."

Tully glared at them. "This time I'm not listening to either one of you. Remember, I'm counting on Wynton to be a better place because of your plans. I'm getting out of here. You two scare me. See you in the morning. Don't want to miss Queen's surprise."

Canty traced the scratches and stitches on Burke's ravaged face with a feather touch. "I'm sorry."

He held her close. "Hey, it's done. We did it. Scars to prove it. Partners?"

"Forever, I hope!" She hugged his neck and nibbled on an ear.

"Whoa now. I've got too much work to do tonight to mess around with a sexy lady like you. No fair." He buried a hand in her thick hair and pulled her head back gently. "To the court house, woman, and get that Deed recorded. I've got some big numbers to start tossing at Hearn Guilford, the sooner, the better."

DAGMAR MARSHALL

CHAPTER 28

The next morning, Canty, Tully, and Burke met at the café for breakfast. Patsy brought three plates filled with scrambled eggs, grits, sausage, and bacon. The sides were canned peaches, softball-sized biscuits and a crock of fresh butter.

"You must be Burke MugWire," Patsy smiled. "Heard you had a run in with a plate-glass window. You look bad, but I'm glad you're okay." She turned quickly, and headed back to the kitchen.

Burke sputtered, his anger fused. "What the hell was that all about? Everything I do around here, published and distributed? And what is this MugWire thing? You been coaching these people, Sheriff? Now that I'm going to be around this town a lot," he looked at Canty, "I think these folks ought to learn how to say my name right."

Canty laughed out loud, echoed by a guffaw from Tully. Burke glowered at both of them.

"Burke, you don't get it. They just say it like that. It's okay." Canty smiled.

"Bullshit." Burke kept his eyes off Canty and continued to work on his eggs.

Tully took a large gulp of coffee. "Mr. MugWire, and I can say McGuire but it doesn't sound right. We mountain folk have our own ways of saying things. I believe it has a nice ring to it, don't you Canty?"

257

"I do indeed." Canty blotted her lips carefully. "Where's your sense of humor, Burke?

"I don't have a sense of humor when it comes to mutilating my name. A man's name's important to him. Mispronouncing it is as bad as spelling it wrong, in my book.

Canty reached across the table and put a hand on Burke. "You're going to be very unhappy here, which makes me very unhappy. I don't like being unhappy."

Burke pulled off a piece of biscuit and slathered butter on it. He took a bite and chewed. Canty and Tully remained silent. He finished the bite, wiped his hands on his napkin and took a large swallow of coffee. Burke raised his eyes and looked at Canty and then Tully. "I've got to tell you something."

Canty tucked a lock of hair behind her ear. Her foot started jiggling under the table. "Serious?"

Burke kept his gaze on Canty. "I talked to Hearn Guilford, at length, last night. He knew what happened before, and during the closing. The man was storming mad. There may be no Secret Creek. I may get my ass fired."

Canty stiffened. "Oh, my God. How did he know?"

Burke cleared his throat. "Seems he tried to reach me in my room and started making some inquiries when I failed to answer. He finally questioned the desk clerk and, of course, the desk clerk knows everything, like everyone in this town knows everything," Burke slammed his coffee cup down hard enough to make Canty jump, "and tells everything to anyone who'll listen."

"No. Not after all that's happened," Canty's voice cracked.

"I'll work it out. Let's go see what surprise old Queen has for us." He slid out of the booth, and started for the door.

"Burke, wait for us." Canty yelped. She caught up to him

and put an arm around his waist. She reached up and pecked him on the cheek. "That didn't hurt, did it?"

"Do it again so I can tell for sure."

★   ★   ★

Tully pulled the truck up close to the front steps of the cabin. Pauly lay in the fetal position on the porch, silent and bloody.

"Pauly!" Canty screamed and ran to him. "He's breathing. Dear God. He's breathing but the blood - -"

Pauly turned to Canty and tried to sit up. "Pauly, you all right?" He shrugged and pointed a blood covered hand in the direction of the cabin door.

Burke yelled as if in pain. Tully bellowed, "Holy shit!" Canty ran into the cabin.

Even in the dim light she could make out the three bodies. Terrell and Smith were slumped down against the wall opposite Queen's rocking chair. They each had a blackened hole in their foreheads. Puddles of thick black blood lay beside each body. Their heads lolled down just enough to see shreds of skull blown into the wall behind them. Queen was slumped over in her rocker, her rifle on the floor beside her. The back of her head was blown away.

"Get out. I hate you. Get out. Go away!"

Canty gazed through the gloom. All this time, she'd thought Queen taught the bird to say those words out of meanness to anyone who came by. It was for her brothers. God, how she must have despised them. She could now discern that every piece of furniture and the TV were smashed to bits. The spinning wheel and loom that Queen treasured had been reduced to a pile of sticks.

Burke held Canty's head while she vomited over the porch rail. They went back inside while Tully checked each body carefully.

"Looks like Queen killed those sorry bastards, and then herself." He reached down and picked up a piece of paper beside her chair. "Look here, the check for the sale. It's made out to Pauly Ponder. My God, no wonder they went nuts."

Outside, the fresh air calmed Canty's urge to be sick. She and Burke tried to clean up Pauly who sat huddled on the porch. He had witnessed it all. He and the bird. He showed no response when they talked to him. He just stared, and pointed at the cabin.

Tully radioed town, and sent for two ambulances. One would come from Wynton, the other would come from Maryville, ten miles south.

Canty spoke to Tully. "Queen whispered something to you at the closing. My God, did she tell you what she was going to do?"

Tully put his large hands on her shoulders and looked into her eyes. "I can't believe you asked me that." Tears glistened in his deep brown eyes, but his voice was harsh. "I was keeping a promise, not a secret."

Canty wrapped her arms around Tully's neck and pulled his head down to her. "I'll always love you, Tully Jones."

Tully hugged her hard. "I know, Canty. It's okay." He inclined his head slightly toward Burke. "I told him I'd always be around."

"You rascal!"

Burke and Tully put Pauly on the back seat of the truck. Canty covered Black, and brought him, perch and all, into the back seat beside Pauly. "I'll find him a home, Pauly," Canty promised. Pauly sobbed.

★   ★   ★

Most of the town seemed to be in front of the police station when they returned to town. A reporter from Gainesville, and another from Franklin were already on the steps taking pictures and asking for comments as Canty, Burke and Pauly walked into the building. Canty held on to Black's perch, with Black tethered close.

Tully interceded, and promised the reporters a short interview in a half hour.

Pop, Toby and Willodene were inside waiting. Willodene held out her arms to Pauly, as awful as he looked. The pitiful creature stared at her blankly, and let her give him a hug. Canty felt tears coming. Pop and Toby hugged her and nearly caused the dam to break.

"You can cry if you want to, Canty. I might myself." Burke was at her side. Relief and love tumbled through her body.

"What have I done, Burke? I loved you so much and I wanted so much for Wynton. I blindly went on killing the Ponders, and didn't realize what I was doing to them. If I hadn't been so determined…"

"From what I understand from your Pop, an O'Neil never turns down a chance to turn a good deal." He held her chin, and looked her square in the eyes. "Canty, the Ponders were dead before you started. Queen jumped at the chance to save Pauly, but I wonder what would have happened if we hadn't come along? She might have killed him, too. She was a dying woman. He had no place to go if she hadn't been able to sell the land and provide for him."

"Lord, I hadn't thought of that. At least not yet."

"Damn smart-ass mountain woman. Now, you have to help me convince Hearn Guilford of those truths or Secret Creek Golf Club will never be."

Canty grinned at him. "You don't believe for one second that we can't do it."

Burke pulled her close. "We'll do it."

Tully told them all to get out of his jail and take the damn bird with them. "Fool thing'll be screeching and dropping bird shit all over this place. MugWire, think you and Canty can get Pauly to that place where he's going to stay? Pop, Willodene, Toby, go on with them."

"We can handle it, Sheriff, " Burke snapped. "How'd you keep your self-control yesterday?. I would've shot those bastards in the first two minutes."

Tully cracked a slight smile. "That's why I'm sheriff and you're not."

Canty whispered in Burke's ear. "Mr. MugWire, I talked to Pop, and he agreed, you need to come home with us, and stay until you heal up. You can't go around looking like that, you'll scare all the prospective clients away."

Burke gave her a squeeze. "Got a problem. I vowed one thing when I met you Canty O'Neil, and that was I wouldn't sleep under the same roof with you unless you were my wife. Better get my butt back to the unremarkable Best Western."

Canty gave him a savage kiss on the lips. She could feel pricks of glass under his lips. "Bullshit. And, by the way, I Do."

EPILOGUE

The Secret Creek Golf Club opened three years after the first bulldozer cleared land for a fairway. It was touted as the most luxuriously elegant golf resort to be found anywhere in the USA, and perhaps, just anywhere. The logo depicting a spinning wheel and a loom is identified with The Secret Creek Golf Club of Wynton, Georgia, by golfers around the world.

On the first visit, all women are presented with a white leather jacket, studded with gold stars and dripping with velvety ribbons of fringe. The label reads, "Compliments of the Queen."

There is a place called Pauly's Rock, which only the agile can climb. The effort is worth it. The view from the top reveals the whole valley, Secret Creek, and the mountains beyond, in one of Mother Nature's most breathtaking accomplishments.

Rabid Press, Inc.

The Closing by Dagmar Marshall at $13.95 each: _____

Up The Devil's Belly
by Rhett DeVane at $14.95 each: _____

The Madhatter's Guide to Chocolate
by Rhett DeVane at $14.95 each: _____

Willing Servants *(available Spring 2006)*
by Eric Turowski at $14.95 each: _____

Sales Tax (if applicable): _____

Shipping: _____

Total: _____

Please include $3.95 for shipping and handling for first book and
$1.25 for each additional. Texas residents must include applicable
sales tax. Payment must accompany orders.

Allow 3 to 4 weeks for delivery.

Name: _____

Date: _____

Shipping Address:

Street: _____

City: _____ State: _____ Zip: _____

Phone: _____ Fax: _____

Card Type: VISA ❏ MasterCard ❏

Name on Card: _____

Card#: _____

Exp. Date: _____

Signature: _____

Make your check payable to:

Rabid Press, Inc.
P.O. Box 4706
Horseshoe Bay, TX 78657
www.rabidpress.com

Dagmar Marshall received her Associate of Arts Degree in Journalism from Green Mountain College, VT. A Northeasterner by birth, a Southerner by choice, Dagmar and her family have been residents of Georgia since 1963. She is the proud Mom of three and proud Grandmom of five.

After twenty-five years in Real Estate in the Atlanta area, retiring meant putting writing first – at last. She has had several short-stories published and is working on another novel.

Photograph by Jill

a preview of

WILLING SERVANTS

BY

ERIC TUROWSKI

Available Spring of 2006

Bridgett Halloway turned off the television and stared out the window at her garden, obscured by the heavy rain sluicing down the panes. January had been quite the month. She considered the weeks one at a time. First, the entire world ushered in the new millennium (although she herself really didn't consider it new until the following year, but she was definitely in the minority according to what she'd seen on TV). The Y2K bug had been all but exterminated by diligent system managers like herself around the globe. The planet continued to spin, and no new messiah had appeared on the news to judge the living and the dead. Quite a relief, all around. Week two, Mike announced that his small contracting firm, not half as old as their marriage, had landed a contract refurbishing and remodeling the interiors of houses for a huge real estate company. Work for him had started almost immediately, and the money poured in (especially considering the season). At the beginning of the third week, the line turned pink on her home pregnancy kit, confirmed two days later by her OB-GYN. They were having a baby.

This sent Bridgett into a frenzied nesting mode; one which proved most unfortunate for Michael's waistline, especially in this post-holiday season. Week four, Mike celebrated in his own, manly way by beginning a project to refinish the basement into a new workspace. He wanted the baby to have a room of her own. Or his own, maybe, but Bridgett was already certain the baby was a girl.

She raised the footrest on the recliner, and draped the afghan hanging on the chair-back over her shoulders. Rain sizzled in the yard, tumbled across the roof, steamed along the street, and she snuggled hard into the blanket, taking in all that she could from the storm before the gray day faded. Bridgett would talk her husband into building a fire when he got home. Two could snuggle better than one.

A tiny life was growing inside her. Bridgett's hands unconsciously slid to rest on her abdomen as she pondered this little miracle. A future little person was depending on her fully, on the very functions of her body. It frightened her a little, this benevolent parasite lodged inside her. At the same time, she felt a soft warmth that spread from the exact center of her outward, and she swore she would see herself glow if she gazed at herself sideways in the mirror.

For the fifth or sixth time that day, she considered baking bread. She'd thought about it from time to time at work. Michael had bought her a new bread cookbook as soon as her nesting phase kicked in. Though not thoroughly familiar with pregnant women, he certainly knew how to best take advantage.

Bridgett smiled at this thought. She then sat bolt upright, sending the footrest back into the La-Z-Boy bottom with a reverberating thud.

Pork?

She turned her head, lifting her nose to test the air like a dog. Definitely, that was the smell of cooking pork hanging in the air, the precise odor shifting from the realm of bacon to the kingdom of pork roast to the distant hold of barbeque. Not ham, that was for sure.

Okay, she'd had a few cases of the cravings, but she had a snack as soon as she got home from work. A bowl of soup, the last of the homemade bread, a small bowl of ice cream and … So call it a sub-meal.

At any rate, she wasn't hungry. The meaty fragrance in the air did nothing to make her feel any hungrier. She glanced at the window, and decided not even the most determined barbequer could be out in that cold rain. The closest rib restaurant was at least three miles away, and besides, the wind blew in the wrong direction.

Bridgett slowly rose from the recliner. Sliding into a pair of slippers, she padded from the living room into the kitchen. Had she left on a burner, or maybe the oven? She twisted each knob counter-clockwise, but none had any play. In the kitchen, she noticed, the scent had disappeared. She walked back into the living room, where the smell was strong, then opened the front door and stuck her head out. No porky smell outside.

This is really weird, she thought to herself (she remembered thinking those words very clearly, and related it to Mara verbatim), not knowing the weirdness had barely begun.

When she closed the door, a breath of hot air caught her in the face, lifting her hair with the force of a good hair dryer. The atmosphere in the living room suddenly seemed fully comprised of cooking, burning, smoking pig. Oily, hot, smoky air rushed through her nostrils, down her throat, scratching its way to her lungs where it clung like mustard gas.

Bridgett bent double, hacking. There was no overpowering smell nearer the floor, and she gasped deeply, hands on her knees. She raised her head, tentatively tasting the air as she did. It was clear. There was no fleshy smell at all.

What the hell was that? She wondered, gazing around the quiet living room. The day was all but gone. She turned on the overhead lights.

The moment the bulbs flared, she felt it again, a blast of wind hot enough to prickle sweat along her hairline, and again the smell. Bridgett jerked away, her shoulder impacting the door. The flow of air blew past. Missed me, she thought, wildly. And then doubled back, whipping hotly through her hair, gagging her with the greasy odor.

Batting the air in front of her wildly, she darted from the door to the corner occupied by the television set. A hot blast shot past her arm.

Suddenly, the TV came on, full volume, drawing a shriek from Bridgett. Almost immediately it snapped off again. The overhead light flickered and died with it. She strained her eyes, teary and sore from nonexistent smoke, at the iron gray rectangles of the windows, but saw nothing.

"Bridgett," a voice, deep and rough, whispery yet perfectly clear, called her name, making her spin around in a circle looking for the source. She couldn't identify the voice, not even whether it was male or female, but it carried undertones sounding like steam in a kettle before a full boil. Her hair raised on her arms, her neck.

"Bridgett. You belong here with us."

Panic seized her. She scrambled for the front door, slamming it behind her. Standing in the driving rain, eyes locked on the door, panting, she waited. For what, she had no idea.

After a few minutes, her heart rate slowed. Her eyes moved to the window. She could make out the silhouette of the armchair against the dim front windows.

"Working late?" Mike's voice made her nearly jump out of her skin. He received a fierce embrace that nearly knocked him off his feet.

• • • • •

Mara looked up from her quick scribbling on the forms.

Bridgett gazed off toward the living room, her eyebrows bunched, frowning.

"And since then?" Mara prompted.

"Same kind of thing."

"Regularly?" Mara asked, "Daily, weekly?"

Bridgett shrugged. "Every now and again. When Mike's not here."

Mara reached over and turned off the video camera, pressed the stop button on the DAT recorder with her pen. Her friend was holding back something. It may have been something she didn't believe herself (or thought Mara wouldn't believe), or maybe she was distressed, recounting her odd story. Either way, now was not the time to press.

"Okay, this isn't anything I haven't heard before," she said.

Bridgett looked at her in disbelief. "Really?"

"Similar stuff, yeah. A few times. Here," Mara dug in her case, and found a bound notebook. "Write down the other events. Give me dates and times, if you remember them. Do it while you're at work. Anywhere you feel comfortable."

"Right," Bridgett said, seeming more at ease at writing it out than telling it face to face with a woman she'd known for years.

"It's getting pretty dark. Why don't we pick this up again tomorrow? I'll get an interview with Mike then."

Mrs. Halloway readily agreed, as Mara knew she would. The interviews always went best in the daylight, in situations less likely to bring about a reoccurrence of the phenomena. And when people were less afraid.

Lugging her case down the driveway, she turned right on Eucalyptus Road, walking toward the tight bend in the looping street. With her gear piled in the trunk, she climbed in the Toyota and started the engine. Mara jumped as the radio blared static loud enough to hurt her ears. As she turned it down, she noticed the writing on the windshield. Though hard to make out, it had been written so that she could read it from inside the car.

Cut you bitch Stay Away Piglet

Those letters were written largest, though smaller cuss words, even more difficult to read, surrounded the most prominent message. Leaning close, she tried to make out the medium. Reddish-brown, shining with the light from her dash, much of it oozing down the glass, she clicked the mist button on her windshield wipers. Thankfully, it brushed away after several squirts and wipes.